Finding L

After stints working in entertainment and advertising, Amy True turned to chasing her one dream: writing romance. She can often be found in her local writing spot sipping her favorite iced tea (with a touch of lemonade) and putting together playlists for her next books. When she's not daydreaming about her next cinnamon roll hero, Amy is traveling with her family, reading good books, and plotting her next small-town romance. While she grew up only ten minutes from Disneyland, which inspired her love for storytelling, she now calls Arizona home.

Also by Amy True

Ivy Falls

Meet Me in Ivy Falls
Finding Love in Ivy Falls

AMY TRUE

Finding Love in Ivy Falls

hera

First published in the United Kingdom in 2024 by

Hera Books
Unit 9 (Canelo), 5th Floor
Cargo Works, 1-2 Hatfields
London SE1 9PG
United Kingdom

Print ISBN 978 1 80436 802 2
Ebook ISBN 978 1 80436 799 5

Look for more great books at www.herabooks.com

Printed and bound in Great Britain by Clays Ltd, Elcograf S.p.A.

For Julie…

Who has the biggest heart and gives special meaning to the word sisterhood.

Chapter One

MANNY

Encased In Nothing But Tight Blue and Red Polyester

Bright. Royal blue. Tights.

Why, why, why had I agreed to this costume?

I clutched the vacuum-sealed package, glaring at the image of the deceptively happy guy on the cover. There was only one person in the world who could get me to play superhero, and she was currently standing in front of me with her hands on her hips, lower lip set in a determined pout.

'Superman always wore blue tights, Pop. You have to put them on!' Lou adjusted the plastic gold crown on her head, her matching Wonder Woman wrist cuffs sliding down her arms.

'What about letting me be Clark Kent? I could wear a suit and fake black glasses,' I practically begged my pint-sized daughter, who had all the determination of an orca pod flipping a fishing boat.

Lou tapped her foot. Shook her head. She was a month past her eleventh birthday and already as stubborn as I was. I could only imagine how much trouble I'd be in once she was a teenager. High school. Driving. First love and broken hearts. My pulse rocketed up, and I quickly shook away all the worries of what was yet to come for my only child.

It was times like these my heart ached for Gina. With each passing day I saw more of my late wife in Lou. The way she tipped her head to the side when she was curious. How her black hair looked almost blue in the early morning light. The fire in her eyes when she saw any kind of animal. Dog. Cat. Hamster. It didn't matter. If it had fur, Lou loved it and usually wanted to bring it home.

Our house was already a menagerie of creatures. Our old Irish setter, Fergus, whose eyesight was so bad he constantly bumped into walls. A rescued African grey parrot named Mr Peepers who constantly demanded raisins and sang out the F-word – an unnerving habit I didn't know about until we got him home. Then there was Lou's beloved ferret, Reggie, who currently stunk up the entire house. I'd tried to keep our three-bedroom Craftsman neat and tidy, but with a small child, animals and a busy work schedule, that was nearly impossible.

I moved around the kitchen collecting day-old coffee cups and food-encrusted plates, loading them into a dishwasher that had seen better days.

'Did you clean Reggie's cage like I asked?'

'Pop!' Lou huffed again. 'The fall festival began an hour ago, and you promised we'd be superheroes together.'

I must have been out of my mind when I'd agreed to this costume. Flustered was more like it. My renovation business with my partner, Torran, was booming. Our TV show, *Meet Me in Ivy Falls*, was doing well in the ratings after being on the air for nearly six months.

According to our producer, Lauren, the show was continuing to get good buzz (whatever that meant). We'd begin shooting a second season in a few weeks and were waiting to hear if the Hearth and Home network would sign us for a third. All of that amounted to a lot of distraction, which explained why I'd absentmindedly agreed to this Halloween pairing.

Lou loved the festival held in the town square every year, and the trick-or-treating that followed in our friend, and my partner's sister, Tessa's neighborhood. We never walked our own block because Lou swore they handed out the best candy – Sour Patch Kids and Twizzlers – near Tessa's house.

Tessa. I groaned, glancing at the package again. What would she think when she saw me in the ridiculous outfit? If I had to guess, she'd press a hand against her beautiful mouth and do her best to stifle a laugh. Too worried she might hurt my feelings.

In years past, I'd agreed to be the Scarecrow to Lou's Dorothy. Luke Skywalker to her Rey. Those were all fine costumes to be seen in, but the tights were pushing me to the limit. I wanted Tessa to think of me as a warrior. A fighter. Although Superman was one of my favorite DC heroes, the thought of her seeing me, and my nuts, encased in nothing but tight blue and red polyester, was messing with my already anxious brain.

'Come on! You promised.'

When Lou pushed out her lower lip, she was hard to resist. Lately I'd been so busy with work that guilt wore me down. As much as I grumbled about the costume, I owed her this.

After we restored the house on Huckleberry Lane, I thought I'd have some time to breathe, but offers to fix other run-down historical homes in Ivy Falls, and nearby towns, came flooding in. Torran and I agreed after talking with the town council that our next project had to be the old Thomas Place that'd been vacant for way too many years. We'd just started work on it last week, and wood rot, termites and corroded pipes had forced us to take what was left of the skeletal structure down to the studs, giving me barely enough time to run Lou to school and make dinner at night.

'Fine, Lulubean. Give me a minute.'

I walked into the bathroom, my hooded eyes revealing the toll of the last few years. Shoving a hand through my black hair, I grimaced at the small bits of white popping up near my ears. *Dammit.* I was only thirty-three. How was it possible I was already going gray?

I'd never been much into my looks. In college, I'd spent hours studying, and in the weight room training for football. My hair grew long and shaggy until I finally gave in and went to the barber. Once I'd married Gina, I'd tried to keep my hair cropped short the way she liked it. Honestly, I'd have shaved my head if she'd asked. She was my whole world before Lou, and I never thought I'd be single again. Now, nine years after Gina's sudden death, here I was in the bathroom contemplating if Tessa would see my premature grays as sexy or a total turnoff.

'Hurry up!' Lou knocked on the door. 'We gotta go, or all the special donuts will be gone from Sugar Rush.'

Great. Just what she needed. More sugar.

My thoughts wandered back to Gina. She'd tell me to take a breath, close my eyes and remember this moment. That Lou wouldn't always be this age.

I yanked off my T-shirt and jeans and tore open the package. The feet of the tights dangled in front of me. I turned them in my hands trying to figure out the front from the back. How the hell was I going to get the thin material over my thighs?

One day Lou would go to a dance and want to wear tights. This was a test to teach me how to do it right so that when the time came, I'd be prepared. She came first – now and forever. At times like these, pride didn't matter. I had to be both mother and father, and I wouldn't let my daughter down.

My phone squawked on the counter, and I refused to pick it up. Torran had set my ringtone to the sound of a growling bear every time I got a notification, telling me it was exactly how I sounded when I complained about another change she wanted in a house.

Usually it only went off for two reasons: a text from Torran or the ESPN app alerting me to the latest college football scores. But since the show started airing, the social media apps had gone berserk. At first, it was simple comments or questions about the changes to the house on Huckleberry Lane. People asking for renovation tips or inquiring about the stain used on the refinished staircase. In the last couple of weeks it'd gotten, well, a little weird.

People had started asking personal questions. How tall was I? Were my eyes really that gray or was it a filter? Most uncomfortably, was I single? And let's just say that once that floodgate opened, the propositions started flying.

I took in a long, slow breath and tried to push that worry out of my head. Tonight my only job was to follow through on my promise to Lou.

Once I was seated on the edge of the toilet, I cursed under my breath and worked the blue material up my hairy legs. Proof that I was willing to do just about anything to make my daughter happy.

Chapter Two

TESSA

In Hibernation For Way Too Long

'That's a good look on you. Please tell me where you found blue tights in your size,' I teased Manny as we walked past the tables set out in front of the Sugar Rush Café.

Only seconds after the owners, Barb and Susan, appeared with a tray of ghost-shaped donuts, the kids were gobbling them down. As Manny's daughter, Lou, and my girls, Iris and Rose, reached to take one, we both shoved napkins in their direction. We'd started doing this lately. Anticipating the exact same thing our kids needed. It was nice. Comforting.

'You're one to talk.' His gaze moved down my polyester blue-silver gown that pinched at my chest and hips. 'Although I have to admit in that wig you do make a pretty good Elsa.'

He gave me that familiar look. The one that said he was trying to be serious but instead made a laugh bubble in my throat.

I tried not to stare, but, man, he could give Henry Cavill a run for his money. And don't get me started on the blue tights, and the way the bottom half of his costume, which was about the size of a man's Speedo, hugged his thick thighs and other parts of his gorgeous body.

I quickly looked away, pretending to tug on my white wig that had shifted when I'd chased Iris and Rose down the sidewalk toward the town's main fountain. At seven and five, neither of my girls could make a decision on who would be Anna and who would be Elsa from *Frozen*. In a compromise, I'd agreed to be the older sister so both girls could be Anna.

'Pop, can I go check out the games with Iris and Rose?' Lou asked.

Poor Manny did look uncomfortable in his outfit, but Lou beamed at him like he was the real Man of Steel.

'Yes,' he said. 'But stay close by.'

She took off with the girls, her little cape flapping behind her. Manny's eyes held that hint of pain I'd learned to recognize over the last few years. He was thinking of Gina, his late wife, and what she was missing. I nudged his shoulder, needing to get him out of his head.

'That costume does suit you, Manny,' I said as we kept walking.

Inflatables of ghosts, goblins and vampires bobbed and swayed on every corner. Orange twinkle lights hung across big picture windows of the businesses that faced out to the square. Older folks sat in rocking chairs in front of the hardware store. Cauldrons filled with candy were perched on their laps as they waited for kids to stop.

'Since when is dressing in costume for Halloween a requirement for adults?' he said, shoving back his own red nylon cape.

Again, he did the Superman thing justice. His broad shoulders filled out the costume nicely, and the slicked-back black hair was a sexy touch, especially with the slight grays poking through. Most days, I only saw him in paint-splattered jeans and a ratty baseball cap when he was at a worksite with my sister.

'Don't get too far ahead,' I called to all the girls as they rushed past Minnie's Market, their dresses sweeping past stacked bales of hay and several carved jack-o'-lanterns set along the sidewalk.

This was one of the many reasons why I loved Ivy Falls. There wasn't a holiday people didn't celebrate, but Halloween was when my hometown went all out. Even the local business signs, usually filled with humorous sayings for our town contest, were holiday themed. The one outside Mimi's Pizza said *Witch Types of Toppings Do You Want?* and the Dairy Dip's read *Selling Over Twenty Flavors of Ice Scream!* My girls giggled at that one.

In front of the Ivy Falls Community Bank, my father stood with his bank manager and girlfriend, Isabel. They were dressed as Gatsby and Daisy. Dad looked perfect in his black starched suit. Isabel wore an elegant white flapper dress. Her lips were so red they rivaled the roses in the town's community garden. When they spotted the girls, they bent down and opened their arms, cradling all three of them and fawning over their costumes.

I stopped for a minute, watching the scene. Manny stood beside me, a bright smile lifting his ridiculously carved cheekbones.

'It's a perfect night,' he said, inching in closer, his hand twitching at his side like he wanted to lace his fingers between mine.

We'd been doing this dance for the last several months. Gently brushing past each other, poking sides when we told jokes. Doing anything and everything we could to innocently touch each other without actually committing.

Whenever we were with my sister Torran and her boyfriend Beck, they watched us with eager anticipation. Waiting for that moment when Manny and I would finally talk about what had been simmering between us since we'd first become friends.

I'd been ignoring the way my skin hummed every time he came to my bookstore, the Pen & Prose. How when we walked through a door together, he'd gently press his hand to the small of my back. The dormant parts of my lower body finally waking like they'd been in hibernation for way too long.

Every time I thought I'd be brave enough to say something, make the first move (which I knew he was waiting on), I hesitated. My soon-to-be ex-husband, Billy, had burned me so badly the scorch marks on my heart were just beginning to form scar tissue.

All the rational parts of my brain understood Manny would never hurt me, but when I let myself imagine what that future might look like, my bones went cold, and my stomach tumbled. From the beginning, he'd been a confidant, a friend, and I couldn't bear to lose what we'd built over the last year.

'Tess, did you hear me?'

I shook my head, shoving away all my fears, and met his fervent stare.

'You all right?' He gave me a steady look.

'Yes,' I stuttered. 'Just thinking about how much this town means to me.'

His lips thinned, and his hand twitched at his side again. His gentle sweetness was like a gravitational force pulling me in. I began to inch closer when a young woman I didn't recognize beelined down the sidewalk in our direction.

'Hi,' the girl gushed, tossing back her long blonde curls. 'Could I get a selfie? My friends and I are fans of your show, and they'd die to see you dressed like that.'

Manny's Adam's apple bobbed up and down. His panicked gaze shot to where Lou stood.

'I'm sorry,' I said, stepping in front of him. 'He's needed immediately at another event. Maybe another time.'

Before she could protest, or hold her phone up to take a picture anyway, I gripped his hand and raced toward the bank. When we reached our families, Dad arched a brow at me. 'That excited to bob for apples?'

'Yes, sure,' I said roughly.

As if sensing something was off, Isabel corralled the girls to the old wine barrels placed at the edge of the building.

'Let's go, Miles. Think we're going to need those towels too. Rose has been telling me for weeks she plans to submerge her entire head.'

Dad chuckled and said, 'That's the spirit,' before grabbing some beach towels off a wrought-iron bench and chasing after her.

Manny glanced down to where our hands were still clenched together. 'Thanks. Should I just call you my bodyguard now?'

'Can you afford me?' I teased.

He paused. Gave me that knee-wobbling hint of a smile. I'd caught him doing this a lot lately. Looking at me like he wanted to press the outline of me into his memory. As if I might disappear at any moment. A sad side effect of grief. Of losing someone you loved much too soon.

'We better go,' he finally said, releasing my hand. 'Lou is very competitive. If we don't moderate, she'll put her entire body in that barrel just to win.'

I jokingly hip-checked him. 'Gee, I wonder where she gets that from?'

'What?' he said innocently.

'Come on. I have never seen anyone get as invested in Rummikub as you do. It's like an obsession.'

Lou took off her crown and wrist cuffs and eyed the barrel with a grave look.

'Yep. We better go,' he said.

We hustled down the sidewalk and reached the corner at the same time as Beck and Torran appeared on the other side of the square.

They took one look at us and burst out laughing.

'Now that is what I call commitment, you two.' Beck grinned at us.

'Seriously, Manny. You are the only guy I know who can actually do that costume justice,' Torran joked.

'Oh, that's for sure.' Old Mrs Vanderpool appeared from out of nowhere and gave Manny an appraising look, which made all of us burst into another round of laughter.

Manny and Beck went to help Dad and Isabel with the apple bobbing. I tried to follow, but Torran grasped my arm and pulled me a few steps away.

'Costumes, huh?' There was a gleam in her eye I did not like.

'Yes,' I sighed. 'It *is* Halloween, you know.'

Her gaze moved to Manny in that costume that hugged him in all the right places. 'You two look good together.'

'Come on, Tor. Are we doing this again?'

'Doing what?' She feigned innocence.

'Trying to insinuate there's something between Manny and me. You know I'm still tangled up in all the legal stuff with Billy.'

She crossed her arms over her chest. Her defensive move every time the subject of my ex came up. 'Has he signed the divorce papers yet?'

I looked down at my dress and played with the edges.

'Tessa, it's been nearly two years.' Her voice went rough.

'My lawyer can't find him.'

Her mouth went hard. 'What do you mean?'

'He disappeared from that apartment he was living in with...' My throat went dry. 'With... her.'

Torran let out a deep sigh and rolled her eyes. 'Just when I think he can't become a bigger douche canoe, he proves me wrong.'

The sound of the girls' giggles and cheers floated toward us. 'I'm begging you. For tonight, let's forget all the drama and enjoy the fun. For the girls.'

I knew that would send an arrow straight to her heart.

'Fine, but if that man ever shows his face in this town again, he won't have only me to deal with.'

'Yeah, yeah, I know. You and the townspeople with torches and pitchforks,' I teased even as a knot tightened in my chest.

Chapter Three

TESSA

A True Superhero

Manny, Torran and Beck kept the girls busy with the beanbag toss game, while I went to check on the bookstore. Once I was in the door, I pulled in a shaky breath. With a crowd filling the square, I expected to find at least a dozen customers browsing the aisles, a few kids darting around the shelves with their parents fast on their heels, but only a few patrons sat in the overstuffed chairs. And even worse, not a single person was in line at the register.

Penny, the store manager, kept busy dusting the shelves. Her long blonde ponytail swung behind her as she moved from display to display. When she noticed me, she let out a loud snort.

'Elsa, huh?' she said, scanning me from head to toe. 'The wig is something too.'

'The girls' choice, of course.'

Her bright blue eyes lit up. 'Can I take a picture? It would be perfect for the store's social media accounts.'

She went for her phone in her back pocket, and I said, 'Don't you dare.'

'Okay, okay,' she laughed. 'Where are Rose and Iris? I was hoping to see them all dressed up.'

'They're out in the square with Manny and my sister.'

'What's his costume? He looked all kinds of hot in that Luke Skywalker outfit last year.'

Penny harbored a small crush on Manny that she was not very subtle about. When he came into the store, it was amusing to watch the two of them as he looked like a giant next to her almost uncanny resemblance to a tiny Alice in Wonderland.

When I looked away, pretending to straighten a display, she clucked her tongue.

'Oh, wow. With how red your cheeks are, this has to be good.' She ran to the window in front of the store and pressed her face to the glass.

I followed and quickly dragged her away. 'Fine, if you must know, he's dressed as Superman.'

'No, he is *not*!' There was that snort again. She tried to move back to the window, but I stepped into her path, needing to redirect her enthusiasm.

'How are sales today?'

Now she was the one who looked away.

'Penny,' I pressed.

Her freckled cheeks paled. 'Not great.'

'Even with all the work we did on that big window display? I thought all those cute Halloween picture books would bring people in.'

She gave a sad shake of her head. 'There's still time. We don't close for two more hours.'

She forced her voice to be hopeful, but I understood how the next few hours would go. If the store was this dead during the height of the festival, once the sun fell, traffic would slow to a crawl.

'You should go back outside and have fun with your girls.'

'All right,' I said reluctantly. 'There's extra fives and ones in the safe if you need more change.' I gave another cursory glance around the store. 'Not sure you'll need it though.'

'Go have one of Susan's ghost donuts. Maybe two. Things are under control here.'

'Thanks.'

I walked out the door and headed in the direction of where the games were set up near the fountain. A walnut-sized lump filled my throat as a group of teenagers sped past me. In front of the stores, people took photos of the decorations. Swapped gossip with their friends. The warm feeling in the square made me think of my mother. How much she'd loved Ivy Falls. I felt sick every time I considered how she'd entrusted her beloved bookstore to me and that I was failing her.

When I finally found my family, Manny was holding a thick beach towel and drying off Lou, who'd gone back to the apple-bobbing booth. According to him, she'd fully immersed herself in the barrel this time, intent on grabbing a shiny red apple.

For the rest of the afternoon, we kept the girls busy with more games and crafts, trying with no luck to steer them away from Miss Cheri, who ran the town theater, and Mrs Vanderpool, both of whom kept slipping them extra candy.

As soon as the sun faded into a night sky, the festival wound down. Torran and Beck said their goodbyes, along with Dad and Isabel. All three girls pulled us toward the neighborhoods to begin trick-or-treating.

The deeper we waded into the center of Ivy Falls, the more historic the houses became. The street before mine had more than one home that was built in the late nineteenth century. Some of them were in good shape. Others looked like if a good storm hit the town, they'd collapse into a pile of wood and bricks.

Manny and Torran's restoration work was a real gift to this town. I'd hoped the attention from their show would turn into more tourism and sales for the downtown shops like mine, but so far none of the businesses had seen a real change. When I asked Torran about it one night at dinner, she told me that Lauren, the show's producer, said it often took a while for a new program to find its audience. So far the numbers were trending up for *Meet Me in Ivy Falls*, but a second season would be where the town would really see a change. Sadly, I wasn't sure my store could hold on that long.

Dried fall leaves crunched beneath our feet as we tried to keep up with the girls. A few of the more festive neighbors had set up haunted houses in their garages, but my girls weren't quite old enough for that type of fright yet. When we were kids, Torran dragged me into one. I had nightmares for weeks after. Rose was already having issues at night, and I didn't need to add to that problem.

'Girls, don't run, you might fall,' I called.

'They're okay, Tess,' Manny said.

'I know they're fine, but it's hard not to be a helicopter parent when you're doing it alone.'

'A fact I know all too well,' he sighed.

I blew a wayward white hair away from my face. Maybe the Elsa wig was a little much. 'Sorry, if anyone understands my challenges, it's you.'

I hated the tremble in my voice. This was supposed to be a time for our kids to run free. Laugh. Play.

'Hey,' he said gently. 'What's going on?'

'I want the girls to enjoy today. The last thing they need is memories of their mother being sad and defeated, but it's hard to put on a brave face when you feel like your world is crumbling around you.'

'Any word from the bastard? I mean Billy.'

'No,' I huffed. 'And please don't call him that. Although it's accurate, I can't bear to have the girls hear it. They deserve to believe their father is a good man.'

'Tess, you can't hide the truth from them. They're both smart like you. Eventually, they'll understand what their father did was wrong. That his choices, especially taking off just before your mom passed, were selfish and cruel.'

'They're little girls,' I choked out. 'They deserve to believe, even if it's only for a short time, that their father is not a complete waste of space. That he decided a box-dye redhead with big boobs, a tight skirt and a cheap silver nose stud was more important than his own family. My job is to protect them from pain, and no matter how long I have to juggle the reality of our lives, I'll do it to keep them happy.'

Iris and Rose hopped down the steps at the next house. The gleam in their eyes was all that mattered. My soon-to-be ex-husband may have disappeared in the middle of the night, leaving only a note saying he was sorry he couldn't be a better man, but my children didn't need to know that cold, hard truth. They needed comfort, security, safety, and no matter how hard I had to work, I'd give it to them.

We continued to follow the girls down the street, and Manny let out a slow breath. 'Can I ask you one more thing?'

'Even if I said no, would it stop you?'

'Probably not,' he said with a teasing edge to his voice. 'Go ahead.'

'Has he at least sent you money to support the girls?'

'How about those Titans? Aren't they undefeated this season?' I mumbled, hoping he'd drop this topic.

'Tess, I'm not talking football with you.' His voice went firm. 'Billy should be helping, or you have to go to court without him. Tell a judge you need help. If you can't track him down, make him pay, he needs to go to jail.'

Jail. It was the last thing I wanted for my ex. When we first met in high school, he was such a sweet guy. Thoughtful. Attentive. At least when we were alone. Once we were around a crowd of people, he became a jerk. Like he thought he needed to perform in order to keep his friends.

When I got pregnant at nineteen with Iris, I thought he'd settle down after we got married, and he did for a while, becoming a good father to Iris and then Rose. He played dolls with them. Strummed his guitar to soothe them to sleep at night. But as time went by, and I took on more hours at the bookstore, something changed. He became angry. Distant. The note showed up on the kitchen counter just weeks before Rose's fourth birthday, and we hadn't seen him since.

'Please, can we *not* do this,' I said, suddenly very weary. 'For one night, I don't want the ghost of my idiot ex to ruin everything.'

Manny lifted his hands in surrender. 'You're right.'

'Thank you,' I said over the growing knot in my throat.

'Are you still thinking about changing the hours at the bookstore?' he asked, regret lingering in his tone.

'Nice change of subject. Real smooth.'

His lips twitched as he rubbed a hand behind his neck. It was hard to be annoyed with him. Since Billy left, he'd become our rock. Like he had a sixth sense, Manny would show up with Lou and a gallon of Caramel Ribbon ice cream when we'd had a rough day. When a hinge broke on a cabinet, or the garbage disposal leaked, it only took a single text before he showed up at my door with his toolbox.

When you trusted someone with your every breath, and they crushed your soul, how were you supposed to recover? Sure, you could move through the motions of life, but that didn't mean you were truly living. From the moment I'd read Billy's note, I'd felt trapped inside a bubble of despair. Unsure if I'd ever be able to force my way out of that existence.

'I'm still talking over more options for the store with my dad,' I said. 'We're trying to figure out ways to bring in new revenue but haven't come up with any good options.'

It was hard not to let my shoulders sink. The bookstore had been my mother's dream. At first, it had turned a regular profit, but in the last two years, foot traffic had stalled. We'd tried special programs like reward cards that would earn you a free book after ten punches. Added another story hour. Narrowed our hours on Sundays. But with their busy lives, people found it easier to order online now. At one time, the store had been the real hub of the square. Where everyone in town would come to relax, hold their book group meetings, but without my mom as the anchor, interest began to fade, and I didn't know how to turn it around. She'd been the warmth you needed on a cold winter's morning. The smile that turned an otherwise horrid afternoon into one you could manage. When she was gone, my family not only felt her loss, but the entire town did too.

'Don't worry,' Manny said, interrupting my thoughts. 'You're one of the smartest women I know. If anyone can figure this out, it's you.'

'I'd rather talk about anything else right now.'

'No, let's not avoid this.'

We walked down the sidewalk, and every few feet, a woman gave him the same look the young woman in the square did. Like they wanted to tear off his costume. See what was underneath. It made my skin itch in a way I didn't like. Those stares saw the man on TV who walked around in perfectly worn cargo pants. A baseball cap turned backwards when he was focused on a carpentry project like a new dining table or a refinished staircase. They had no clue he could sing on key to most of his favorite country songs. That his deep gray eyes always softened whenever he watched his daughter at play.

'What other ways can you bring in money?' His urgent voice brought me back to the conversation.

I ignored his question and countered with my own. 'Are we going to talk about *it*?'

'I thought we were talking about *it*.'

'No, I mean the looks you're getting from women as they pass. And that selfie request in the square was a little wild. Has that been happening more often?'

He turned away, hiding how his face flamed. *Meet Me in Ivy Falls* had turned him into the internet heartthrob known as 'Manny the Zaddy', and Torran and I teased him about it relentlessly.

'Quit changing the subject and tell me what you and your dad discussed.'

He flashed me a look of intensity that made the hairs on my arms stand on end. We were just friends, but when he stared at me like he'd slay a dragon to protect me, it was hard not to go weak-kneed. I pushed the thought, and wobbly feeling, out of my head. The two of us were buddies. Jokingly, I'd even started calling us SPPs. Single parent pals. That was all we could ever be.

'We haven't settled on anything yet,' I said, giving in. 'There's more research to do.'

He seemed satisfied with my answer, but it wasn't completely honest. Dad had laid out a few options for the store. Pull inventory back even more. Cut our hours again. Let go of a few staff members. Even closing the store altogether. That idea alone made the two mini candy bars in my stomach want to revolt.

Books had always been my thing. The tether that still connected me to my mother. The thought of doing anything else was so foreign I couldn't wrap my brain around it.

'Have you considered adding things that could complement the store? Candles or stationery? Even high-end paper for résumés and letters?'

I couldn't help the snort that left my mouth. 'Do people even write letters anymore?'

'I do. Well, I did. When Gina was alive, I made it a point to write her love letters.'

I was convinced Manny was the last romantic man on the planet. Billy thought if he did one load of laundry or emptied the dishwasher, he should be given some kind of medal. Or a blow job.

As we trailed behind the girls, Manny kept pushing back his cape. His chiseled jaw set like he was still mulling over ideas.

'What if I offered my services for free?' he said, almost too low for me to hear.

'To do what? Work the cash register?' The image of him trying to fit his bulky body behind the counter made me laugh.

'No. What if I built more seating? More spots for people to stay and read?'

'That's not the issue. It's them actually buying books.'

He tipped his chin down, chewing on his beautifully full lips.

Besides being a great contractor, Manny was also an amazing craftsman. What he'd done with the staircase in the house on Huckleberry Lane was truly a work of art. My mind spun with several ideas, and a jarring thought hit me.

'Could you build a coffee bar in the store?'

He arched a thick brow. 'Coffee bar?'

'Yes. It would encourage more people to come in. Hang out. Buy drinks *and* books.'

The idea spooled out in my mind like a fish taking off once hooked. It would mean more work. Getting a food service license. Finding a spot in the small store to put it. But it would entice people inside to spend money, which was not currently happening. Only problem was where was I going to get the funds for that kind of project? Maybe I'd spoken too soon.

'It's a good idea, Tess.' He placed his hands on my hips suddenly, steering me around a big puddle on the sidewalk. I tried not to react, but he smiled as he watched my arms dot with goosebumps. Once we were past the water, his hands lingered for a torturous moment before he pulled away.

'I don't know.' My voice trembled. 'Maybe I should come up with other options.'

'Hey,' he said in a warm voice that made my toes curl. 'It's just a thought, not a commitment.'

I shook away the tingling in my fingers and toes that always happened when he pinned me in place with his steely gray gaze.

The sound of a witch's cackle coming from a nearby speaker dragged me back to reality.

'Slow down. Don't get too far ahead,' I called to the girls again as they started to round the corner.

Manny nudged me with his elbow. 'Don't overthink the store, okay? It'll all work out.'

When I first met him, I didn't like his gruff tone as he worked side by side with my sister. But then I ran into him at the park one day with his daughter – a coincidence that felt more like a setup from Torran. It was hard to ignore how he followed Lou down the slides. His muscled body barely fitting along the plastic edges. The way he gently pushed her on the swings, encouraged her across the swinging bridge, melted my heart. He may have been built like a tank, but there was a sweet abandon to how he chased Lou through the grass. Circled her into a hug once he caught her. After that day, our single-parent status brought us together. We arranged play dates. Started relying on each other for free babysitting when one of us needed a break.

Manny and I had a good thing going. Adding anything physical would ruin it. And what would happen to our kids? Lou was like an older sister to the girls, and they, in turn, adored her. Besides, the idea of dating again sent another nauseous rumble through me.

'Lou and I were thinking about going apple-picking over at Breyer's farm next Sunday. You and the girls want to come along? They have those fried apple hand pies you love so much.'

'Are you trying to distract me from all my problems with promises of one of my all-time favorite foods?'

'Maaaybe,' he drew out, giving me a devious grin that made my mind race with very non-platonic thoughts.

'We're in,' I said a little too quickly as the girls raced to the next house. A few days before, Manny told them pillowcases held much more candy than their small buckets. Now they struggled to carry their loot as they moved to ring the next doorbell.

'When I was a kid, we'd run home, dump out our full bags, and hit the neighborhood for another round. We had candy all the way until Christmas most years.' His smile quickly brightened my mood.

'Only one round this year. Rose is already dragging.' I tipped my chin in the direction of my tiny blonde child, who dragged the weight of her bright purple pillowcase along the grass.

Three more houses and the girls agreed it was time to head home. Manny picked up a sleepy Rose and tossed her up onto his shoulder, looking like a true superhero. We walked in silence for a few breaths before he said, 'I can picture that brain of yours churning, thinking about all the reasons the coffee bar isn't a good idea, but I think you should discuss it with your dad. I bet he'd even help you get a small loan.'

His words fueled my racing brain. Great. Even more debt.

'What if I come by tomorrow morning? Walk the space and see if we can figure out a plan.'

A plan. It was a start, but the biggest challenge was getting my dad on board, which was never an easy task.

Chapter Four

MANNY

Teenagers Have No Clue

We walked the four blocks back to Tess' house as Rose began to snore quietly.

'Here, let me take her.' Tess tried to pull her from my arms, but she had enough of a challenge corralling Iris and Lou through the throngs of trick-or-treaters racing down the sidewalks.

'No. We're almost home,' I stuttered. 'I mean, we're almost to *your house*.'

She gave me a small grin as Iris said something about wanting to tear into her candy. Tess warned she'd get a tummy ache if she ate any more.

A few minutes later, we reached the front walk of Tess' house, a small yellow bungalow with a gray slate roof and crisp white shutters. Our eyes locked for a moment, and she cocked her head toward the house, inviting us in. I followed her up the brick path and through the front door.

'Go ahead and lay Rosie in bed. I'll be in after I get the girls settled.'

I walked down the short hall with Rose cradled in my arms. Pictures of Billy still hung on the walls. Tess had been through hell since he'd left, and although I wanted her to be angry with him, I couldn't force her to act in a way that wasn't in her nature.

Torran claimed Tess was ready to date, but the heart-breaking ache in her voice as she talked about her ex warned she was still nursing a bruised and battered heart. A part of me understood her hesitation about us. We had a good, solid friendship. Even so, I found myself dreaming about how she and the girls could become a larger part of our lives. We were already leaning on each other for babysitting and moral support, but I wanted more. Yet every time I toyed with the idea of telling her about my feelings, I pictured her pulling away, shutting me out, and that was the last thing I wanted.

I moved into the room the girls shared and set Rose on the bed with the dark purple bedspread covered in sweet pink flowers. In the corner sat another piece of Billy – an old Gibson acoustic guitar. Tess told me he used to sing the girls lullabies at night when he was actually home. When Tess tried to remove it one day, Iris had what Tess called a DEFCON 1 meltdown, and so it stayed. A bitter reminder of one man's poor choices.

Rose's small, sleepy murmurs sent another sharp ache through me. Everything about her, from the pale shade of her gold hair to the warmth of her brown eyes, reminded me of her father. How could a man leave behind this perfect life Tess had built for them? Two little girls who needed him so much? And Tess herself, who, to me, was the brightest star in the whole damn sky.

I stood and found her watching me from the doorway. The adoration shining in her eyes pulled all the breath from my lungs.

'The girls went to the family room to sort their candy.' She moved close, brushed against my side, and I almost lost my mind. 'Let me tuck Rose in and then how about some popcorn and a movie?'

'Sure,' I managed to choke out.

She gave me that smile like she'd climbed inside my head. Could tell that all I wanted was to snake a hand around her waist, pull her in and unleash the most devastating kiss on her lips.

'Pop, can I eat these Pixy Stix?' Lou called from the other room.

'Do not eat another piece of candy, Louisa Marie!'

'Uh-oh,' Tess laughed. 'It's the double name. You better go and check on them.'

I reluctantly pulled myself from the room and walked toward the kitchen. The tights were starting to chafe my legs, and the damn cape kept catching on doorknobs and chairs.

Lou and Iris sat on the floor in the family room, negotiating a swap between Skittles and peanut butter cups.

I headed into the kitchen to start the popcorn, and it only took a few steps before all the blood in my body drained to my toes. The back door sat open. A single pane in the leaded glass was deliberately shattered.

I spun around and lowered my voice. 'Lou, I need you to take Iris out the front door. Don't touch anything. Wait for me on the walkway.'

'What? Why, Pop? We're not done sorting our candy yet.'

'Right now, Louisa.'

She recognized the grave tone in my voice and pulled Iris back down the hallway.

My senses were on high alert. I scanned every corner of the room. Except for a random box of cereal on the counter, nothing looked out of place.

27

'Tess!' I called. She rushed down the hall and I met her halfway. 'I need you to pick up Rose and follow me outside.'

'But I just tucked her in,' she protested.

'Now. Please.' I forced my voice to be taut so she understood the seriousness of the situation. She went and scooped up Rose, and I followed her out of the house. With my hand curled around the material of my cape, I slammed the door shut. I'd watched enough cop shows to know I shouldn't touch anything.

Tess stopped ten steps from the door with Rose curled against her chest. 'Manny, what's going on?'

I held up a finger and spoke into my phone, reciting Tess' address to the sheriff's department. After the dispatcher confirmed a deputy was on his way, I ended the call.

Tess shook under the weight of worry. Instinct had me laying a warm hand against her back and encouraging her to take full, deep breaths.

'When I walked into the kitchen, I found the back door open. The center pane was busted out. Did you lock up before you left?'

'Of course I did. Ever since Billy, well, since we've been alone, I triple-check the doors and windows before we go anywhere. It's kind of dumb because it's Ivy Falls, but I do it anyway.'

'Mommy.' Iris' voice trembled. 'I'm scared.'

'Me too,' Lou echoed.

'It's okay, girls.' Tess did her best to keep her voice level.

'We're just being cautious. Don't worry,' I added, trying not to let panic tinge my own voice.

As we waited on the front lawn, Tess begged me not to call her sister, but before I could even get my fingers back on my phone, Torran blazed into the driveway, her old truck sputtering and coughing like usual. She jumped out of the driver's seat like her ass was on fire and Beck was right behind her.

Rose lifted her sleepy head, while Iris and Lou raced toward the couple's outstretched arms. I'd had some issues with Beck at first, and he'd made a few mistakes when he'd come back to town, but Torran was happier than I'd ever seen her. That made him okay in my book. It didn't hurt that Lou had a special fondness for him and the way he always asked about her animals and soccer games.

Before Tessa could utter a single word, Torran had her wrapped in a hug with Rose still clinging to her neck.

'Are you okay?' she asked.

'I'm fine.' Tess squirmed out of her sister's grasp and pulled the wig off her head. Her beautiful auburn hair tumbled over her shoulders. Even in the opaque haze of the outdoor lights, she was stunning.

'How did you know what was happening?' Tess asked.

Torran and Beck swapped a measured look.

Tessa grimaced. 'Let me guess, Deputy Ben called you?'

Torran's shrug was all the answer Tess needed. In small-town Ivy Falls, your business was pretty much everyone's business.

Torran's eyes locked on me. 'What happened? Tell me the full story.'

'Um, hello,' Tess said with an irritated huff. 'I'm right here. You can ask me.'

'You? The Queen of Everything Will Be Just Fine?' Torran shook her head. 'Manny will give it to me straight.'

Just as I opened my mouth, an Ivy Falls sheriff's car pulled up to the curb. Deputy Ben jumped out and hurried up the path.

'What's going on here, Manny?' His eyes pinched at the corners as he took in my costume.

'Someone's been in the house. When we came home from trick-or-treating, I found the back door open. Windowpane looks like it's been deliberately smashed out.'

'Did you see anyone lurking around when you came home?' Ben asked, adjusting his radio as it squawked.

'No. All I knew was I needed to get Tess and the girls out,' I said.

He gave a nod. 'That was the right thing to do. Let me go in and look around. For now, move closer to the street and wait there.'

He walked past us and entered the house with his hand pressed against his gun belt.

Torran coaxed Rose out of Tess' arms and held her niece softly against her shoulder. Beck clasped Lou's shoulders, giving her the reassuring comfort she needed. As a group, we shifted away from the house like Ben had instructed.

'Tessa, have you had problems like this before?' Torran asked firmly, like she knew her sister hid a lot of issues from her not wanting to cause any worry or trouble.

'No. My guess is it's neighborhood kids messing around. Remember when we were in high school, everyone used to egg houses? Toilet paper the trees. This was probably an accident. Not intentional.' Tess held Torran's steady stare, confirming she was telling the truth.

We waited in silence on the front lawn until Ben strode out the front door.

'It's all clear inside. Do the neighborhood kids know you're here alone with the girls, Tessa?'

She popped out a hip. 'It's Ivy Falls, Ben. What do you think?'

He shoved a hand through his dark hair. 'I'll write out a report, but I'd say this is a Halloween prank gone wrong.'

'Is it okay to go back inside?' Tess asked.

He rubbed a hand over his mouth. 'Maybe we should get a team out here. Look for fingerprints.'

'You just said this was a prank gone wrong,' Tess countered.

'I believe it was, but it's up to you what comes next.' Ben's gaze wavered between Tess and the door. 'Uh, after, well, you know, after Billy… did you change the locks?'

'Yes,' Tess said sharply. 'My father insisted on it.'

'The mayor's a smart man,' he said.

Rose's little snores grew louder as Torran began to rock slowly from side to side. Beck glanced her way and couldn't hide his look of adoration.

'I'll head to the car and write things up. Go inside and look around. If you notice anything missing, come out and let me know. I'll include it in the report for insurance purposes.'

'Thank you,' Tess sighed. 'And please… don't tell my dad. I'll let him know the details in the morning.'

'Oh, of course.' He shifted uncomfortably on his feet. Gave a guilty glance to Torran. 'But you know how quick news travels around here.'

He offered a weak smile and strode back toward his patrol car.

'Tessa,' Torran said with a firm tone. 'Did you really change the locks?'

Fire built behind Tess' eyes. 'Yes. It was hard to do, but necessary.'

'Hey,' I said, interrupting their tense moment. 'Tor, why don't you go inside and help her take a look around.'

'We'll all help.' Beck pointed to his back, and Lou quickly jumped on. She giggled as he trotted into the house. Torran was right behind him with Rose in her arms. A sleepy Iris trailed after them.

As soon as they were gone, I walked down the brick-paved path to Ben's patrol car. When he saw me approach, he stepped out.

'Tell me the truth. Do you think it was a prank or a break-in?'

He rubbed a hand over his mouth. 'If I had to guess, I'd say it was kids. We haven't had a burglary or vandalism incident since...' He broke off like he didn't want to broach a touchy subject.

After we'd almost finished restoring the house on Huckleberry Lane, it was trashed by vandals because of Piper Townsend, Beck's sister. She was doing well now. Been sober for over a year and was working at Sugar Rush. It was an incident we all wanted to put behind us.

'She's okay here, Manny. Safe. I've known Tessa since we were kids. If I thought she was in any danger, I'd let you know.'

I blew out a rough breath, and Ben smiled.

'You're good for her. She knows it too. Just give it time.'

'Did I ask you for relationship advice?' I said with a little too much snark.

'Nope, but you know Ivy Falls. There is a little bit of busybody in all of us.'

He chuckled and went back to his car. From the front lawn, I watched Tess and Torran move around the kitchen.

I'd worried for a while how Tessa would hold up after all the things in her world began to crumble. I was glad she had so many people around for support, even if she didn't always say yes to it.

I got it. She was trying to figure it out all on her own. I'd tried to do the same after I lost Gina, and it sent me to a dark place. A dark place that almost cost me Lou. I knew all too well that without family and friends, things could go downhill fast.

Next time I saw Tessa's dad, I'd have to thank him for insisting she change the locks. He could be a pain in the ass at times, but he always had his girls' best interests at heart, even if he didn't deliver those sentiments in exactly the kindest way. He had lightened up, though, over the last year, especially after he and Torran agreed to be easier on each other.

Once I walked back inside, I checked the back door, ensuring the bottom lock was intact.

'The glass will be a pain to fix.' Tess said, her quivering chin tipping to the jagged shards littering the wood floor. She moved around the small kitchen, picking up the box of cereal on the counter. Her mouth thinned.

'Problem?' Torran asked.

Tess stared at her sister for a long minute. 'No, it's only that I didn't think we had a box of this anymore.' She turned and smashed the entire carton into the trash.

Torran shot me a worried look before she tapped Tess on the elbow. 'Let's go tuck in the girls.'

'You go ahead. I want to ask Manny a question.'

Torran gave a nod and disappeared down the hall.

'There's extra scraps of lumber in my truck,' I said. 'I'll patch the window tonight. Come back with a new pane tomorrow and fix it. It'll be okay, Tess.'

'Why'd they have to break it? Don't they know custom glass is expensive?'

'I'm pretty sure teenagers have no clue what glass costs.'

'Well, they should,' she huffed. 'If I find out who did this, they are in a world of trouble.'

I couldn't help but smirk. 'Love your tough side, Tess.'

She bumped my shoulder, and her smile faded. 'I did change the locks, because even if he returned to Ivy Falls, I wouldn't want him here.'

All my instincts screamed that I should ask to stay on the couch tonight. Have Lou bunk with the girls. But acting overprotective said I didn't think she could handle this situation on her own. That was the last thing I wanted her to believe about me, even if the troubling scene nagged at me. Warned the break-in was much more than a teenage prank.

Chapter Five

TESSA

Coffee Has A Hell Of A Markup

The low beeping of the alarm bounced against the walls of the Pen & Prose. I moved to the panel located near the front door and punched in the code. I waited a beat, looking at the lit-up numbers. Maybe I should have an alarm installed at the house.

I shook off the ridiculous idea. This was small-town Tennessee, where the most dramatic thing that happened was when someone had one too many at the Pool and Brew. Hardly anyone locked their doors. The more I thought about it, the more I believed the break-in was a prank done by teenagers, who had way too much time on their hands.

I headed back to the office, turning on lights as I walked past velvet-covered love seats and thick upholstered high-back chairs. My mother had a knack for interior design, and this store was proof of that talent. Torran often said the space felt like an old English study with its dark paneled walls and warm furnishings in shades of scarlet red and thunderstorm gray. The solid dark walnut shelves always polished and dust-free. Mom even set up the register in the center of the room, so it was easy to find, and highlighted a row of displays that featured the new hardcover fiction releases.

This place felt as much like home as my own little bungalow did. A creeping ache filled my throat as I paced around the store and headed back to the non-fiction section. I let my gaze wander along the exposed brick walls, considering how I'd move the shelves, possibly use the space for a coffee bar.

A quick thought doused the idea. Would having coffee here hurt Barb and Susan's business over at Sugar Rush? Competing with them in any way sent my stomach into a swirl. I'd already lost enough money to the chain stores and online retailers. The idea that I could take anything away from them made me doubt this plan again.

After dropping my bag and keys in the office, I went to the safe and pulled out the cash for the register and returned to the front of the store. When I reached the counter, the bell over the door jingled. I expected Penny's round, freckled face, but the sound of firm footsteps made my pulse speed up. I'd have known the cadence of that stride anywhere.

'Hi, Dad,' I said before he could round the corner.

When he stepped into view, I braced myself. The corners of his eyes pinched. His mouth sat in an unpleasant line. He didn't have to say a word. It was clear he already knew about the break-in.

'Tessa.' His shoulders went tight around his ears, but he waited a beat like he was talking himself out of whatever churlish response was forming in his head. That talk he and Torran had a while ago about easing up on his 'Mr Mayor' attitude was taking root nicely. 'How are you?' His voice hung heavy with worry, and it knocked me back a bit. He had enough happening in his life with trying to run the bank *and* the town.

'By the grim look on your face, I'd say you know about last night.'

He slid his hands over the polished wood on the counter. 'I may have heard something about it at town hall this morning.'

'Deputy Ben,' I cursed under my breath.

'No. It was actually Stina, last night's dispatcher. She came in to bring Isabel coffee this morning. She thought I already knew. That my daughter would have called and told me.'

There was the 'mayor' voice.

'Don't freak out. It was kids playing a Halloween prank. That's all.'

'I know it's kids being dumb. Remember when you and Torran were in high school, and those football boys terrified all the old ladies in town by planting scarecrows in their front yards? Heard about that nonsense for weeks.'

I bit my tongue, not wanting to remind him that even though he didn't play football, Billy was a part of that stupid stunt.

'Is it true they broke out a pane in your back door?'

'It's fine. When I left the house this morning with the girls, Manny was already there measuring for a new piece of glass.'

'Still, it wouldn't be a bad idea to put one of those camera doorbells up at your house. Here too for safety purposes. Maybe Manny could help with that.'

His gaze lingered too long. Like Torran, he'd made more than one comment about Manny's crush, but I ignored it. I was concerned with exactly three things in my life right now: my home, my business and my girls. There wasn't room in my life for anything else.

'About him,' I started, and his eyes lit up.

Yep. He was definitely Team Manny.

'Last night after we left the festival, we started talking about new sources of revenue for this place. I mentioned that if we built a coffee bar, it'd bring in more money.'

'A coffee bar?' He arched a brow. 'I think it would be simpler to start with cutting staff. Lowering your inventory numbers.'

'This is a *book*store, Dad. Not buying inventory only means people will come in, not find what they want, and turn around and purchase from online retailers. Or, they'll drive to Nashville and buy from a big box store. The key is to get them in the door and keep them here.'

He ran a hand over his perfectly combed silver-white hair and started to pace. I was sure if I cracked his head open I'd witness his brain smoking from all the overthinking he was doing.

'How would you pay for it?'

This was the part I did not want to broach with him. I'd been up most of the night thinking about it. After Deputy Ben left, along with Torran and Beck, Manny boarded up the hole in the window. A hesitant look, like he wanted to stay, keep us protected, crossed his face, but I pushed him out the door, insisting he take Lou home.

In the late-night hours, I went through my business finances. Pulled out the paperwork on my mortgage. After my mother passed, she'd not only willed me the store but given me a small chunk of money that had been an inheritance from her own parents. With Dad's blessing, I'd used that money to pay off the mortgage on my little bungalow.

'I was thinking I could use the house as collateral for a small business loan.'

His pacing in front of the register grew more frantic. 'I guess that could work, but have you done any research? There are permits required, and you'd have to work with the state on getting a food service license.'

'Yes, I already started looking into it.' I moved around the register and walked right into his path. 'This makes sense. I can operate on a tight budget, and after reading a few things online last night, I learned the markup on coffee is eighty percent. That's thirty percent higher than the markup for books.'

'And the construction? It would slow down business here even more. Are you sure that's what you want?'

'Manny offered to do the work at night and on weekends when he's not at the old Thomas Place.'

'And my guess is your sister would pitch in too.'

'Not sure I could keep her away,' I admitted.

His grimace morphed into a faint smile. 'You're right about that.'

'There is one issue I'm worried about though.'

'Just one?'

I expected his mood to turn sour again, but there was a hint of teasing in his voice. Yeah, the changes in him were still a bit shocking.

'Barb and Susan. Do you think they'll be upset about me having a coffee bar?'

He tapped a finger against his sharp chin. 'They're only open until two in the afternoon. And I imagine you wouldn't start serving coffee until late morning, which would mean you're not taking away their breakfast business.' He hesitated. 'But, as a good neighbor and business owner, I suggest you talk to them before you make any firm plans.'

I bounced on my toes, not expecting this kind of response from him. 'So, you think it's a good idea?'

'Let's run some numbers and see how things look,' he said in a cautious tone.

'That's not a no,' I said with a little too much hope in my voice. 'But I insist you treat me like other customers. Put me through the regular loan application process.'

'Tessa,' he sighed. 'Let me give you the money. Consider it an investment.'

'No. I need to do this the professional way as a small-business owner. And if you won't consider that, I can talk to some banks in Nashville.'

'All right.' He heaved out a weighted breath. 'I can never win an argument with you girls anymore.'

The bell over the door jingled again. Manny walked into view with Penny on his heels. Her eyes narrowed at the way his butt filled out his cargo work pants.

I pressed my hand to my mouth, shook my head. She wasn't the only one stunned by the sight.

'Manny, glad you were there with Tessa and the girls last night.' Dad stepped forward and shook his hand.

'Of course, sir,' Manny replied, fully knowing where Penny's eyes were still focused. He finally looked over his shoulder, and Penny giggled before rushing off to put her purse down in the office.

Manny shot a quick look in my direction. The pinch to his brow said he was curious as to why my father was here so early.

'Stina, the police dispatcher,' was all I had to say.

He gave an understanding nod. 'I already ordered the glass for the back door, sir. It'll be fixed by the end of the day,' he said, anticipating Dad's next question.

Manny's phone buzzed in his pocket, and he ignored it.

'To be on the safe side, I'll have Deputy Ben ask around,' Dad said. 'See if he can pin down who broke in. At least if we discover the culprits, we can get them to pay for the cost of the glass.'

'Dad, please let it go. I'm sure you have other "mayoral" things on your plate.'

That grimace flashed at me again. 'Yes, that's true. That Lauren woman from the TV network is coming to the office after lunch to talk about closing the streets to shoot some more footage for,' he turned to Manny, 'your second season.'

I expected Manny to smile. He and Torran had been talking about plans for the old Thomas Place for a while. Instead, his face went tight, and his phone continued to buzz in his pocket.

'Do you need to get that?' I asked.

'No,' he said too quickly. 'Did you tell him about the coffee bar?'

'Yes. We've already agreed I'm going to apply for a small loan.'

'I can do the work with limited funds, sir. It'll only take a small crew. We'll get it done quickly.'

'Don't you have a lot on your plate right now?' Dad said. 'And for heaven's sake, stop calling me "sir". You're making me feel ancient.'

'I can always make time for Tess, sir.' Manny paused. 'What I mean is, it should be an easy build. And the bar will create the influx of cash Tess needs.' This time, his watch beeped, and again, he ignored it. 'What spot were you thinking about, Tess?'

'Over near the non-fiction shelves against the wide brick wall.'

'Good. I'll head that way.' He gave a nod to Dad and strode toward the back of the store.

'It's nice you have someone like him on your side.'

'Goodbye, Dad. I'll call you later, and we can talk more about the loan.'

'Tess,' he started. I waited for him to say something about how I was in over my head on this. How I should make better business decisions. Instead, he said, 'I'm glad you and the girls are all right. I was worried.'

'We're okay. Thanks for coming by.' I reached out and squeezed his hand. He gave a quick squeeze back and left out the front door.

Penny moved out of the office and headed for the register, getting everything set up for the day. She'd graduated from Lipscomb a little over a year ago and still wasn't sure what she wanted to do. She was into reading and had a pretty robust online presence where she talked all things books. I'd have loved to keep her as an employee for as long as possible, but there was a sparkle in her eye that warned she was meant for bigger things than Ivy Falls.

I met Manny at the back of the store. He mumbled under his breath as he took notes on his phone.

'Thanks for your help with my dad.'

'He's a good businessman. Give him time, and he'll get on board.'

'I hope you're right.'

Even though I tried to hide it, he heard the tremor in my voice.

'Tess, I've got your back on this. We can make it work. Once it's done, it's going to be perfect.'

I gave him a reluctant smile, and turned my attention to the shelves and displays that would have to be moved.

Another quiet beat passed before he said, 'Okay, what's really bugging you?'

I held on to my spiraling thoughts, not wanting to sound defeated or scared. This was my business. I should be confident. Self-assured. But there were still moments when I questioned whether my mother had made the right choice in giving me the store, running something that was precious to both her and the community.

'Tess, you can tell me anything.' His intense stare said I didn't have to hide what I was feeling. That he was always a safe space to land.

'Do you think people in this town believe I'm weak? That they tell all the details of my life to my father because they feel like I can't handle my own problems?'

'No. People don't see you that way.' He brushed back a stray hair from my cheek, sending a snapping heat across my skin. 'They're like me. They care about you. Want to make sure you're okay.'

'I guess you could be right.'

He tipped up my chin. His breath soft on my cheeks. 'You've got this. We'll do it hand in hand. You won't be alone.'

We stared at each other for a long beat. The flicker of many things washing across his face. Hope. Encouragement. Desire. I wondered if he could see the same things in my eyes.

His phone buzzed in his pocket again, and he let me go. The heat of him slowly fading in a way that made me ache. He turned away, focusing back on the wall. That faint buzz continued in an annoying rhythm.

'Why aren't you answering your texts? Torran will be mad if you keep ignoring her.'

'They are *not* texts from your sister,' he grumbled like a tired old bear.

'Who are they from?'

'No one important.'

I didn't like that he wouldn't look at me. A sudden thought made my heart skip a beat. Was he dating someone? Torran told me the guys on their crew kept saying he needed to set up a profile on a dating app. I tried not to picture him with other women, but he was an attractive guy, and I was sure he was tired of waiting on me.

'Manny.' My voice went thin. 'What's going on?'

'I've been meaning to ask you about how to do that Dutch braid. Lou keeps talking to me about it.' He frantically scratched his hands through his dark hair. 'I swear I've watched those YouTube videos dozens of times and still can't figure out how they get the hair to look good.'

Another deflection.

I finally reached out and touched his hand. 'Who are the texts from?'

His shoulders gave just enough for me to know he was carrying so much weight. Guilt clung to me. He was already busy with the new house, and Lou, and here I was asking him for one more thing. Taking up even more of his time.

'They're not texts but social media notifications,' he finally confessed.

His phone buzzed again. Once. Twice. Three times. I hated to admit his answer was a relief.

'How many are you getting a day?'

'I'm not sure if there is electric or water behind this wall. I'll have to look at the original plans to see.'

Did he really think I was going to let this go?

'Manny.' I stepped into his space. The delicious scent of him – soap and steel – washed over me. 'How many notifications?'

He held out his phone like it was a poisonous snake. As soon as I touched it, the screen lit up with over two dozen alerts.

Well, shit.

Chapter Six

MANNY

Do Not Slide Into My DMs

'I can't believe you're tagged in all of these.'

I didn't like the quiver in Tess' voice. Hell, I hated any time she wasn't smiling and happy. And those bluish shadows under her eyes warned she hadn't slept well last night. Maybe I should have asked to stay, but I was taking my cues from her, and by her body language, and the way she shuffled me and Lou out the door, it was clear she'd wanted to be alone. Needed time to think.

'Yep. The alerts have been going off all morning,' I confessed. 'I'd turn off the damn phone if I didn't need to stay available in case Lou needs me.'

'That girl from the square who wanted a selfie.' Her voice went firm as she stared at my screen. 'Even though we asked her not to, she still took a picture of you at the festival and posted it.'

I should have known better than to wear that costume in public. Usually I only had to deal with town gossip, but thanks to social media, my choice had turned into a total nightmare.

'She wasn't the only one,' I huffed, not wanting to discuss the dozens of other images I'd been tagged in. Thank God Lou wasn't in any of them.

'Can I scroll through?' she asked.

I gave a curt nod. From her sudden stuttering breaths, it was obvious she'd gotten to the numerous propositions and requests for inappropriate photos.

'Did you see this one?' she said with a roughness that chilled me. 'You're not tagged, but there's a specific hashtag the fans use for you.'

Yeah, I knew about the 'Manny the Zaddy' bullshit.

'The picture is a candid. It was taken from across the square, but it's clearly you pulling Lou out of the apple-bobbing barrel.'

'What?' My voice broke as I took the phone.

Sure enough, @mannyfan912 had posted a picture of Lou in a towel after her apple-bobbing escapade. The caption read:

Manny the Zaddy is really the cutest daddy.

'No,' I spat out. 'How can people be okay with posting pictures of my child?'

'Unfortunately, there are people who have zero morals when it comes to posting anything about a celebrity.'

'Celebrity?' I choked on the word. 'Tess, I am *not* a celebrity.'

She ran a warm hand down my arm, and I wished it slowed my racing heart, but seeing the photo set off alarm bells in my head.

'Can I get the person to take it down?'

Her lips thinned. 'Probably not.'

'I could reach out. Say I don't want pictures of my child shared online.'

She gave me a pained gaze. 'Sadly, I think any communication with this person could only lead to more issues. Encourage her to be even more thoughtless.'

When Torran and I agreed to do our TV show, I never thought people would take notice of me. I wore ratty baseball caps. Wood stain usually colored my fingers and nails. And most days, I didn't shave because I was too busy feeding our animals. Making sure Lou had her backpack and lunch before we raced out the door for school.

I purposefully stayed in the background while Torran did most of the on-camera work. There were a few situations when I had to explain how we'd refinished the kitchen cabinets, or talk about the hours it took me to restore the home's staircase, but for the most part, I let Torran be the face of the show.

Unfortunately, my attempts at anonymity hadn't worked. As soon as Episode Two – titled 'To Replace or to Refinish; That is The Question' (corny, yes, I know) – aired, both our business and social media platforms blew up. One day I had 140 followers, the next it was closer to 15,000. I hadn't bothered to look recently – too afraid, I guess – but Torran's account was close to 400,000. Thinking about that number made my head hurt.

The majority of the comments and direct messages made me shudder. Some people were kind. Wanted to compliment the show. But most of the DMs were so inappropriate, I started locking my phone, too afraid Lou would see some of the propositions which ranged from marriage proposals to sexual positions I was sure weren't possible, no matter how flexible you claimed to be.

I'd spent most of my life flying under the radar, keeping my head down and giving Lou the most normal childhood possible. The show was a way for Torran and me to save the important houses in Ivy Falls, as well as bring business to our little town that had been struggling financially for years. Never in my wildest dreams had I thought the attention would become this overwhelming or ridiculous.

Now that someone had posted a photo of Lou, the whole situation made me more uncomfortable than the rash I got after I bought that generic laundry soap at Minnie's Market.

'You can start calming things down by asking Lauren to turn off the show's comments,' Tess said.

She chewed on her bottom lip. The nervous twitch in her cheek was barely visible if you didn't know to look for it – but I knew all of her tells. When she was nervous, her leg did a little bounce. If she was deep in thought, she'd pull some hair off her shoulder and twist it around her pinkie. Each day I noticed something new about her, and I loved every moment she let me be in her orbit.

'Do you still have that account you made so your in-laws could see pictures of Lou?'

'Hell, is that a problem too?'

She grimaced and tapped at my phone again. A second later she turned the screen to me. 'I set it to private. No one can get access now unless you approve them.'

'How do you know how to do that?'

She went back to scrolling. 'Once I took over the store, I started social media accounts to promote events, new releases and author visits. Every once in a while, we get an inappropriate comment or direct message, which I quickly block and delete.'

'I didn't think about people being so... bold. This all happened so fast. Too fast.'

'I'm sure Torran is getting this kind of stuff too. Both of you should discuss this with Lauren. Ensure the Hearth and Home network is protecting your privacy.'

'We're supposed to see Lauren later today after she finishes meeting with your dad. She wants to talk about the "run and gun" style the film crew wants to use to shoot this season.'

'Look at you being all fancy with the lingo,' she teased.

I shrugged. 'When you're around the crew for long hours, you pick it up.'

'Well, *now* you're learning about the dos and don'ts of social media.'

She handed me back my phone, giving me that sweet-as-sunshine smile that made my brain go fuzzy. I followed her to the back wall, where she ran her hand over the exposed brick.

'What do you think about this space for the coffee bar? We'll have to move some displays and shelves. Rearrange a few things about the layout of the store.'

Light flooded in through a small transom window, turning her hair a deep red as she kept talking. It would be so easy to reach out and cup my hand around the back of her soft neck. Pull her into a deep kiss that made her breath hitch. It was something I'd been dreaming about for a while. Wanting for much longer than that.

I must have stared at her for too long, because she reached out and waved a hand in front of my face. 'Manny, did you hear me?'

'Yeah,' I lied. 'But say it for me one more time.'

She gave an exasperated sigh. 'I asked if the space would work. How much demo there'll need to be.'

'Who's the one throwing out the lingo now?' I teased.

She laughed, and I swear a squadron of jets took flight in my chest.

'I'll get the original plans. Take a look at this section and make sure there isn't an issue with load-bearing.'

'I trust you with whatever you need to do.'

She beamed that bright smile again, and I nearly lost my mind with ache. With each passing day, it grew harder to be around Tess. The light in her eyes, her bubbly laugh, were things I craved. I knew she was still struggling with raising her girls alone. Hurt by what her ex had pulled. But I wasn't sure how long I could continue to stay in the friend zone with her. Stand so close as her rose and spice scent washed over me and not touch her, not whisper in her ear all the ways I wanted to show her how I felt.

I'd lost Gina nine years ago, and my heart had fewer cracks these days. Time spackling over the parts that used to have dark, deep crevices. I was ready for companionship, possibly love. I wanted that chance with Tess. She'd woven her way into our lives so seamlessly. I woke up thinking about her and all the ways I could make excuses to stop by the bookstore. How we could take her girls and Lou to a movie, or to the Dairy Dip for their favorite ice cream. At night, her gentle blue eyes were the last thing I pictured before I went to sleep.

It was getting increasingly difficult to keep my mouth shut, swallow down my growing feelings while I was around her, but there was an unseen line she'd drawn for us, and I refused to cross it until she invited me into a more intimate part of her life.

'You sure you're okay?' she said as if sensing my mood change.

'Yeah, I'm all good.' I swallowed back all the things I wanted to say. 'Are we still on to take the girls apple-picking on Sunday?'

'Of course. We can't wait.'

The sweet tone in her voice shot heat to several spots in my body. My mind racing back to that kiss I wanted so badly.

'Gotta go,' I mumbled. 'Your sister is waiting for me at the old Thomas Place.'

I shoved my phone back into my pocket, ignoring the continuing alerts, and not letting myself wish that one of those proposition texts was from her.

Chapter Seven

TESSA

Keep It Simple

Fall was my favorite season. Once Halloween was over, there was a sudden bite to the air in Ivy Falls. Russet and gold leaves fell lazily from the trees. Instead of summer smells like lemonade and ice cream streaming out of stores, the air turned rich with the scent of brewing coffee and wood-burning stoves.

With Dad's help, I'd applied for the loan for the coffee bar. It was easier than I expected, but one problem still thrummed in the back of my head. Before I could truly move ahead with changes for the store, there was an issue I had to resolve.

A car rolled through the town's single stoplight as I walked past the antique store and around the square where Mrs Vanderpool was taking her regular rest from walking Baby, her Teacup Yorkie. She'd slowed down a bit over the last year, and I was glad to see she was still getting outside with her dog, who was more like a child than a pet.

You couldn't walk past Sugar Rush and not pause to read the sign. Barb and Susan had won the town's 'The Sign Says It All' competition for the last two years. Today's read: *A little bit spicy. A little bit sweet. Come inside for a tasty treat!*

The scent of cooking dough and warm spices instantly drained the stress from my bones as I walked inside the café. My mother loved this place. The way the steel tables and peony-pink wallpaper made the space feel homey. How the domed glass cases were crammed with dozens of sweet treats. When Miss Pat owned the store, we came here with Mom every Saturday morning. She called it her 'daughter time', and Torran and I soaked up every minute with her.

'Hey, Tessa!' Piper greeted me from behind the counter.

Beck's sister had endured a lot of trauma in her life, been to rehab several times, but somehow she'd moved to the other side of it. Settling down in Ivy Falls, taking the job here with Barb and Susan, even signing up for classes at the local community college. More than once at family dinners, she'd mentioned wanting to find a place of her own. Beck and Torran always objected, saying they enjoyed having her around the big, rambling house on Huckleberry Lane they now called home.

Piper's gaze darted around me. 'Where are the girls today?'

'In school. They don't get out until two.'

'Oh, that's right.' She paused, and I knew that look. Thanks to the Ivy Falls gossip train, she'd heard about the break-in too.

'Are Barb and Susan here?' I said quickly.

'Yep. They're in the office squabbling over new table-cloths. Barb wants to order the same ones we already have. Susan wants to spruce things up a bit.'

Ever since Barb and Susan purchased the shop from Miss Pat, this had been an ongoing issue. Barb was a traditionalist. Said that people liked the way the café was now. That it shouldn't be fixed if it wasn't broken. Susan, on the other hand, had a vision for a new and shinier version of the café. Tablecloths were only the start of their squabbles.

This was a bad idea. They were busy. I'd come back another time.

'Oh, okay. I shouldn't interrupt.'

'It's not a problem,' Piper chirped. 'I'll go get them.'

Before I could protest, she was weaving her way past the stainless steel ovens and walk-in refrigerator, stopping at an open door and poking her head inside. Less than a minute later, Barb appeared. This week her hair was the color of grape soda and piled high atop her head.

'What's going on, Tessa?' Her eyes darted to the racks of treats cooling behind her. 'I've got sugar cookies fresh out of the oven. Want to take some to the girls?'

'Thanks, Barb. I appreciate you thinking about them.'

This was going to be a nightmare.

'Uh, I was wondering...' My throat went dry. Having this conversation with her and Susan was the last thing I wanted to do. What if they got angry about me building a coffee bar? Thought I was trying to take business away from them?

Since they'd come to Ivy Falls, they'd become an important part of the community. Their leftover pastries always went straight to the local food bank. On Sundays, they held dinners at their house for the older widowed folks in town like Mrs Vanderpool and Silvio from the hardware store. They never missed one of the girls' soccer games, and they'd held viewing parties here for Torran and Manny's show.

Barb quirked a thick penciled-in brow at me as she waited.

'I was hoping you and Susan might have a minute to talk to me about an idea I have.'

Barb called to Susan, who walked out of the back office. Her black bob, sprinkled with flecks of silver, swayed against her shoulders.

'Hey, Tessa!' she crowed happily, her warm brown cheeks bunching up into a smile.

The knot in my gut twisted into a pretzel. Not the small ones in the chip aisle at Minnie's Market, but a thick, twisty one like you bought at a Titans' football game.

'Can we talk at a table? Maybe one with a little privacy?'

They gave each other a weighted stare before moving to a quiet back corner of the café. Before our butts fully hit the seats, Barb said, 'What's wrong? Is it the girls? Did someone try to break into your house again? Are you locking your doors?'

Susan reached out and pressed her hand to Barb's arm, covering her shiny mermaid tattoo. 'Give her a minute, babe. She'll tell us why she's here.'

I clasped my hands in my lap. Took a solid breath. Mom always said the best way to ask for something was to keep it simple.

'I know the gossip around here is fierce, and you both already know I'm having some financial troubles with the P&P.'

They kept their faces schooled like they didn't know, but the tic in Susan's cheek, and the way Barb's lips thinned, gave them away.

'Sadly, yes,' Barb finally spoke. 'What can we do to help?'

'Well,' I hedged. 'I have a plan to generate more busi-ness, but it's complicated.'

'Oh, sweetheart, we'll support whatever you want to do,' Susan said sweetly.

'I need to bring in more customers. Figure out another revenue stream. Manny and I were talking, and he offered to help build a coffee bar. I discussed it with my dad. He agreed that it might help get more people in the store.'

The color drained from Barb's rouged cheeks, and Susan let out a conflicted squeak.

As if the entire café was listening, the room went pin-drop silent.

This was bad. I was an idiot. Why did I ever think they'd say it was okay?

Barb drummed her fingers on the tabletop. Susan looked at her shoes. She was about as good at conflict as I was.

'It wouldn't draw too much business away from here because I don't open until ten, and you close around two.' Even to my own ears, I sounded weak and desperate.

Barb stayed quiet, which made me all the more nervous because she had a comment for everything. She yelled at contractors when they walked muddy boots across the café floors. Wagged a finger at Silvio when he put too much sugar in his coffee, because she knew he was having issues with his health. More than once, she'd whispered not so quietly to Beck that he should get off his backside and 'put a ring on it' with Torran.

'Well, uh, that's uh, great, honey.' Barb's brittle tone said she thought it was anything but great. 'Susan and I appreciate you discussing it with us.'

'Your friendship means a lot to me, and I wanted to be honest about what I was planning.'

Barb gave a firm nod and pushed back from the table. 'We've got more paperwork to go over in the office.'

Susan stood and hesitated. 'Are you…' She shoved her hands into the pockets of her carnation-pink apron. 'Will you serve food too?'

'No. Just coffee and maybe a few varieties of tea.'

'Okay,' she said quietly and followed Barb back to the kitchen.

I sank lower in my seat. Stares from the other tables flicked in my direction, and I swore I saw judgment in everyone's eyes. This was a total mess. The coffee bar would never work if people in Ivy Falls didn't accept it.

An out-of-towner moved into the square five years ago and set up a smoke shop. Mrs Vanderpool let everyone know through the town whisper network that she'd skewer anyone who went inside. The place lasted less than six months before it closed.

I pushed back from the table and raced out the door, swallowing down my tears.

It was times like these I needed my mother. The ache of losing her was still rooted so deep in my bones that the grief often made me lose my breath. I rushed down the sidewalk, not bothering to look where I was going, and slammed straight into a wall of hard muscle.

'Hey.' The low growl of a voice I'd know anywhere forced me to look up into stormy gray eyes. 'Where are you headed like your tail is on fire?'

I sank deeper into Manny's chest, not caring that I was blurring my boundaries with him again. I needed someone to hold me. Tell me that my life was not swirling straight down the toilet. That all my choices weren't ruining my girls' lives.

'I'm going back to the store and hiding out for a while after the mess I just made of things.'

'Mess?' He pulled back and stared into my eyes. 'What's going on, Tess?'

Every time he said my name it sent a shot of warmth through my center. It was equal parts honey and gravel, and I could listen to him say it all day long.

'I talked to Barb and Susan. Let them know I was planning to build the coffee bar. It wasn't right to go ahead without telling them about it. How it might affect their business.'

'And I take it from the way you're buzzing through town, head hung low, it didn't go well?'

My shoulders sank, and he gripped my hand and pulled me to a metal bench in front of the Dairy Dip.

'It wasn't like they argued about it,' I gulped over the rawness in my throat. 'They just looked hurt.'

Manny waited for a minute. Scrubbed a hand behind his neck. Kids sped by on their bikes and scooters. A few cars rumbled past the square.

'No one can expect to be the only game in town,' he said to soothe me. 'We still have so many empty storefronts down here that it'd be easy for someone to come in and set up a competing shop. Even the Ivy Falls Inn serves breakfast, which takes business from Sugar Rush.

'That's different.'

'How?' He slid his hand over my face, pushing back a hair stuck to my cheek. We shared a gentle look that made my heart slow. How did he always know the right time to touch me so I could take a breath? Calm down.

'Because the Ivy Falls Inn was here before Barb and Susan,' I said softly. 'Me, I'm sort of infringing on their business afterward.'

'You caught them off guard, that's all. Give them time to think it over. They want you to be a success. For all of Ivy Falls to thrive.'

'I don't know.'

He slid closer like he could sense my fear, my slow spiral into panic.

'Tell me what else has you worried.'

'Do you think my mother would be disappointed that I've messed things up so badly? That I even have to consider building a coffee bar?'

'This town's been floundering for a while, and you inherited a store caught in that storm. I'd say you've done a damn good job of running the P&P, all things considered.'

His steady stare was always a comfort to me. The voice of reason to my frenzied panic. These moments were why I couldn't risk a relationship with him. What we had in this moment, our steady friendship, wasn't something I could afford to lose. But still, when he looked at me with that sweet gaze, it was hard not to lean into him. Let him hold me until my heart beat out a steady rhythm again.

'Let me walk you back to the store,' he offered.

'What are you doing down here anyway?' I said, letting him pull me to my feet.

'Silvio ordered a specific paint sample for the interior of the old Thomas Place, and I was headed to pick it up.'

'Go take care of that. I can get back to the store on my own.'

'Tess.' He moved behind me and gently pressed his mitt-sized hands to my shoulders. Heat licked through me, and I reveled in it. It'd been so long since someone had really touched me. 'Silvio can wait five minutes.'

He steered me across the brick-paved street, past the memorial fountain, and in the direction of the P&P on the corner.

Chapter Eight

MANNY

Brave and Beautiful Woman

If I could envision the perfect day, it would be this one. The temps hovered in the low sixties, but the blossoming yellow sun made the air warm. Lou, Iris and Rose sat in the back seat of my truck, tucked in shoulder to shoulder like books resting on a shelf. Their sweet little voices sang along to their favorite country songs.

Tess sat in the spot I loved, right next to me, as the open windows blew back her auburn hair. She usually wore it tied back from her face, but today it was loose and floating in the wind like glistening copper. She'd looked so shaken after her conversation with Barb and Susan a few days ago, and it was good to see her relaxed now. The tension gone from her shoulders and perfectly pink mouth.

Dried brown and yellow leaves crunched under the tires as we flew down the small two-lane highway that led to Breyer's farm. My hand lay open on the seat. I itched to reach out and place it on top of hers, but I needed a signal, some sign, that we'd reached that point in whatever was growing between us.

A few yards up the highway, a bright red sign directed us to turn left to enter the farm. We took the narrow road barely wide enough for two cars. Along the fence line was a handful of horses, some gray and others a tawny brown. The girls squealed and jockeyed for position to see them.

'Keep those seat belts on!' I warned.

The road ended at a large dirt parking lot that was already filled with two dozen cars. The sweet scent of freshly baked pies, and ripe apples, floated in through the open windows.

Once I parked the truck, the girls unbuckled and scrambled out. They cheered when they saw a large tractor pulling a long bed filled with several families.

'Can we do the hayride, Mommy?' Iris bounced on her toes, and Rose nodded along like she wanted to ask the same question. That heavy weight Tess had been carrying since Billy left, since the store began to have issues, melted away. This was what she needed. What *we* needed. To make special memories with the people we cherished. The ones who wanted to spend time with us. Who would never run away.

'Let's get your coats on first,' Tess said. 'We'll pick some apples and then do the hayride.'

'And then, of course, the corn maze.'

Tess smiled at the way my voice was just as giddy as the girls'.

I slid Lou's coat on over her T-shirt, and Tess helped the girls with their sweatshirts.

'What kind of apples are we going to get?' Lou said to Tess once I'd zipped her up. 'Daddy buys the ones that crunch, not the ones that go all mushy in your mouth.'

'We have to go to the stand near the entrance. They'll tell us what trees are available for picking.' Tess pointed to a makeshift wooden booth with a sign that said, *In today's orchard...*

Lou raced over to Tess and slid her hand into hers, and my heart swelled. Iris and Rose rushed up beside them and held on like a beautifully loving chain. As the four of them walked in the direction of the booth, I yanked my phone out of my back pocket and snapped a picture. A thought breezed through my head, and my breath went unsteady.

This could be my family.

I was jumping way too far ahead, but my mind had already put the picture of them in a frame. Set it on the mantel as a reminder of this perfect day.

After selecting two baskets to collect our apples, we followed the small wooden signs leading to the orchard. The breeze picked up, and the girls rushed ahead, jumping and singing a made-up song about fall and the taste of apples.

Tess let her head tilt back, and the sun danced over the top of her pink cheeks. I couldn't help but move in and gently bump her side. She turned to me with one brow arched. 'Did you just hip-check me, sir?'

I inched in closer and brushed my hand over hers. 'Do you have any idea how stunning you are? That you have this gorgeous dotting of freckles sprinkled over your cheeks and nose, like a beautiful set of constellations.'

'Manny.' She flushed. 'That's very sweet.'

Her eyes lingered on my lips before she quickly looked away. I wanted to believe in that moment that she wanted to kiss me as much as I wanted to kiss her. In an act of bravery, I reached out and linked my pinkie with hers. I looked forward, too afraid to see the reaction on her face. That she might want to pull away. Instead, she gave a little squeeze, and it sent a sweet rush of blood to my head, and, well, other places.

'Pop!' Lou came running back in our direction, and Tess quickly released me. The pain of losing that connection was visceral. 'The painted sign next to the trees up ahead says "Gala" – is that the soggy or crisp kind?' Lou asked.

'You like the kind called Fuji.'

'Oh, okay.' She looked to the spot where I once clasped Tess' pinkie, and her smile faded before she raced back to Iris and Rose.

'Thank you for today,' Tess said as we kicked at rocks and gravel, trying to keep up with the girls.

'No need for thanks. I'm glad we made time to do it.'

She went quiet and chewed on her bottom lip. I'd known her long enough to understand something else was weighing on her mind.

I reached out and gently tapped a finger to her head. 'What kind of things are swirling around in that brain of yours?'

'There's a lot going on, and I hope…' She pulled in a rough breath. 'Well, I hope I can handle it all.'

'You're strong. Smart. You've got this, Tess.' I held her gaze, needing her to know that I was right there to support her.

'Thank you, but I must admit I feel unmoored right now. With the store and now this new loan the bank just approved, it feels like I'm walking this unknown path, and I'm not sure what's around the next corner.' She tugged on the end of her hair. 'All of it scares the hell out of me. If this goes sideways, I could lose everything.'

I hated the quiver in her voice, wanted to do anything I could to reassure her, but I also needed to listen. Let her know she could tell me anything.

'It's in my nature to be thoughtful, prepared,' she went on. 'But it's like I keep trying to grasp for something solid, and all I'm getting is air.'

She gave the ends of her hair another tug.

'Because of Billy, I almost didn't agree to take over the bookstore after my mom got sick.'

'What?' I bit out. 'Why?'

'Since we were teenagers, he's had this uncanny ability to get inside my head. Make me doubt myself. It's not like he ever came out and said I didn't have the brains to do it, but he'd drop small, cutting comments like I wasn't a math person, so how could I run a business? He'd needle me about my personality. The fact that I didn't like confrontation. How that'd make it tough to be a good boss.'

The longer she talked, the more I hated her ex. It wasn't just that he ran away like a coward, it was that he made her doubt her abilities and her intelligence. That he made her think she wasn't the brave and beautiful woman the rest of us saw. If it took me a lifetime, I'd prove to her that she was an angel on earth. That her presence in Ivy Falls made the town so much sweeter, better. That she deserved to be loved unconditionally, and supported in everything she did.

The question was, would she let me in to be that shoulder she needed? And even if she did, what would that mean for our friendship, which had become one of the most important things in my life?

Chapter Nine

TESSA

Everyone Needs A Little Vitamin D

With the girls dragging after a long day and eating way too many fried apple hand pies that Rosie declared 'delicious', we made our way toward the farm's exit. Only steps from the parking lot sat a large white shed that housed an antique mart. We started to walk past it when I came to an abrupt halt, turned into the building and made a beeline for a stall at the far back.

The girls and Manny tried to keep up as I raced past booths filled with handmade quilts and not-so-antique vases. My focus stayed on my target: a massive turn-of-the-century mahogany buffet with a black and white marble server.

'Are you thinking what I'm thinking?' Manny said when I stopped a few feet from the stall.

'The answer is yes if your idea is to refurbish that piece and turn it into part of the design for the coffee bar.'

'It's perfect, and now that you've got the loan, you can start thinking about how to put it all together,' he said, appraising the rare and beautiful piece.

A man with a thick beard and matching snowy-white hair moved out of the stall to greet us. The girls stared and I had to agree that he did look a little bit like Santa Claus.

'She's a beauty, isn't she?' He shoved his hands into his worn jeans and walked closer. 'Belonged to my great-grandmother. It's been sitting in storage for years. Thought it was time to bring it out. Sell it to the right buyer.'

'Do you know the year it was made?' I asked.

'If I had to guess, I'd say late eighteen hundreds.'

'May I get a closer look?'

'Sure, go ahead.'

I took my time running my hand over the white marble server with thin gray veins. 'It's in good condition. What's your asking price?'

The man scanned our little crew like he was trying to figure out a number. 'Is it going in y'all's house?'

'Uh,' I mumbled at his assumption. 'We're all friends.'

The man's brows went up.

'The piece, it would be perfect for my business.'

He rubbed at the whiskers on his chin. 'What kind of business?'

Before I could utter a word, Rose said, 'My mama sells books. The store used to belong to my granny. She died.'

The man's eyes went sad. 'I'm sorry to hear that.'

'My business is…' I bit away the words 'in trouble' and said, '…about to add a coffee bar. This piece would be part of the design.' I cocked my head to Manny. 'Part of *his* design.'

The man's face lit up. 'Oh, you're a carpenter? So am I!'

'I'm mostly a builder. My partner and I restore old homes.'

I loved the proud tone in Manny's voice. How he was such a good foil for Torran. When my sister first intro-duced us, he stood in the doorway of their first project, and I swore I almost swallowed my tongue. His muscled body filled the entire frame. The ratty old baseball cap he loved was turned backward, allowing only a small bit of black hair to poke out.

At first I thought he might be a good fit for Tor, but over time, his patient voice, the way he gently jabbed back at her quick wit, told me they were good friends. It wasn't until Billy was gone that Manny appeared at the park one day with Lou while I was there with the girls. I was pretty sure Torran had put him up to it. When I asked about the timing, he ignored me, insisting in that gentle, soothing voice I'd come to adore, that it was important to get outside. That everyone needed a little vitamin D.

As the girls played with Lou that day, it was like they'd woken from a long, deep sleep. They laughed, smiled, cheered as they chased Lou around the equipment and down the slides.

It'd been months since I'd smiled, had a bit of warmth fill my body again. That warmth only grew as I spent more time with Manny. It felt good to settle into that feeling. To know there was a chance that, despite all the chaos in my life, he might be mine if I was brave enough to take that first step.

There was clearly a wild kind of chemistry between us, but every time I considered crossing that line, I thought about our friendship. What we could lose if things between us didn't work out romantically. The idea of him not being a constant in my life always had me hesitating, waiting another day.

The owner of the buffet pressed a hand over his mouth as he sized up Manny. 'I thought you looked familiar. You're that guy on the Hearth and Home show. The quiet one to the lady who does all the talking about her love of saving old homes.'

'That's our Auntie Torran,' Iris said quietly. 'She's really smart and good with her hands.'

The man gave Iris a sweet smile. 'Bet you're just as smart?'

Iris blushed and turned into my side.

'Would the piece be on TV? I think my great gran would have loved that.'

'No, but if you sell it to me, it'll be handled with loving care,' I reassured him.

The man's gaze moved over us, and I held my breath in anticipation. 'Let me show you more details about the piece, and we can talk numbers.'

Manny turned to me. 'Tess, I can handle this. In the bed of my truck are some moving blankets. Why don't you and the girls go grab them?'

It would have been easy to let Manny step in. Fall into old habits. When we had plumbing issues at my house, I let Manny or Torran take over. If my car needed repairs, my dad always knew what to do. But I needed to make changes. Take charge of my own life.

'Sir, can you excuse us for a minute?' I said.

'Sure. Take your time.'

I pulled Manny a few steps away while the man made small talk with the girls.

'I'm not sure how much I can spend. There's a budget, and I haven't figured out all the details yet.'

He gave me a warm smile. 'I'll negotiate a good deal.'

'But…' I started, my voice trembling. Buying the piece made all of this real, and it scared the crap out of me. The store was mine. The coffee bar would be mine too. It was my job to negotiate this deal – not his.

'Trust me. You won't pay a penny over what it's worth.'

'I appreciate your help, but it's *my* store. I need to handle this.'

He searched my gaze and then stepped back. 'Of course. It's all you, Tess.'

My heart swelled as I looked into his eyes. He never pushed. Undermined me. There was a calm tenor and acceptance in his tone. Like he understood that I had to do this on my own.

'I'll head back to the truck with the girls. Grab those blankets so we can move it safely.' His eyes went fiery as he stepped in close. 'But just so you know, I'm a good negotiator too.'

His smile went deliciously wicked for a second, and then it vanished as he called for the girls to follow him back to the parking lot.

Chapter Ten

MANNY

Badass Businesswoman

When I returned from the truck, Tess was still working the negotiations. I'd never seen this side of her. She was so resolute. Hands firm at her sides. Jaw jutted out. She'd never looked so gorgeous, and I bit into my tongue to keep from actually cheering for her.

I set down the blankets on a nearby bale of hay as she continued to haggle with the antique dealer.

'Let me go talk to the missus right quick. I'll be back in a jiffy,' the man said, scurrying to another side of the tent where a woman with gray hair threaded with white stood behind a table.

Tess stepped back toward me, hands twisting anxiously in front of her. Again, that instinct to reach out, do anything to calm her, raced through me, but I had to settle for distraction.

'Looks like you're working your charm on him,' I teased.

'We'll see if it's enough,' she said looking around me. 'Where are the girls?'

'I sent them with Lou to the playground near the petting zoo.'

She toed at the ground nervously. 'I think, well, I hope, we're at the right number. He definitely doesn't want to let go of the piece easily.'

'You've got this, Tess,' I said softly.

She locked eyes with me, and for a flash, I saw that same ache and need I'd been battling for nearly a year. I started to reach for her, needing to touch her if only for a minute, when the man reappeared.

Before he could say a word, Tess unleashed a sweet smile. No one could resist her when she looked at them like they made the moon rise and fall.

'Mr… uh…'

'Sturridge. But you can call me Edmund,' he said.

'Oh, I like your first name. It reminds me of one of the children in *The Chronicles of Narnia*.'

His face lit up. 'That's who I was named after! Although, I have to say when my mother read me *The Lion, the Witch and the Wardrobe*, I wasn't sure why. He wasn't the most loyal fellow. Well, at least not until the end.'

'You're right, but he did get better in the later books.'

'That story turned me into a reader. Didn't much care for books when I was young, but then those kids walked through that wardrobe and I was hooked.'

'This piece of your history will look lovely in my bookstore in Ivy Falls,' Tess said like she was eager to turn the conversation back to her offer.

'Ivy Falls? I know that place. The Pen and…' He tapped at his lip, and then snapped quickly, 'Prose. Pen and Prose. Haven't been there in a while, but I do remember the lovely woman who owned it. Was that your mother?' he asked sadly.

'Yes.' Tess took an uncomfortable gulp. 'And she was lovely. Thank you.'

'Your mother had the patience of a saint. She turned me on to that Brad Thor fella. Boy, can he write a good military thriller.'

'She was pretty good about matching a reader with a book.'

He had a far-off look in his eye like he was remembering that time, and Tess' mom, who was a hard lady to forget.

'So, about the buffet?' Tess urged.

He scribbled out a new number and handed it to Tess. I looked over her shoulder and tried to keep a poker face. She wrote down a different number. Edmund pulled the paper toward him. Tapped that finger back to his lip again.

In the distance, Rose and Iris' laughter filled the air. It was the perfect sound for this negotiation. As soon as he heard their giggles, his shoulders gave a little, and he held out his hand. 'I think my great-granny would be happy that her beloved buffet is going to a place full of books.'

'Thank you, Mr Sturridge. I swear we'll take good care of it.'

I couldn't help but look at her with awe as she firmly shook the man's hand. I loved this badass businesswoman side of her.

Once we had the buffet loaded, I called to the girls and hustled them all back to the truck. They asked a bunch of questions, whined about leaving, but I only gave them a smile and told them it was time to go.

Not more than twenty minutes on the road, all three girls were sound asleep.

'Today was really special. Thanks for inviting us,' Tess said.

There was so much I wanted to say. Tell her about my earlier thoughts as I had snapped that picture of her and the girls. Whisper that I'd almost come out of my skin with her single pinkie touch. With the girls still snoozing in the back, I held my tongue though. But one day soon, we'd have to talk about what was brewing between us.

We sped down the highway, nothing but the sound of the wind moving through the windows. She glanced over her shoulder to where we'd laid the buffet in the back of the truck.

'I think I might be having buyer's remorse.'

'Why?'

'It's hitting me now that this is happening. That I'm going to take this leap.'

'Do you trust me?' I asked quietly.

'Yes. Implicitly.' There was such ferocity in her voice that I pushed on.

'If I thought for one second that this was a risk, a bad choice, I'd have told you.' I held her gaze before returning my attention to the road. 'Reach behind you. My sketchpad is under Iris' feet.'

She turned and grabbed the spiral-bound drawing book. Over the years, I'd filled it with design ideas for furniture and built-ins I wanted to install in future renovations.

When we were weeks into shooting the first season, Lauren had found it laid across a sawhorse in the kitchen. Mentioned how much she loved the farmhouse table I'd designed. That maybe it could be a side business Hearth and Home could promote. I laughed off the idea. I already had a full plate. Designing for the houses Tor and I worked on was more than enough.

I told Tess to flip to one of the last cream-colored pages, and she let out a gasp.

'Oh, Manny, it's exactly what I pictured.' She ran her finger over the sketch I'd created for the coffee bar.

'Now that we have the buffet, I'll readjust the design for the counter. I can mimic the piece's intricate scroll so they'll look like a matching set.'

'That'll be beautiful!' she gushed.

It was good to see her shake away her worry.

'We could use some white remnant marble with gray veins so it will match the server. I also looked at the measurements for a top-quality espresso machine while you paid Mr Sturridge. There's one from Italy that will fit perfectly on the marble server.'

'I love it! What about the design above the upper shelf? It looks like it's ridged.'

'I'm planning to shape the bracketed pieces up to the top tier with a traditional C-scroll, making it have that classic feel.'

She blinked rapidly, like she was holding back tears.

'I didn't mean to make you weepy,' I teased.

'They're happy tears. Seeing this on paper. It makes it all feel possible.'

'It's going to happen, Tess. I'll make sure of it.'

She bit her lip and inched her fingers across the seat until they were entwined with mine. For a minute my mind went blank, my throat dry, as I sank into the feeling of her touch. I swallowed all the things I'd wanted to tell her, like 'I want you' and 'Let's not be afraid to try', because even though she'd crossed that small line between us, I didn't want her to overthink it, or push my luck, on such an incredible day.

Chapter Eleven

TESSA

Through The Wringer

Dr Sheridan's office was always a flurry of activity. Nurses moved in and out of doors. Older patients sat on one side of the room, thumbing through old issues of *Architectural Digest*, or watching whatever cable TV news program was on the big-screen TV. In a small back corner, children drove plastic toy trucks and cars over the massive rug made to look like a small city. Other kids moved in circles, chasing the toy train that ran on a small track built over-head.

I sat in a wooden chair and held Iris' hand. Rose was beside us, kicking her feet back and forth in a nervous motion.

'Why do we have to see the doctor today?' Iris asked in a voice that always went tight when we had to come to the Ivy Falls Community Health building.

'Just a regular checkup,' I said to her in a calm tone. 'There's nothing to worry about.'

A nurse in bright pink scrubs called out their names. I clasped both their hands and followed the girl with electric-blue hair back into the office area. She guided us to a room with the number four attached to the door.

Once inside, she asked basic questions about the girls' height and weight. If I had any concerns at the moment. I did, but that was a conversation for after the exam.

After she was done tapping on the tablet in her hand, she reassured us the doctor would be in to see us soon.

I kept the girls busy with coloring pages left on a nearby table. A few minutes later, there was a knock on the door, and Dr Sheridan walked into the room. His white curly hair hung past his chin. Instead of a stiff lab coat or scrubs, he always wore jeans, a Hawaiian shirt and shiny white sneakers. Around his neck hung a stethoscope with a small koala bear toy gripped around the rubber tubing.

Dr Sheridan had spent the last twenty years treating most of the town's residents. He'd gone to high school with my parents, and then Vanderbilt for college and the rest of his medical training. Mom always laughed at his bad jokes. Said his own funky style landed somewhere between Jimmy Buffett and an old hippie. He even drove an ancient yellow VW bus that we often saw sputtering around the square. Years ago, teenagers started calling it the 'Flying Banana', and it stuck.

He gave a bright smile to Iris and Rose and said, 'How are the two loveliest flowers in Ivy Falls today?'

Rosie giggled while Iris remained her quiet self.

Dr Sheridan noticed and gave a quick tip of his head to the exam table. 'Rosie, want to go first?'

He did a quick exam. Looked in her eyes and nose. Talked to her about soccer and school. The minute he asked about her sleeping, her little lips pinched together, and my heart squeezed.

When Dr Sheridan finally coaxed Iris to swap spots with her sister, she sat stiff as a board as he asked the same questions. He also prodded about her stomach. What were her favorite foods? How much water was she drinking after soccer practice?

She gave quick, muted answers, her worried eyes glued to my face as she did.

Once he was finished, Dr Sheridan opened the door and called to his nurse. She led Rose and Iris back to the waiting area with promises of blowing the train's small horn.

As soon as the door closed behind them, Dr Sheridan gave me a pointed look. 'You need to stop worrying. They're perfectly healthy.'

'But the nightmares and stomachaches,' I insisted.

He sat in the chair next to me. It was hard not to stare at the bright blue and black toucans splattered all over his shirt. The way his white curls puffed out around his head like dandelion fluff.

'We've done all the pertinent tests, checked on Iris and Rose quite a few times over the past year, and everything has been normal. Your girls,' he paused, '*and you*, have been through some rough patches. They lost their beloved grandma.' His voice went thin. 'Then, well, Billy. It was a confusing time for them.'

'Not just for them,' I muttered.

'You've *all* been through the wringer,' he sighed. 'But I want to reassure you that the symptoms happening to the girls are a side effect of all that loss. You've done right by them, Tessa. You did family therapy. Helped them understand as much as possible that they are safe and secure.'

'Yes, but how can I make the nightmares and stomachaches stop?' I said with a trembling voice.

'They're less frequent now, correct?'

'Maybe once a month or so.'

'Compared to what?'

'A couple of times a week.'

'That's progress. Keep going about your day. Stay with a routine. Surround them with love and support from your family. From the folks here in Ivy Falls. I know you've been spending time with Manny and Louisa.' He gave me an approving smile. 'Keep building a life. Let them play with their friends. Explore new activities. Slowly, but surely, those manifestations will fade for good.'

'Promise?' I said more as a tease.

'You're a good mother. Keep the girls on track, and everything will be all right.'

I gave him a quick nod. 'Thank you, Dr Sheridan.'

'Now.' He arched a wiry eyebrow. 'What's this I'm hearing from Barb and Susan about you building a coffee bar at the P&P?'

I couldn't help but groan. 'Yeah, they're not too happy with me right now.'

He rubbed at the white stubble on his chin. 'The only way this town is gonna stay alive is if we keep its heart beating. That means breathing new life back into the shops. Giving people new and exciting reasons to come to Ivy Falls. Manny and Torran's show has helped with that cause. I think adding coffee as an offering at the bookstore will too. Barb and Susan know you have to diversify to keep a business fresh. They'll come around. Older folks like us, we just need a bit of time to adjust.'

'You're not old,' I protested.

'My wife might not agree,' he chuckled. 'She keeps telling me to retire. That I need to take her on that trip to Scotland and Ireland I've been promising since she became my bride.'

'You should listen to her, because you never know when you won't have time anymore. I sadly learned that with my mom.'

'That's fair advice.' He gave me another steady look. 'You know it's all right to move on. To find joy and happiness again. She'd want that for you.' He hesitated before saying, 'She'd approve of you and Manny.'

'No,' I sighed. 'Not you too.'

He shrugged. 'All anyone in this town wants is for you to be happy, Tessa.'

'I love this town too, but y'all need to start minding your own business,' I said halfheartedly.

'Not sure that's ever going to happen, especially as long as Mrs Vanderpool keeps tabs on everyone around here.'

'That woman needs a hobby,' I laughed.

His face went solemn. 'Greta is getting older. Most of her family is gone. I think her sticking her nose into other people's lives is what keeps her going. Well, that and her little dog.'

He gave my hand a firm pat and left the room. I pulled in a full breath, trying to be soothed by his reassurances.

My mind fluttered back to Manny and me in the truck. The way it felt so easy to slide my hand over the top of his. Things were certainly changing. Maybe it was time I listened to the doctor's orders and moved on.

Chapter Twelve

MANNY

I'd Wait For Decades

Torran was at it again.

Her face was fixed in that intense, unrelenting gaze, and I tamped down the urge to groan.

'We are not refurbishing the cabinets,' I said, keeping my tone even while Tina, the Steadicam operator, kept the shot focused on me.

'Come on, Manny. You know how I love to keep things as close to period-accurate as possible.'

I walked to the cabinets and placed a finger against one of the doors. The small hint of pressure made the hinge moan. With a low creak, it broke away, and I caught it before it crashed to the floor.

'Get my point?' I set the cabinet panel on the ground, which was already covered in dirt, old leaves and droppings from animals I worried were scurrying around this house.

'All right,' she sighed. 'You win. This time.' She gave me that smirk that said she enjoyed being a pain in the ass.

The director called cut, and the small crew moved out of the kitchen.

'I heard the apple-picking trip was a hit. The girls won't stop talking about the corn maze or those little apple pies. You made extra points there, for sure.' There was a teasing hint to Torran's voice that always lingered when she talked about her sister.

'I hope so.'

She gave me a steady stare that said she knew there was more.

'You know I have feelings for your sister. Strong feelings. They only grow the more time I spend with her.'

'Then why aren't you acting on it?'

'Because I understand her heartbreak. Her hesitancy. After Gina…' I let loose a low breath. 'It took me a long time to get in the right headspace. To even think what might be next for me. I want to respect that process for Tess. Not push her into something she might not want.' I kicked at a loose piece of tile on the floor. 'Her friendship means a lot to me, and Lou loves her. I have to make sure she wants to be more, because it would kill me if things went sideways and I lost her friendship.'

'Manny, I get it, but Tess, well, sometimes she needs a little nudge.'

'Not in this case,' I countered. 'It's got to be something she wants one hundred percent. No doubts. No regrets.'

'Fine, I'll stop meddling. But just for the record, I think you two are perfect for each other.'

I shook my head. She'd never let up, but Torran also understood her sister was in a vulnerable place. The last thing I wanted to do was take advantage of it. Tess had taken my hand in the car, and it was a start. It may take a while to get beyond those tentative touches, but I'd wait decades for Tess.

A crew walked out of the house, tucking tape measures into their work belts.

'Are they measuring for the glass estimate?' I asked.

'Yes, double-paned. I want this beauty to be as energy efficient as possible.' Her gaze moved back to me. 'Speaking of glass. Thanks for getting the door repaired for Tess.'

'Sure.' A question floated through my head as the guys went back to their truck. 'You've lived in this town most of your life. Do you think what happened at Tess' house was a Halloween prank?'

'There are a lot of teenagers on that street with too much time on their hands. My guess would be yes,' she said.

'They did a lot of damage for a prank.' I cut myself off, keeping my other suspicions to myself.

'Manchester Riley Parks, what are you not saying?'

Crap. Tor only used my full given name when I'd hit a nerve. Her gaze remained unflinching, and I knew I'd never get out of the house without admitting my worry to her.

'The whole scene still feels weird to me. Why break in and not take anything?'

She flailed out a hand like she could wave away my worry. 'You're overthinking this. I'd bet those kids were throwing rocks and one happened to hit the window.'

What she said made sense, but I couldn't shake the feeling that something else was going on.

'Let's talk about the porch issues on the back of the house,' I said, not wanting my spinning thoughts to distract us from the work that needed to be done today.

'It's a total gut,' Torran said, following me out of the kitchen. We walked through the front door and around the side of the house. Navigating our way across the warped and crumbling wood was like playing Jenga. One wrong move and the whole floor could go.

'We have to tear out all the rot and start with fresh lumber,' I said.

'How long do you think it will take? We need to make it a priority so we can safely get the crew in and out through the back kitchen door.'

'I'd guess about two weeks. I already have a crew lined up to start in a few days.'

Her phone pinged, and she glanced at the screen. Tension built in her shoulders, and she worried her bottom lip.

'Problem? Is it Tess?' I said, way too panicked.

'No,' she said in a teasing voice. 'It's Beck asking about when we are going to set up a meeting with Teddy Ray. He's anxious about finding the perfect spot in Ivy Falls for his next restaurant.'

The edges of my chest tightened. I wasn't good at juggling too many projects at once. We'd agreed to work on this house as a follow-up to the first season of *Meet Me in Ivy Falls*, and it was a good choice because we were going to have to build the whole dang house from the foundation up. It had to be my only focus if we were going to do it right, but in the back of my mind, I thought about Tess. How she lit up when we talked about the coffee bar. I'd do everything in my power to make her look like that every single day, and helping her revamp the store was a good start.

'Manny, what else is wrong?' Torran's voice drew me out of my thoughts.

'I'm not sure I can take on another thing right now.'

'Another thing?'

I tore the hat off my head. Scrubbed at my messy hair. 'Tess has been talking to your dad about how to bring more revenue into the store.'

'Yeah, I've been bugging the two of them about it constantly.'

I hesitated. Since we'd first started working together, we'd done every project as a team. Even though it was her sister, I didn't want her to think she had to take on this too. 'I might have promised Tess that I'd build her a coffee bar at the P&P.' Torran's brows shot to her hairline, and I quickly said, 'It won't interfere with what we're doing here.'

'A coffee bar?' She let out a whoop. 'That's a fantastic idea! She could definitely get more people in the door that way.'

'Don't get too excited yet, there's a lot to be done. I'll have to work mostly at night, so I was wondering if you and Beck might be willing to rotate with Barb and Susan to look after Lou for me?'

Her bright green eyes shined. 'Of course. We'll all work together to watch Lou.'

'Good. I can't imagine it will take too long getting the structure set up for it. The issue will probably be the permits. Know anyone who can help with that?'

She rolled her eyes. 'I'm sure the mayor can help.' Her face quickly sobered. 'Thank you, Manny.'

'For what?'

'For supporting Tess. Standing by her. With Billy...' She blew out a rough breath. 'Well, she deserves someone believing in her. I'm glad that's you.'

She gave me a warm smile and went back to inching her way around the shaky porch. I stood surveying the mess, hoping Lou would understand my taking on one more project. That even though this was important for Tess and the P&P, I'd have to spend more time away from her.

Chapter Thirteen

MANNY

Walking Sunshine

I may have worn a Superman costume for Halloween, but I'd have done anything to turn into the Invisible Man right now.

Two women I didn't recognize sat in the bleachers two rows below me. More than once I heard the click of the camera button on their phones, and their quiet whispers about where they'd post the pictures.

Who were these people? And a more terrifying question was: how had they known I'd be here?

Blood began to race in my veins. If either of the women mentioned Lou, took a picture anywhere near the field, I wasn't sure I could hold it together.

The crowd cheered as Lou's team stole the ball away, and all I could do was tighten my fists at my sides. All this attention was more than confusing to me. It made zero sense. At the moment, I wore two days of scruff, an old MTSU baseball cap and a pair of cargo pants that had seen better days. Why would they want pictures?

I stood to get away from the women when Torran appeared at the bottom of the bleachers. Without a second look at me, she climbed the steps toward the women.

In her sweetest 'bless your heart' voice, she asked if they knew anyone playing. When they shook their heads, she politely asked them to leave. The two women agreed as long as she'd take a selfie with them. Torran obliged, and the women scurried away.

'Eight in the morning, and you're already causing a stir,' she teased, sinking onto the row in front of me. Every time one of the little girls on the soccer field shouted or cheered, she flinched. Pushed up the dark sunglasses hiding her eyes.

'Late night with Beck?' I taunted.

Her cheeks flamed, probably remembering how I almost walked in on them the first time they were together while we were still renovating Beck's house on Huckleberry Lane. If I hadn't noticed her kiss-swollen lips (and the condom wrapper wadded up in the corner of the room), they probably would have gotten away with it.

'Why do they have to make these soccer games so early?' she muttered. 'I didn't even have time to stop at Sugar Rush and get coffee.'

I reached to my left and grabbed the extra-large cup I'd ordered for her, as well as two of her favorite crullers. When I walked inside the café today, it was teeming with Saturday morning traffic. Things were definitely picking up thanks to our show. Barb was her usually prickly self, but when she saw me, she turned downright surly, like she knew I'd be helping Tess with the coffee bar.

As soon as she saw the to-go cup, Torran swiped it from my hands. 'God bless you,' she murmured before taking a giant swallow.

My phone buzzed in my pocket with another social media alert. I would have turned it off, but I was waiting on a call from the roofers about availability of the slate tile we wanted for the old Thomas Place.

I scanned the field for Lou, and my gaze caught on a corner of the park where there was a long line of trees. Pacing between them was a guy dressed in a dark hoodie and black pants. Thick sunglasses covered his eyes. A baseball cap sat low over his brows. There was something familiar about his cocky type of walk too. Shoulders back. Jaw tight. For a minute, I waited to see if his eyes stayed on a specific field, thinking maybe he was watching a child at play, but his head kept swiveling, his stride growing more frantic.

With *Meet Me in Ivy Falls* regularly playing on the network now, all kinds of strangers were showing up. Another side effect of the show I had not anticipated. I loved our quiet little town. That everyone watched out for each other. Yes, the gossip was annoying, but there was a kind of safety in knowing people had your best interest at heart. That they'd protect your child at all costs. With strangers suddenly appearing, it felt like we were losing that tight-knit feel, and I didn't like it one damn bit.

'Where's Beck? At home still recovering?' I focused back on Torran, needing to steer my mind in a new direction.

'Get your mind out of the gutter, Mr Parks.' She could act tough, but there was no hiding the blush in her cheeks. 'He and Pete are meeting with Teddy Ray in Knoxville to look at the new restaurant. Talk over media plans for its grand opening.' She held my gaze. 'And just so you know, Teddy Ray is still asking about a meeting.'

I let out an irritated huff at the reminder, and she held up her hands.

'I told Beck he had to hold him off. That there was too much on your plate right now. But Teddy Ray, he's like that piece of popcorn that gets stuck in your teeth and is nearly impossible to be rid of.'

When I'd agreed to Beck's plan to lure a restauranteur to Ivy Falls as part of his advertising agency's pitch, I didn't think the guy would become a permanent pain in my backside.

I ignored Torran's stare and focused on the only thing that kept me calm.

Lou trapped the ball at midfield and dribbled toward the goal. My heart sped up as she weaved in and out of the little bodies. She took a shot at the corner of the net. The goalkeeper easily snatched it away and kicked it back to the opposing team's side of the field. Lou hung her head low. Her shoulders hunched in a defeated pose that bothered me. When the referee blew the whistle for halftime, all the girls raced to the sidelines for a water break and orange slices.

'What's up with Lou? She's usually the first one in.'

'I don't know. She's been acting weird lately. Arguing over small things like brushing her teeth. Putting her dinner dishes away.' I rubbed a hand behind my neck. 'The other night she said she was too old for bedtime stories. That one punched me in the gut.'

'She's growing up, Manny. That's normal.'

'There's more to it though. I know she's upset about something. She won't talk about it, and it's driving me nuts.'

'Maybe it's a girl thing. I could talk to her, or Tess could.'

'No. I want her to be able to come to me if she's upset.'

'She's only eleven,' Torran offered. 'Some days she just might be off, but she'll talk eventually.'

'I hope you're right.'

My mind went back to when Lou was ten months old and cutting her first tooth. She'd cry and cry, and Gina would rock her until she fell asleep. When I'd come into the room to help transfer Lou to the crib, Gina would jokingly say, 'Teething is bad. Puberty will be worse.'

Puberty.

The word shot ice through my veins.

How was I going to do it all without Gina? First heart-break. First kiss. First period.

'I can sense you spiraling,' Torran said. 'You don't have to do any of it alone.'

'Yes, I know, but it still terrifies the crap out of me.'

Torran patted my knee. 'Enjoy today, Manny. That's all you can do.'

A laugh burst from my lips. 'Really? Who turned you into Little Miss Bright and Shiny?'

She smiled into her cup. It was all the sex. It had to be.

I shook my head, trying not to think about the last time I'd been touched or kissed in an intimate way. Like clockwork, Tess filled my field of vision, and I swallowed a groan. She looked like walking sunshine in dark blue jeans and a bright yellow cardigan. Who was I kidding? She could walk across the field in nothing but a garbage bag, and I would still think she was the hottest woman on the planet.

Tess caught my eye and waved in my direction. I jumped off the bleachers and raced to the edge of the field where she was pulling Rose and Iris in a collapsible wagon. Two big camp chairs hung from her arm.

'Hey, let me take those,' I said, nodding to the chairs.

She gave me that solid blue stare that made my blood hum. 'I can do it, Manny.'

'I get it, but I'm here now, so let me help.' She begrudgingly let me pull the chairs off her shoulder.

Rose hopped out of the wagon and threw herself at my legs. 'Mommy brought snacks and juice pouches for the entire team!'

'Oooh. If there are any leftovers, can I have a juice pouch?'

She stepped back and propped her tiny fists onto her hips. 'No, Mr Manny. Juice pouches are for kids only!'

I laughed as she took off in the direction of the bleachers. As I watched her speed toward Torran, my gaze caught on the man in black again. He continued to pace until he slid behind a tree like he didn't want to be seen. A part of me thought I should walk casually by him. Try to act friendly. Find out if he was here to see his child. Make sure he wasn't someone who didn't belong.

'Manny!' Tess called to me as she pulled the wagon to the field where Iris' team was playing. 'Are you coming?'

I rushed after Tess, letting the man, and my dumb worries, disappear.

Chapter Fourteen

TESSA

Vanished Into Thin Air

Manny paced back and forth in front of the brick wall at the back of the store. Several pages of blueprints lay across the top of a table. He kept glancing at them and then back at the wall.

'Hoping your X-ray vision will kick in soon?' I teased.

'Ha. Very funny. I'll have you know that damn Superman costume chafed in all the wrong places.'

I barked out a laugh. 'I bet it did!'

'Like you're one to talk. You still have scratches on the back of your neck from that awful wig.'

My hand flew up to my skin. 'What? Scratches? Where?'

He gave me that slow smile that said he was full of it.

This conversation was the reason why Manny and I couldn't be anything but friends. Romantic entanglements made things too weird. All the little innuendos tossed back and forth became awkward when kissing or sex was involved in a relationship. We could be idiots together. Tease each other and not have it be uncomfortable. That was exactly what I needed in my life. Friendship. Now if only my heart, and my damn hormones that made me feel sixteen again, would get the message.

'You're way too gullible, Tess.'

'Says the man whose daughter barely has a cough but convinces him she needs to stay home from school the last two days.'

His bright smile faltered. 'You think Lou's faking?'

'Oh, Manny,' I sighed. 'Does she have a fever?'

'No.'

'What about a rash?'

He rubbed a hand over his mouth. 'No.'

'Headache or nausea?'

This time, all I got was a shake of the head.

'Thank you, people of the court, I rest my case,' I said, doing a little bow.

'Why would she lie to me?' he sputtered.

'Children play sick for all sorts of reasons. Is a kid bothering her at school? Did she have a fight with her friends? Is she struggling with any subject?'

The wind picked up outside, sending a low whistle through the windows. Trees in the square bent and swayed as another whirlwind whipped through the dark, empty streets.

He shoved his hands into his pockets. 'Not that I know of.'

'You should talk to her and see what's up. Maybe all she needed was to spend a little one-on-one time with you.'

'She has been extra grumpy lately. I can't figure it out.'

'Has anything changed with your routine? One week, I had a lot of author events here, and I missed dinner a few times. It threw Rose off her schedule, and she was a total cranky pants because of it.'

'Everything is the same. Well…' He hesitated.

'Well what?'

'The old Thomas Place is a lot more work than we expected. A few days Barb and Susan have had to watch Lou. Feed her dinner. Put her to bed.' He gulped. 'In fact, they're at my house right now so I can be here.'

'We can do this another night, Manny. I refuse to put anything into motion until Barb and Susan come around anyway.'

'Tess,' he grumbled in that bearlike way. 'Stop worrying about what everyone else thinks. The buffet fits perfectly, and you like the bar design. Let's move forward. Build it. Once we're finished, and it's up and running, Barb and Susan will see it's not a big deal.'

He was right, but it still didn't untangle the knot in my stomach every time I remembered the way Barb looked at me like I'd insulted her signature raspberry scones.

'I'm sure what's happening with Lou is just typical kid stuff. Someone said the wrong thing, or she didn't get to sit next to a friend at lunch,' I said, purposefully changing the subject.

'I hope it's that simple. The last thing I want is for her to be upset and not be able to talk to me about it. I want to lay that groundwork early, because I know when she becomes a teenager, the last thing she's going to want to do is talk to me about her issues.'

Another burst of wind shook the trees outside. I crossed the room and gently touched his arm. 'You're doing a great job with her. Don't get inside your head and believe any differently.'

'Thanks,' he said. 'I'm trying really hard.'

'Lou knows that.'

He placed his hand over mine. We held on to each other for a long beat. I wasn't sure what kind of mental state I would be in without him. He sensed my every worry. Was always quick to build me up when my resolve started to fade. Unlike my ex, he didn't assume he'd be rewarded when he did something kind. Or require some sort of praise for simply being a decent human.

As I gazed into his slate gray eyes, I considered how easy it would be to slide into his arms. Let him caress me in places where I ached to be touched. But deep in my heart I understood that once that boundary was crossed, there'd be no going back. That if things flatlined between us, the friendship we'd built would never be the same. I was willing to risk loneliness in order to keep that from happening.

'Back to the coffee bar,' I said, letting go of him.

'Oh, yeah. Sure.' He let out a shaky breath and moved around to the opposite side of the table.

'The blueprints show there's water and electrical access behind these walls. That means we won't have to install any new lines, which will help with costs.'

The antique buffet we bought sat in a corner, still covered in gray moving blankets. Manny suggested we leave it there until his team could cut into the wall and get an idea of all the access points. He warned that they'd probably have to drill into the back of the piece to run electrical cords and a line for water.

I tried to picture the setup as he kept talking about construction. How the built-out wall of shelving and the sideboard on the buffet could hold stacks of white coffee cups and thick, leaded glasses, all branded with the P&P logo. In the center, we'd place a chrome espresso machine, as well as three cylinders that would hold freshly brewed coffee: light, medium and dark roast. On the other side of the buffet, I'd place several glass containers to hold all the different types of tea I'd offer: chamomile, ginseng, Earl

Grey, a flavored green, like pomegranate or blackberry jasmine. The ideas and flavors spun through my head. The more I thought about how it would look in the store, the more I wanted this to happen.

We stood shoulder to shoulder, and I told him my ideas. He smiled. Said he'd done some research and discovered some of the best coffee beans came from places like Colombia, Jamaica and Hawaii. It was hard to explain how the low rumble of his voice set me at ease. I cocked my neck right and then left.

'Still have that uncomfortable pinch?' he asked.

'Yep. It won't go away.'

'That's because you keep falling asleep in the girls' beds at night.'

'It's not like I mean to, but Rose continues to have those nightmares. She wakes up screaming and won't go back to sleep unless I'm there.'

He pressed his lips together. After having one too many glasses of wine after a family dinner, I'd told him about Rose's nightmares. What I hadn't said was that when she was in the throes of one, she called out for my ex to save her from whatever monster was chasing her. I felt like such a failure when I finally got her to wake up, and it was me she saw and not her father. But Dr. Sheridan said things would get better, and I was holding onto that reassurance for dear life.

Manny reached out and, with a soft touch, he kneaded the solid knot above my right shoulder. My eyes shuttered closed at the relief his hands brought to the tender area. An embarrassing groan escaped my lips as he dug his capable fingers deeper into the tension corded in my neck. His heavy breath warmed my skin.

It would have been so easy to spin around. Press my lips to his and let go. I'd have been a liar if I didn't admit that Manny had made more than one appearance in the spicier dreams I'd been having lately.

As the knot began to unwind, he whispered against the cuff of my ear, 'Am I getting the right spot?'

I turned around as heat started its slow, torturous journey up my body. Manny stared at me with wild abandon, like he could sense what was building between us. He moved in and slid a hand through the hairs that escaped my braid. With a small but delicious tug, he pulled me to him. Our hips pressed together, lips only a breath apart. I inched in closer. Our lips almost touching when a splintering crash made me jump back.

'What was that?' I shrieked.

Manny immediately yanked me behind him. We waited for another sound. Any other noise that would give us a clue about what was happening. Another frozen silence passed before he said, 'Wait here.'

'Um, no. In horror movies, the girl that gets left behind always dies first.'

He cursed under his breath but didn't stop me from following him around the corner toward the front of the store. Settled on the ground only inches from the door was a black rock the size of Manny's fist. Splintered glass from the single pane in the center of the door spilled out around it. The sound of shards cracking beneath his work boots sent a shiver through me. Waves of memory from Halloween hit me in an icy shock.

Before I could stop him, Manny threw open the door and sprinted into the small parking lot in front of the store. I chased after and skidded up behind him, my black ballet flats sliding along the gravel sprinkled across the asphalt.

The air was eerily quiet. Wind ruffled what was left of the leaves in the trees. The clock tower made its familiar *click click click* noise before it was ready to chime the nine o'clock hour. Manny spun in a circle, trying to locate who threw the rock, but there was no sound of trailing footsteps or a car racing away.

'First, the house. Now the window here,' Manny said. 'There's something not right going on.'

'This doesn't make any sense. Maybe it was just a rock tossed by the wind.'

He let out an aggravated sigh, grabbed my hand, and led me back into the store. 'I'm calling Deputy Ben.'

While he was busy on the phone, I walked back to the door. Outside, the emptiness in the town square rattled something deep inside me. If it wasn't the wind, then the person who'd done this had vanished into thin air, and that fact frightened me more than anything else.

Chapter Fifteen

MANNY

Impossible For The Locals

'Manny, if you swing that hammer any harder, you're going to drive the nail straight through the structure wall. Stop taking your frustration out on the poor lumber and talk to me.'

Torran crossed her arms and leaned against the new entry frame to the house. We'd built it with an impressive arch that would be filled with leaded glass. Below it would sit two massive side-by-side wrought-iron doors. We wanted this house to make an impression when you first saw it. The doors were a good start.

I stood and used the bandana in my back pocket to wipe the Sheetrock dust from my hands. 'We've got a lot of work to do. The film crew is supposed to be here soon to start shooting more interiors. It can wait.'

'No. Tell me what's bothering you.' She tapped the toe of a dirty black boot. Crossed her arms. She wasn't letting me off that easy.

I didn't have to tell her about the rock incident at the P&P. Ivy Falls gossip again. She also knew that when I wasn't squabbling with her for more than a half-hour, something was troubling me.

'The break-in at the house, and the rock at the store.' I hesitated, trying to put into words what I was worried about without freaking her out. 'Is someone trying to bother Tess? Did she unknowingly make someone mad?'

'Did you ask her?' she flipped back at me.

'Of course. She swore she has no idea what's going on.'

'Then that's her answer.' She paused and slid her hands into the pockets of her paint-splattered overalls. 'Although all of it is sort of weird. This is Ivy Falls. Usually when a person has an issue, they'll just stomp right up to you on the street and have it out.'

Torran knew better than anyone how much that was true. When Hearth and Home shot our first TV pilot, an entire can of green paint fell on her head, and she shouted out enough F-bombs to make even Roy Kent blush. The footage made it to YouTube, and people in Ivy Falls weren't shy about letting her know how angry they were that she'd told the entire internet that she hated the town. It wasn't true. She loved this place more than anything, but in a fit of rage and fear, she'd said the wrong thing.

'If it's not related to Tess directly, then what in the hell is happening? Is it kids getting a vandalism thrill?' I said.

'If that was true, wouldn't we know about it by now? People around here can't keep a secret for very long.'

My mind went to that day at the soccer fields. The man pacing behind the trees.

'You don't think this is related to the show in any way? Like out-of-towners trying to stir up trouble?'

'I get why that might make sense for the incident at the store, but Tess' house? Why there?' she asked.

I shrugged, and the worry lines around her mouth tightened.

'I can talk to my dad. Make sure Deputy Ben makes more frequent passes by her house.'

'That'd be great. I might just drive by a few times too.'

'Manny,' she sighed. 'Why don't you just ask her out? It doesn't have to be a big deal. Go and have a drink one night. Beck and I will watch the kids. We can do a campout in our backyard before it gets too cold.'

A brief flash of Tess and me standing close in the P&P, a kiss only seconds from happening before that rock came through the window, sent heat through my bones.

'I thought you promised you'd stop meddling.'

She gave me a shrug. 'This is my sister we're talking about. I want her to be happy.'

'We've been over this, Tor. She needs to be ready. I can wait for however long Tess needs.'

She held up her hands in surrender. 'Okay, message received. I won't push anymore.'

'Liar,' I said with a smile. 'But for now, can I get back to work?'

'Thank you for looking out for her. She needs it,' she said in a soft voice.

'Don't let her hear you say that. More than anything, Tess wants to prove to you and your dad that she can stand on her own.'

'She knows we believe in her.'

I'd already said too much. What Tess shared with me on Halloween about Billy not providing any money to support Iris and Rose felt like a private, vulnerable moment. She didn't need me exploiting it now, even if I thought it would help her. I turned away and tried to get back to work.

'Hey.' Torran tugged on my ragged work shirt. 'Is there something else going on with Tess?'

'Tor, you should talk to her, not me.'

'No. You brought it up.'

I hated that I'd opened my mouth, but Tess needed to know that she wasn't alone in any of this. That she had support if only she'd ask for it.

'When was the last time you talked to her about the financial state of the store?' I was in it now, may as well let out the rest. 'Did you know Billy still hasn't paid a dime to support the girls?'

All the color drained from her cheeks. 'Shit. I've been so busy with the business and Beck…' She rubbed at her tired eyes. 'I guess I haven't talked to her much, and that makes me a seriously crappy big sister.'

'She knows you care, but a little reassurance from you, and your dad, couldn't hurt.'

'You're right.' She tapped the wrench she was holding against the leg of her overalls. 'I'm telling you right now that if Billy shows his face again in Ivy Falls…' She paused, her jaw clenching. 'Well, I just hope you have bail money.'

'Me? Why isn't Beck bailing you out in this little made-up criminal scenario of yours?'

'Because he loves Tessa as much as I do, and he'd be in the cell right next to me.'

'Oh, like Bonnie and Clyde?' I teased.

'Nope. More badass like *Mr. & Mrs. Smith*.'

Her phone pinged, and she pulled it from her pocket. 'Crap.'

She turned the screen to me. It was a text from Lauren saying she was two minutes away.

'You ready to hear the offer for Season Three?'

I shrugged. The last year had been a whirlwind. And while I appreciated that the show might make tourism pick up soon, help Tess' store, I wasn't loving the stares pointed at me when I walked through the square, or the small group of onlookers who lingered outside the house right now. The way phones were pointed in my direction every single time I walked into a public place in town.

We'd talked to Lauren about the uptick in uncomfortable comments, and she'd promised Hearth and Home would protect our privacy, and luckily no one had figured out where I lived.

Tor was a different story.

After the second episode of our show aired, people started showing up in front of the house on Huckleberry Lane to take pictures. We knew it might happen after she and Beck decided to keep it and move in. What we didn't expect was people trespassing on their front lawn. Knocking on her front door at all hours of the day and night, scaring Piper, who was still a little too fragile.

Discussion had gone back and forth with the Ivy Falls sheriff about the trespassing. Now Torran and Beck were discussing putting up a privacy fence for safety.

A freaking fence.

That was not something I ever wanted to consider for Lou and me.

Like she could read my mind, Torran said, 'I get that the attention has grown a little intense, but we really are helping the town. Hell, the other day Silvio actually smiled at me when I grabbed my coffee at Sugar Rush.'

'It has been good. I just want things to stay calm for a little while longer, because once Season Two is done and starts airing, it's going to bring in a lot more people.'

'Yes.' She looked up at the framing that was going up for the second floor. 'But the extra funds are letting us do a lot more for this house than we'd be able to do with our own budget.'

Her response brought up yet another worry for me. The upgrades we'd planned would put this house in the highest price range for anything on the market in Ivy Falls. I wasn't sure anyone local would be able to afford it, which meant a possible out-of-towner buying it.

Over the last few months, I'd read articles about shows similar to ours that'd brought attention to their towns. The result was the cost of homes skyrocketing, making it impossible for those original to the area to purchase properties. I wanted people to come to Ivy Falls. Taste the deliciousness that came from Barb and Susan's café. Browse the shelves at Tess' shop. I just didn't want them to move here and make it impossible for the locals to buy and live in our community.

'Let's not get ahead of ourselves, Manny. Wait until Lauren presents the deal, and we'll go from there.'

Her phone buzzed again, and a slow smile slid over her face.

Must be Beck.

'I'm going to head inside and take this.'

'Tell Beck I said "Hi".'

She smirked, and her voice took on a golden tone as she answered. She and Beck had been through hell, and I was glad that Tor was finally happy. After the long, agonizing period of grief she'd gone through after her mom passed, she deserved it.

I went back to hammering, focusing on the framing for the doors. A few minutes later, the familiar click of heels on the pavement warned Lauren had arrived.

'Manny,' she said in that soft Georgia twang. I'd been around her enough to know that was her I-want-something-from-you voice.

'Lauren.' I kept working in the hope that she'd go inside and chat with Torran first.

'How's that sweet little girl of yours?'

Yep. She definitely wanted something.

I set down the hammer and tried not to smirk. It always blew me away how dressed up she was when she came to the sites. Today she was wearing a bright pink pantsuit with a crisp white shirt underneath. Her heels were the exact same shade of what Lou, I think, called Barbie pink. She'd slicked back the hair from her face in a perfect ponytail. I tried not to grimace. I'd been doing Lou's hair for years now and still could not get my ponytails to look that good.

'What do you need?' I finally said, giving a good yank on the brim of my hat.

'The show is still getting great buzz, and we really want to amp up the promo for Seasons Two and Three.'

'Isn't that something you take care of back at the network?'

She pinched her lips into a thin line. 'What we need is for you to make a personal social media account that ties into the show. Your fans are being relentless about getting updated photos of you.'

I gave my hat another good yank so I wouldn't have to see her eyes when I said, 'That would be a big freaking no, in fact, we need to talk again about moderating the show's account and limiting the comments. They're still way out of hand.'

'Manny, work with me here. If we limit comments, the fans will get upset.'

'I'm more than happy to let your publicity team take photos when we are shooting here. Put them on the show's account. But I won't agree to anything more.'

She propped a hand on her hip. 'Is this a negotiable or non-negotiable item with you?'

I swallowed a laugh. After Tor and I finished the first season and started having talks with the network about Season Two, they made a lot of ridiculous requests. First, they wanted us to get on a big bus and spend the summer going to home and garden shows around the country to do speaking engagements. I shut that one down quickly by saying that was a 'non-negotiable' item. Then they asked if we could do one or two within the state. That became something 'negotiable'. We went back and forth for the entire day until everyone involved was beyond exhausted. Now, whenever we spoke, Lauren thought it'd be funny to throw in my turn of phrase to poke the bear a little.

'Non-negotiable,' I said.

She bent down next to me. The hem of her expensive pants picking up bits of sawdust and dirt.

'Come on, Manny. The network is really on me for you to do more promotion.' She pulled in an uneasy breath. 'In fact, they require it as part of the next contract.'

I rose to my full height. Even with those heels on, she barely reached the center of my chest. 'Does Tor know about this?'

'Are you kidding? I know better than to try and talk around you. That woman turns into a fire-breathing dragon when it comes to protecting you.'

Tor did sort of go all 'big sister' when it came to anything dealing with me. At first I was shocked by it, but I'd learned to appreciate it since I was an only child. I hoped Lou had a friend one day who'd look out for her the way Torran did for me.

I picked up another set of nails and clutched them between my fingers. 'Lauren, I know you have a job to do, but I'm not changing my mind.'

'At least come inside and let's talk it over with Torran.'

There was a plea in her voice that made guilt twist in my stomach. She wasn't trying to be difficult, only doing the network's bidding.

Like she was sure I'd follow, she walked through the front door and into the cavernous house, which at the moment felt like the inside of the belly of a whale, all wide gaping hollows and thick wood framing for structure.

I set down the nails and pulled in a full breath, because I had a sneaking suspicion this conversation was far from over.

Chapter Sixteen

TESSA

Rough Edges

The boxes in my office had been piling up for over a week. Dad kept telling me I had to think about scaling back inventory to cut costs, but I could not be a *bookstore* without books.

I tore into the first box. Highlighter-yellow tape stretched over every inch of it warned the books inside could not be displayed until their release date. It was always the same song and dance with publishers and any book that could be a 'potential' bestseller. Of course, I had to shelve these kinds of books, but where I focused most of our stock was on our children's area, as well as a wide section in the corner of the store where I'd curated one of the best collections of romance titles in the state.

I could mark some of the biggest moments in my life by what romance book I was reading at the time. The day I got my period, Gayle Forman's *Just One Day* was tucked underneath my pillow. When I found out I was pregnant with Iris, I was deep into Lisa Kleypas' *Cold-Hearted Rake*. Sitting on my bedside table, when my water broke with Rose, was a copy of Sarah MacLean's *The Rogue Not Taken*. And then, of course, after Billy left, it was the entire *Bridgerton* series that kept me from crying every minute of the day.

Books were more than fictional tales. The delicately inked, slightly faded, sepia-toned pages had become a soothing balm to my tired soul. And now, I was living my dream by bringing those same beautifully woven stories to the most important people in my life.

After fighting the box for another few minutes, I pulled a straight edge out of a drawer in my desk and sliced through the tape. A shiny stack of hardcovers from the hottest British mystery author sat stacked inside. I breathed a sigh of relief. Mrs Vanderpool had preordered ten copies for the women's book club a month ago, and she'd stormed into the store four times this week to make sure she'd get them on release day.

I was tearing into a second box when the door to my office swung open, and Torran stood on the threshold. She was wearing her favorite dark denim overalls. A fleck of yellow paint sat in the center of her right cheek like a bullseye.

Oh crap. What time was it?

Like she recognized my panic, she stepped further into the room and gripped my shoulders. 'Don't worry. I picked up the girls from school. They're with Barb and Susan.'

I covered my face with my hands. 'I am the worst mother ever.'

'Hey.' Torran pulled down my hands. 'You are the *best* mother ever, and I'm sorry I don't tell you that more often.'

'Where is that coming from?' I choked out.

'A good friend reminded me today that I'm currently doing a sucky job of being a big sister.'

'Manny,' I sighed. 'I know he means well, but…'

'He cares about you,' she interrupted.

I took two steps and collapsed into the rolling chair behind my desk. Torran gave me a weighted look but didn't speak.

'Are you also here about the rock through the window? Because it's already been repaired.'

'It's not about the window entirely.' Torran sank onto a corner of the desk. It was hard not to smile at the rainbow array of paint splattered on her overalls. Did she ever get any of the paint actually on the walls? 'It's about all the other stuff connected to the window. Manny said you swore you weren't having issues with anyone in town, but I wonder if you're not being totally honest. I know how much you break out in a rash any time you have to discuss conflict.'

I looked into her eyes so she'd know I was being serious. 'I am just as much in the dark about this as you all are. Who knows, maybe someone is pissed at me because I sold them a book they hated. In case you haven't read the news lately, anyone who works with books, whether they sell them or they work in a library, is currently public enemy number one. Which is a bunch of horseshit.'

Torran's eyes went wide.

'What? I can curse when the topic is warranted.'

Torran flung her hands wide. 'Please go on. What else do you need to get off your chest?'

There was something leading in her voice I didn't like.

'Nope, I'm done ranting.'

'Tessa,' she groaned. 'Talk to me. I know things are tight here and you've got other troubles on your mind.'

She narrowed her eyes and instantly I knew she was talking about Billy. She only got that Medusa

I-want-to-turn-him-into-stone look when he was the topic of conversation.

'Dammit. Does Manny tell you everything?'

'What everything are you speaking of?'

I hated when she acted coy, but I sort of deserved it because Manny kept me in the loop about what was happening with her too. The minute Beck first blew into town and bid the house on Huckleberry Lane away from her, I was the first person he called, though, at the time, he didn't know Beck was Torran's high-school ex.

'No, I have not gotten any kind of child support from Billy. There, are you happy?'

My voice cracked, and I willed away the tears building in the back of my eyes. We'd agreed a long time ago that I was done putting up with his shit, but it still hurt that he was ignoring his girls.

'I'm sorry to push, but this isn't right. The girls are his too. He needs to carry some weight. Not put all the responsibility on you, because you're already carrying too much. Let go of the past, Tess because he clearly has.'

'I get that, Tor, but it's like every time I try to move on, a little piece of him, some reminder, drags me back. And I know I shouldn't forget how many times he's said he'd show up for the girls and then flaked. It's just one more thing that I should hate him for.'

I loathed that after all this time Billy could still cause so much pain.

'Please stop worrying about me. I have another appointment set up with my lawyer. He says Billy doesn't need to be present to have a judge issue a divorce decree.'

'That's a good start.' Torran slid off the edge of the desk and knelt beside me. 'What else can I do to help?'

'Nothing. You're just as strapped for cash as I am.' Torran's right cheek ticced. 'Okay, maybe not so much anymore because of the show, but I don't want or need your money.'

'Tessa, don't take all of this on your own shoulders. I can fill in here when you need a break. Help Manny build the coffee bar.'

I arched a brow at her.

'Yes, he may have told me that too,' she admitted. 'Please, let Beck and me help out. We can have the girls stay over at the house more. I'll do additional school pickups. Give me an order and I'll get it done.'

She stared at me with those wide green eyes, and it was hard not to think of our mother. How, if she was here, she'd be able to smooth over all the rough edges of my life. But she was gone, and if anyone was going to figure out a way through my currently rough path, it had to be me. That would have to start with something that'd been eating at me for days.

'Can you follow me to Sugar Rush? Take the girls to my house for a little bit? I need to settle an issue with Barb and Susan.'

'What issue? Did you press your fingers against the domed glass case again? You know how Barb hates fingerprints.'

That made me laugh. Torran was the only one who pressed her hands against the case and literally drooled over the glazed crullers, pissing Barb off on multiple occasions.

'Just wait for me outside while I tell Penny I'm taking off for a bit.'

She pressed her lips together before standing and going out the office door. I found Penny near the registers, building a new display for the mystery title I'd just unboxed. After telling her I'd be back in a few minutes, I joined Torran outside the store.

We walked past the market, candle store, and the Dairy Dip until Torran finally spoke.

'Lauren paid a visit to the worksite today.'

'Was that expected?'

'Yes. She wanted to talk to Manny and me about a few details Hearth and Home wants worked into the next contract.'

She chewed on the corner of her lip, which she only did when something was off.

'What don't you like about it?'

'It's more of a Manny issue.'

'Is this one of those negotiable/non-negotiable things?'

Manny had mentioned to me more than once that this had become a sort of joke with Lauren.

'It's definitely a non-negotiable.'

'What is it?' I asked, too curious for my own good.

'They want him to create his own social media accounts. Make him more accessible to the public. To the fans.'

I placed my hand over my mouth to stifle a laugh.

'What's so funny?' she asked.

'They're asking the man who will barely stand in group pictures, who always tugs down on the brim of his hat to hide his face, for more social media presence?'

'Yes. Come on, Tessa. You must see the looks he gets on the street. And don't tell me he hasn't told you about the propositions.'

'I may have talked to him about it a bit. Showed him how to put his personal account on private.'

Torran rolled her eyes and pulled me alongside her down the street. We were only steps from Sugar Rush when she pointed to a nearby bench, and we sat down.

'It's part of the deal with the show. We have to do this kind of promotion, even if it makes him uncomfortable.'

'You have to admit it's a little ridiculous. On Halloween, the way women looked at him. A young girl even stopped him and asked for a selfie. It was all really weird.'

'That costume, it really showed…' She gulped. 'Well, it showed off his assets. I'm not surprised he got so many looks.'

I snorted. 'True, but some of the comments he gets are seriously inappropriate. He has to lock his phone now because he's too afraid Lou might see them.'

A lick of anger swept through me. Those women didn't know a thing about Manny. Sure, he had a ruggedly handsome face. Beautifully toned forearms and a butt that looked really good in cargo pants, but he was also the guy who carefully saved a bird's nest when it was teetering on a low-lying branch. Who studiously watched YouTube tutorials on how to fishtail braid. Had the keen instinct to arrive at your door with a gallon of ice cream when you were having a crappy day.

'Tessa.' Torran gave me a steady stare. 'Are you okay?'

'Yes,' I said in a too-clipped voice. 'It's weird that strangers would do that to him. They don't know what kind of man he is. That he's devoted his life to taking care of his young daughter. That he gives care and attention to everyone he knows. Those women don't know a damn thing about him.'

'Do I sense a bit of jealousy?' she teased.

Yes.

No.

Maybe?

Manny was gorgeous, but he was more than that. Kind. Thoughtful. Generous with his time. He was a damn catch. And thanks to the show, women were noticing all those attributes. At some point he'd want to date again, and I'd have to stand by and watch. That thought made me more than a little nauseous.

Before I was forced to answer, Iris and Rose pressed their faces to the window of the Sugar Rush and blew fish faces, clouding up the glass. Oh lord, that would send Barb straight over the edge. Not a good thing as I was about to go and have a difficult conversation with her and Susan.

I followed Torran inside the café and gave the girls big hugs. After I'd asked about their days, and heard about how many cookies and donuts Barb and Susan had fed them (so much for dinner), Torran was kind enough to scoot them out the door.

Susan appeared first and hovered near the counter. I didn't like the hesitant stare she gave me. 'Oh! Hey, Tessa,' she mumbled. 'Can I get you something?'

'No, I would like to chat with you and Barb though.'

Susan gave a brief nod and then rushed to the back office. Barb appeared with Susan trailing behind her. I hated the way they both stared at me like I'd given them a one-star review on Yelp.

Barb stopped behind the counter while Susan took the spot beside her.

I pulled in a trembling breath. 'Let me start by saying I'm sorry if I caught you both off guard the other day. It's never been my intention to do anything that would put our friendship in peril. I really love the P&P, and sales are down due to online retailers and ereaders. Nobody wants to do their events at the store because they can generate more business at a chain. I'm spiraling in debt, and desperate to do something to stop the bleeding. I need to build the coffee bar in order to save the P&P. To be totally honest, if I let my mother down, lose the store, I think it might destroy me.'

I didn't know I was crying until Barb plucked a stack of napkins off the counter and moved toward me. She placed a few in my hands before yanking me into a hug.

'Oh, honey. We know how scary it is to run a business,' she whispered. 'To worry about whether or not you're going to be able to pay your rent, your suppliers and your staff every month.'

Susan moved in close and placed her hand on my shoulder. 'We should have handled our response to you better, Tessa. We know you are fighting for the store. That day you talked to us, we should have been more thoughtful and…' She hesitated until Barb gave a quick nod. 'We want to help.'

'How?' I said in between sniffles.

'We think it'd be great if you could serve food along with your beverages.' Susan gave me a wide smile. 'It could be a partnership between our stores. Until you get on your feet, Barb and I could provide the pastries at cost. Once you're on your way, we can negotiate a fair split.'

It was a great idea, and I wished I'd thought of it in the first place.

'Are you sure you're okay with that?'

Barb stepped back and patted my cheek. 'Let's take it one day at a time and see how it all shakes out.'

'You're both angels on this earth. You know that, right?'

'Angels?' Barb chuckled. 'When we first came to town nobody knew quite what to call us, but I'm pretty darn sure *angels* wasn't at the top of the list.'

Susan tapped at her chin thoughtfully. 'I'm pretty sure those first few months I heard poacher. Traitor.' The corners of her eyes pinched in amusement. 'I think Mrs Vanderpool might have even called us "charlatans".'

That sounded about right for her.

'We all learned fairly quickly that Miss Pat knew what she was doing when she handed you two the keys,' I said. 'Ivy Falls would not be the same without you.'

Barb reached out and took Susan's hand. 'We consider ourselves lucky to be part of this community too.'

That made Susan go a little weepy, and they pulled me in for another hug. Their grace and kindness were another reminder why Ivy Falls was special.

This was my home. Manny's home too.

Torran was right. I had to stop holding on to the past. Clinging to the thought that Billy would ever do the right thing. Manny was the person I could count on. The person I could always turn to when I needed a strong shoulder or a rational voice. The other night we were only seconds from that kiss. A kiss I desperately wanted.

My mind went back to Torran's comments about him in that Superman costume, and I couldn't forget the spark of jealousy that burned inside me when a woman tossed a glance in his direction.

It was time to choose happiness, and I knew the exact person who could make that happen.

Chapter Seventeen

MANNY

Rookie Move

The longer you're a parent, the quicker you know when something is wrong with your child. I'd made Lou's favorite dinner, spaghetti and meatballs with Gina's homemade sauce, and she'd only eaten one bite.

'How was school today?'

She gave me a shrug, her black ponytail swinging behind her. This morning I'd suggested a French braid, but she'd waved me off. Besides the whole pretending-to-be-sick scheme, it was one more sign that things were very wrong.

'The old Thomas Place is starting to look like a real house again,' I went on. 'Do you want to go by and see it when it's in better shape? You can tell Torran where she's missed nails in the floor again. You know how she loves that.'

I thought for sure this would get her to smile. She was good at finding small details we'd missed in a house, but her stony stare remained on her plate.

Outside a storm lashed rain against the windows. Shook the remaining leaves from the trees.

'Was soccer practice okay? I thought that was a great shot on goal during the scrimmage at the end.'

Another shrug.

I set my fork down against my plate. Behind us Mr Peepers squawked, '*Raisins! Give me fucking raisins!*'

With the help of our local vet, we'd learned that ignoring a bird's bad language, or teaching it a new word, was the best way to handle his foul-mouthed behavior.

Lou, in a voice as sweet as honey, turned to the cage and said, 'Fiona finds fleas fascinating.'

I swallowed a laugh and said, 'Where did that come from?'

She set her chin like she was still annoyed. 'Fascinating is on our spelling list this week. It's what my teacher said when using it in a sentence.'

Her gaze went back to her plate, but she still didn't eat a bite.

'Lou, I know something is bothering you. Are you having trouble with your classes? Is someone bullying you at school?'

She shook her head. Clammed up again.

'Your mama used to go all quiet when she was angry or upset or confused. She'd tell me she needed to work out her worries in her brain before she could say them out loud. Is it the same for you?'

Her face stayed an empty mask, which scared the hell out of me.

'Do you think we should go back and see Dr Ramirez? She's helped you in the harder moments. Maybe it would be a good idea.'

'No!' She jumped up from the chair, tossing her napkin on top of her plate and splashing sauce all over the table-cloth.

'Louisa!' I said, struggling to keep my voice level. 'What is going on with you?'

'I don't need to go to the doctor! All I want is to be left alone.' She turned on her heel and raced into her room, slamming the door behind her.

I should have followed. Pressed her for more information, but Gina's voice played on repeat in my head.

There will be times when she's going to want to be alone. Give her space.

I paced the hallway for a good half-hour, finally tapping on her door and pushing it open. She was sound asleep on her bed. I inched off her pink sneakers. Pulled the covers over her. It was hard to look at her peaceful face and know that something was hurting her. The feeling was like a white-hot poker jabbing at my chest.

I left the room and pulled my phone out of my back pocket. If I stayed in the house alone with my thoughts for a minute longer, I might explode. Maybe Torran could watch Lou while I went to the P&P and started work on the coffee bar. If Lou did wake up, I hoped she'd talk to Torran because, sadly, I couldn't get anywhere with my daughter.

'Manny? What's going on?' Torran answered my call, not bothering to say hello.

'Lou's asleep, and I need to run out to the P&P. I have a few ideas I want to map out for the coffee bar. Can you come over for a little while?'

'Sure. Beck's working late at the office again. How are you going to get in though? Tess is out to dinner with my dad and the girls.'

'She gave me an extra key just in case she lost hers. I know the alarm code too.'

'Yeah.' There was a knowing lilt to her voice. 'It makes sense she'd do all that.'

'I'm not going there with you tonight. See you in five?'

'Yep,' she said before hanging up on me.

–

Thunder and lightning rocked the skies as another storm rolled in.

I shook the rain from my hair and twisted the key into the P&P's deadbolt. The sad and broken look on Lou's face played like a bad movie in my mind. Had I been naïve to think that I could raise her on my own? Did she need a woman's care and guidance?

Once I had all the lights on in the P&P, I peeled my jacket off my wet skin and set it on a table. The warmth of the space, the scent of old books and a lingering hint of Tess' perfume made my racing heart slow. I walked to the spot where Tess had cleared and moved shelves to make way for the coffee bar. I pulled out my sketchpad, going over the design for the bar again. Even as I worked, measuring and adding to the schematic, visions of Lou's crumpled face kept filling my head.

When Gina's parents visited at the holidays and birthdays, they frequently offered to find us a house close to where they lived in Tampa. I'd always waved them off, but now I worried that maybe they needed to be a larger part of Lou's life. I wanted to give her the biggest support network possible, but the thought of uprooting her from Ivy Falls and all the people we loved here made my gut clench.

I ran my hand over the exposed brick wall, trying to imagine the exact spot where we'd set the antique buffet. Work always soothed my worried mind, and tonight I needed to forget the pained look in Lou's eyes, if even just for a little while.

Turning back to the blueprints, I searched for all the water and electrical lines until a repeated dripping noise pulled me to the back of the store. In a corner near where Tess shelved the architecture books, a slow river of water fell from the ceiling. Most of the books on the shelves were already wet and warped.

Shit. I tugged on my jacket and raced out to the parking lot. Once I was at my truck, I pulled out my ladder and set it against the side of the building. I sprinted back and grabbed some extra tarp from the bed and a few roof nails.

The storm continued to pour from the sky as I climbed to the spot where I thought there was a leak. Thunder boomed in my ears as I crawled over the shingle tiles. I pulled the small flashlight from my back pocket and held it between my teeth while laying down the blue plastic tarp and securing it in place. Lightning arced across the sky, and another boom of thunder rattled my damn bones.

When I was sure the tarp wouldn't budge, I inched across the roof and hit a patch of water. My feet went out from under me. Shingles scraped against my back like sharp nails. I skidded forward, the momentum shoving me to the edge of the roof. In a panic I rolled over and threw my arms out, catching myself before I torpedoed off the side of the building. My heart was in my throat, and I was soaked from my head all the way to my socks. I leaned back, the clouds rolling overhead like a menacing gray monster.

I was such an idiot.

Climbing onto a roof alone during a storm was a rookie move. What if I'd fallen? Who would take care of Lou if

I was hurt? I cursed under my breath and inched my way back to the ladder and climbed down slowly.

When I was inside the P&P again, I tore off my wet shirt, and headed straight to the back of the store. Water still trickled from the ceiling, but it was tapering off. I surveyed the area again, and my stomach dropped.

Shit. Water and books. What a fucking disaster.

I fumbled with my phone as I pressed Tess' number. When she answered with a sweet, 'Hi, Manny,' I closed my eyes and willed my voice to be steady.

'I know you're at dinner with your dad and the girls…' The ambient noise of the restaurant made it hard to hear her. 'But is there any chance you could meet me at the P&P?'

'Why?' she yelped. 'What's going on?'

I didn't want to freak her out. She already had enough to worry about.

'I can't really explain. It's best if I show you.'

The sound of a squeaky chair and low footsteps echoed through the phone.

'Did someone break in? Is it another rock through the window? Dammit! It was expensive to fix the last one because it's leaded glass.'

'No one broke in.' I interrupted her rapid-fire questions. A loud moan like a door being opened made its way through the phone, and all the noise drifted away.

'Are you okay?' I hated the shake in her voice.

'I'm fine, but I found a small leak in the roof.'

She cut me off before I could tell her where. 'I'll be there in ten minutes. You promise you're okay?'

'All my limbs are intact, Tess.'

She let out a relieved breath.

'But there is one thing.'

'Okay,' she said, that frightened tone returning to her voice.

'I need you to bring towels. Lots and lots of towels.'

Chapter Eighteen

TESSA

Hold Me Like A Promise

The only sign someone was inside the P&P was the set of low lights coming through the front picture window where I displayed current bestsellers, romance titles and my favorite children's books. I quickly parked, grabbed an armful of towels and rushed inside, hunching my body over to avoid the rain.

When I found Manny in the back corner of the store, he was pacing, his gaze fixed on a wet patch in the ceiling. I should have been shocked by the leak in the roof, but that wasn't why my throat went bone dry. Why dopamine flooded my veins with a hum of pure pleasure. Manny stood only a few feet away, shirtless and dripping wet. The waves in his dark hair slicked back. Corded muscles on his biceps and forearms glistened. His dark jeans hung low on his hip bones, and a delicate tattoo was inked in lacy script along his ribcage. He resembled a Greek god who'd just stepped from the sea, and I was about to lose my damn mind.

I stood frozen, completely mesmerized (and admittedly turned on) by the chiseled outline of his gorgeous body. At this point I was pretty sure I was drooling.

'Tess.' His voice rumbled through my body, and my core warmed in a way I hadn't felt in a very long time. Maybe never.

A tiny drop of water plunged off the edge of his strong chin and hit the center of... oh my lord, the most perfectly carved chest I'd ever seen.

'Sorry about all this.' His voice shook me from my heated daze. 'You shouldn't have to see the store this way.'

There was such a gutted ache to his voice that I finally looked into his slate gray eyes.

'What happened?'

'I wanted to start on the coffee bar. Thought I'd take a look at the plans again. When I got here, I heard a dripping noise. I followed the sound to this spot. Water was already pouring down and covering some of the shelves.'

I tried to stay focused on his eyes and not the perfectly cut line of his abs that led down to the sharp V of his hips and dropped into his low waistband. My pulse became frenzied, and I forced myself to remember that it would be all kinds of awkward to reach out and trace the delicious lines carving out his pecs. I gripped the edges of my skirt, trying to concentrate on the words coming out of his beautiful mouth, but it was like watching a Roman statue come to life right before my eyes. A statue I desperately wanted to touch.

Another stray drop eased down his dark hairline and slid across his beautiful cheek. I wanted to lean in and lick it away.

Cool it, Tess. Part of your store is currently wrecked.

'There's a tarp on the roof now which should stop most of the leak. I'll get a crew out here tomorrow to do a patch.'

He worked his tight jaw, and my mind still raced with too many inappropriate thoughts.

'You climbed on the roof during a storm? Why, Manny? That's dangerous.'

He dragged a hand through his luscious hair again and my ovaries did a little dance.

Man, I had to get it together.

'I was worried about the damage the water would do to your books.' He looked at me with such devotion that I had to clasp my hands in front of me, because all I wanted to do was reach out and touch his wet cheeks. Place a kiss on his full lips.

'Books are not worth putting yourself in danger. I'd rather have a thousand-dollar loss than see you get hurt. You know that, right?'

That tender look on his face remained. 'I know, but you have to understand that I'd do anything for you.'

We stayed in a frozen haze, his gaze lingering on my mouth.

'I brought the towels,' I managed to mumble, trying to look anywhere but at his lips.

'Good. Let's start laying them down along the back wall to soak up the mess.'

I started to move to where puddles of water were forming when he caught me by the arm. He'd touched me hundreds of times before, but for some reason, tonight, it was more electric. As if, in the shadowed and quiet surroundings of my beloved store, I was finally seeing the true him. Or it could be that I hadn't had sex in what felt like decades, and the sight of him half naked reminded me that I was still a hot-blooded woman with needs.

'Insurance will cover this. Don't worry,' he whispered.

Reality finally shook me out of my sex-deprived stupor. The floors near the leak were soaked. Water covered the top shelves and spilled over two freestanding displays. I'd have to do a better assessment after we sopped up the mess, but at a glance, the loss would be sizeable.

'Let's clean up as much as we can and then figure out the damage.'

He gave me a defeated nod and pulled half the towels from my arms.

We got on our hands and knees, drying up as much of the water as possible. Some of it had reached the children's section, and I used one of the larger beach towels to cover part of the rainbow rug.

'Manny, why aren't you home with Lou?' I finally said.

He tried to hide it, but his hands shook as he pressed a towel down into a puddle.

'She's acting strange. At dinner tonight, I asked if something was bothering her.' He shook his head. 'I mentioned going back to see her therapist. She got angry and stormed from the table.'

He shoved the towel over and over against the hardwood floor, intent on soaking up as much water as possible.

'I asked your sister to watch her because work usually clears my head. Thought it'd be smart to come here and get the demo started…' He broke off, and I hated the sadness in his voice.

I left my spot on the rainbow rug and crossed the room. My skirt pooled around my legs when I sank down beside him. 'It was one bad night. As she grows older, becomes a teenager, there will be more. Lou adores you. She'll talk when she's ready.'

'It kills me to see her unhappy. I'm trying so hard to do all the right things for her. But I'll never be Gina,' he gasped. 'How can my little girl have a happy childhood if she can't have her mother?'

He jammed two more towels against the wall like he needed to stay in motion or he'd fall apart.

I laid my hand over the top of his. He turned to me, his eyes wracked with pain, and I held out my arms. The weight of him collapsed against me. I thought for sure I wouldn't be strong enough to hold him, but he fit perfectly against me. The dampness of his hair soaked into my blouse. I reached up and slid my fingers through the dark strands. His body rocked against mine as I hugged him tighter.

'You're being too hard on yourself. Lou knows better than anyone how much you love her.'

'What if it's not enough? It terrifies me to think that I could lose her if I don't do all the right things.'

'It's easy to fall into that trap,' I said, holding him closer. 'Every night before I go to bed, I second-guess all the choices I've made that day. Last night, I let the girls have ice cream before bed, and then I tossed and turned all night worrying about whether or not they'd brushed their teeth properly. Praying they wouldn't get any cavities.'

His soft chuckle rumbled against my chest. I tried to pretend that having his rock-solid body leaning into mine did not set off all kinds of fantasies in my head, but then I reminded myself that this was Manny, my friend, who at the current moment was in a terrible parenting spiral.

Like he felt me tighten up, he pulled away and sat back.

He tugged his hands through the places in his hair where I'd run my fingers. The wall of muscle rippled across his chest again. I looked away as the lower half of my body lit up like a freaking bonfire.

'I've had a few struggles in my life,' he said quietly. 'But nothing's been as tough as being a single parent.'

'You're not alone in this. We have each other,' I said, finally looking into his eyes. 'I'm so grateful I have someone to talk to. Who understands my worries and crazy fears, like cavities.'

He let loose a slow smile, and I couldn't stop the heat that swept through me again.

'Maybe you should put a shirt on. Aren't you cold?' I said, jumping to my feet.

His low chuckle filled the room. 'Am I making you uncomfortable, Tess?'

'No,' I said much too quickly.

'Sorry again about the mess.' He moved to his feet, all the muscles in his arms rippling.

I bit into my lip, the hunger in his eyes pinning me in place. 'I'm not worried about it,' I said like I could ignore the way his skin glistened in the shadowy light. 'If anything, I know I can count on you to make things right. This past year you've made life bearable for me. Forced me to play and laugh with my girls when I thought those things would never be possible again.'

He waited a beat, his gaze measuring the small distance between us. 'You and Iris and Rose are my family. I will do everything in my power to make sure you're safe and happy.'

There was so much weight to his words that I felt every inch of them deep down in my bones. He'd been there for me when I wanted to rip my hair out, collapse in a pile of tears, scream at the heavens about being so dumb for trusting Billy. Through it all, he'd been rock solid. Never judging my choices or questioning my dreams.

Isn't that what you needed in a partner? Someone who accepted your authentic self. Who saw the good and bad parts of you and still cared all the same. Manny was that person, and I knew if I wanted this, wanted him, I'd have to be brave enough to step forward and claim him as my own.

I moved in and trailed my fingertips across his warm chest. He sucked in a shaky breath as I traced the curve of his left forearm up to his bicep, over his shoulder, and along the sharp ridge of his collarbone. When I started to move my fingers down the line of his chest, he reached out and gripped my hand.

His questioning eyes searched mine like he wasn't sure what I was doing. What I wanted.

My answer was to tug him past the racks of non-fiction books and biographies to the small reading corner with an oversized antique green velvet chaise and a thick maroon rug. I nudged him against one of the bookshelves. My hands returned to the firm lines of his chest, his heart thudding out a wild symphony beneath my palms.

'Are you sure you want to do this? The other night we almost kissed, but then the rock…'

'Since the day we met, I've wanted to touch you.'

My words slid out smooth and easy because they were the honest truth. I'd fought my attraction to him for so long, but tonight, that resolve was gone.

He reached around my waist and tugged me closer. The hardness of him pushed against my center. It was equal parts thrilling and terrifying. That small but vocal part of me that always doubted my choices, worried what came next, forced me to drop my gaze to the floor.

'Look at me, Tess.' The tenderness in his voice drew my eyes up. 'I need you to tell me this is okay. It'd kill me to ruin what we have if you're not all in.'

I ran the pad of my thumb over the dark stubble lining his strong jaw. He closed his eyes. Pulled in a shaky breath. With him holding me like a promise, his solid body a warm cage around me, my doubt and worry vanished.

'Manny.' I made my voice firm. 'I need you to kiss me right now.'

Chapter Nineteen

MANNY

A Man On A Mission

Eight simple words and they electrified every element in my body. I took a thick gulp, needing a beat to convince myself this was real.

Tess' fingers stayed pressed to my heart, and I was sure she could feel how it was about to explode out of my chest. How her touch completely unraveled me. It would be easy to lean in and take what I wanted, but I had to embed this moment into my memory. I'd waited for it for so long, and I wanted to savor it.

Her eyes flashed with hesitancy, and I took a step back. 'We don't have to do this.'

'No,' she said quickly. 'It's been a while though, and I'm not sure...'

I laid my hands against her cheeks. 'I'm here. Listening to your every word. Tell me what you need.'

She gave me a small, wicked smile. 'Maybe I *need* a little practice. A willing partner.' Her eyes filled with a hunger that turned my skin to flame.

'All right, *partner*,' I whispered against the warm shell of her ear. 'Tell me, what kind of kiss do you want?'

'What kind?' Her breath turned rough which made me even harder.

'Soft and lingering like Mr Darcy gives Elizabeth?' I pressed a kiss to her forehead. To her cheeks. Then lightly to her mouth. Her eyes closed like she wanted to remember the heady sweetness of this moment too.

'That's from the 2005 *Pride & Prejudice*,' she said on a stuttered exhale.

'I remember the night we watched it. If I recall correctly, you let out a satisfied sigh at the end. That's the sound I want to spill out of your mouth tonight.'

Her cheeks flushed that gorgeous shade of pink, and my hands went to her waist. I spun her around until her back was flush with the side of a tall shelf. I pinned her arms above her head and stepped in between her legs. I waited for a hint of hesitation. Any sign that she wasn't ready for this. Ready for me. Instead, I was met with a fire that could not be denied.

'How about a kiss like Westley and Buttercup in *The Princess Bride*?' I said, brushing my mouth over her lips again. It was velvety gentle, but it unleashed an ache in me that had been building, gnawing at my soul, since the day we met.

'Or what about that kiss between Han and Leia in *The Empire Strikes Back*?' This time I feathered a soft kiss over her cheek.

'That was a desperation kiss because he was about to be frozen in carbonite,' she said on a ragged breath.

I edged in closer so she could feel the heat of me. 'Everything about this moment is desperate, Tess.'

I leaned in and moved my hungry mouth over hers, my tongue stroking gently against her lips until she opened for me and met me kiss for kiss.

'Only you would know that the way to my heart would be through my favorite kisses from books and movies,' she gasped as I moved my mouth to the edge of her chin, down her beautiful throat, and across her collarbone.

My kisses became harder, hungrier, and she returned the intensity, running her tongue over the curve of my lips, nipping at the corner of my mouth. Another groan escaped as I lifted her up. She wrapped her legs around my waist, and I let my tongue do more exploring.

All the times I'd imagined this happening, it was tentative and slow, but the chemicals firing between us were hotter, more intense, than I could have ever imagined. We were gasoline and an open flame. The breath of oxygen seeping into a burning room.

Her hands trailed down my back like she was memorizing every rise and fall of my spine. When her grip landed on my ass, it untethered the last of my restraint. I set her gently back on her feet. My fingertips skidded down the front of her chest, over her stomach, and landed on the spot between her legs. She was already wet for me, and I almost lost control with that single touch.

'I can stop anytime. Just say the word.'

'Don't you dare stop, Manchester Parks.' Now it was her turn to growl.

I took my time undoing the buttons on her deep green blouse, my trembling hands having trouble setting them free.

'Do you want my help?'

I loved the huskiness to her voice that warned she wanted this as much as me.

'Tess, I've been having dirty thoughts about you for a long time. Please give me a minute to enjoy this.'

She reached up and pushed back the dark curl that fell over my forehead. Her touch like a bolt of lightning. 'Take as much time as you need. I'm not going anywhere.'

Fuck. The silkiness of her voice, the way she looked at me with want, made me speed up my motions. Once I had the blouse off her shoulders, I took a thick gulp. Her bra was sheer black lace with small flowers that hid her nipples. I wanted to touch her everywhere. Feel the heat of her under my fingertips. Show her that she was a beautiful woman worthy of love, care and affection every single day of her life.

Like a man on a mission, I pressed my fingers along the outside of her waist and dragged them up her body until they latched beneath the straps of her bra. I eased them off her shoulders and undid the clasp. Without hesitating, I pressed my mouth to a soft spot at the base of her neck, trailing kisses all the way down until I reached her hard and pebbled nipple. I laved my mouth over her, sucking and licking until the moan she released was not of this world.

'More,' she said on a stuttered breath, and I obeyed her order, taking her other nipple in my mouth while the tips of my fingers worked the other one. She pressed a hand against my hard bicep, holding on as if she needed to stay upright.

'You and I have been this slow-burning fuse on a stick of dynamite,' I said, slowly pulling back. She let out a small protest until I sank to my knees. Everything I did set off a shimmer of want behind her eyes. I trailed a line of kisses down her stomach, moving my hand over the top of her skirt and stopping where I could feel her heat.

'Sweetheart,' I said on a rough exhale. 'This is the time to speak up. Ask me to stop. Because once I see you naked, I'll never be able to forget it.'

I needed one last reassurance from her, because this was the line, and I had every intention of crossing it if she let me. She brushed her hand over mine, slowly stroking the top of my skin, and I almost swallowed my damn tongue.

'I don't want to go in reverse. My life has been in a holding position for too long,' she whispered. 'It's time to put my foot on the gas and speed forward. Having my legs wrapped around you is a good place to start.'

She took a step back and undid the zipper on her skirt, letting it fall to the ground. In one quick motion, she stepped out of her matching black panties, and the sight of her bathed in the golden glow of the room made my head spin.

For a minute I understood Tess' worry. I'd been on exactly two dates since I'd lost Gina. Did *I* even remember how to do this?

The fear must have been clear in my eyes, because she pulled me down onto the soft rug. Maneuvered our bodies until we were kneeling in front of each other. She set my fingers on her waist like she understood I needed reassurance. That she was just as scared as I was.

'Orange-soaked sunsets. Rainbows after a storm…'

She looked up at me under her gorgeous fan of dark lashes. 'What are you talking about?'

'I'm listing all the beautiful things I've seen in my life.' I reached out and cupped a hand against her cheek. 'You and your body are definitely going on that list.'

Her cheeks flamed again with that luminous pink color I'd never seen on another woman but her. It was just one of many things that made Tess special. The way the light captured the threads of copper in her hair. How she scrubbed at her forehead when she was deep in thought. The little squeaks she made when we watched a scary movie, and she was too afraid to look at the screen.

Her gaze raked over my body. 'You're wearing too many clothes,' she said with a rough achiness. I'd never seen this sexy and teasing side of her before.

I liked it.

Before I could reach down and undo my belt, her hands were already there. I bit the inside of my cheek and prayed that once she put her hands on me, I'd last more than five seconds.

Once my belt was off, I helped her with my wet jeans, which was a hilarious kind of struggle. When the only thing left on my body was my soaked boxer briefs, her gaze wandered down, and there was no hiding what her touch did to me.

She tugged down the material until we were bare before each other. I took my time moving my gaze over every inch of her porcelain skin, loving the freckles dotted over her chest and across her shoulders like she'd been kissed by the sun. The little mole shaped like a heart that sat next to her collarbone. She was more beautiful than I'd ever let myself imagine.

I reached up and twirled a lock of her hair around my finger and tugged it toward me. She met me in the middle, and our kiss wasn't hungry or frantic, but so languid and slow that I felt the heat slowly rising up from my toes until I made it known to Tess, my length pressing against her stomach.

I lowered her onto the rug and took my time kissing every inch of her skin. With each press of my mouth, she let out low pants that made me want to move faster. But

I'd pictured – no, dreamed – about this moment for so long that I swore I'd make it last as long as I could hold out.

As I kissed down the length of her, she writhed beneath my lips. When I reached her sweet center, she quickly sat up and shook her head.

'Second thoughts? Do you want me to stop? We can, and nothing will change between us.'

'It's not that.' Her gaze darted to the side like she couldn't look at me.

'Hey,' I whispered, turning her chin so I was staring into her eyes. 'It's okay. You can say anything to me.'

'I've never done that before. Billy was never interested.'

'What about for him?'

'Yes,' she said with a sharp edge. 'He asked for that *all* the time.'

It took everything I had not to curse out Billy. A real man knew that sexual satisfaction equaled pleasure for both parties. That a woman as gorgeous as Tess deserved to have as many orgasms, in as many ways, as possible.

Instead of blurting out all that, I said, 'We'll only do what you want.'

She glanced at how, even with the conversation, my erection was still hard and thick. Scooting forward, she took me in her hands and started to work me up and down. It felt incredible, but I stopped her.

'You first,' I whispered.

Understanding my meaning, she leaned back. I continued my exploratory path of kisses down her jaw, along her neck and across her breasts. When I reached where she was wet, I slid my palm over her. A delicious moan escaped her lips, and I went to work first with my fingers and then my mouth. It was beautiful to watch her writhe beneath me. To trust me enough to give her this kind of pleasure. She slid a hand into my hair and tugged as her hips arched up to meet my tongue. As soon as she found her release, she pulled me on top of her, begging for more.

'Wait. We need protection,' I said.

One of the guys on the crew had jokingly put a condom in my wallet last week, and I'd never taken it out. When I came back to the rug, she watched me in eager anticipation until I was ready for her. I braced my hands on either side of her hips and slid in slowly. Her eyes closed, and her heavenly smile nearly undid me. Threading my hands through hers, we moved in perfect rhythm until we tipped over the edge of bliss together. I wanted to stay buried inside her for as long as possible, but she opened her eyes and gave me a slow smile.

'So much for fixing the mess.'

I pushed back a lock of hair stuck to her cheek. 'Oh, I like this mess much better.'

She laughed and ran her hands up and down my spine, her nails giving my skin a delicious scratch. We shared a few more lingering kisses before I jumped up and raced to the bathroom to dispose of the condom. When I came back to the rug and laid down beside her, she slid her fingertips along the side of my body, tracing the cursive script inked into the skin below my ribs.

'*If you're going to love me, do it well.*' A small sigh left her lips. 'That's lovely. Is it from a poem?'

The minute she saw me naked, I knew this would be a part of me I'd have to share with her.

'It's what Gina said to me the first time I told her I loved her.'

The air went still. I watched Tess' face for any sign of guilt, worry or regret. It wasn't every day you ran your fingers over the loving sentiment of a man's late wife.

She started to reach out again, but her hand hovered over the spot like she needed my permission to touch such a sacred thing. I took her fingers and laid them on top of the ink.

'Is this her handwriting?' she asked with such loving tenderness that a breath caught in my throat.

'Yes. A year after her death, once I'd come out of the really dark place I'd gone, I was cleaning out her closet and found a box with all the cards and love letters we'd exchanged over the years. I saw those words of hers on the page, it was what she said in our quiet moments together, and I knew I wanted them written on me forever.'

I finally looked into Tess' eyes and found them brimming with tears.

'What does it feel like to be loved that deeply?'

'Tess.' I used my thumb to swipe the tears from her cheek. 'You're an amazing woman. I'm sorry you weren't treasured the way you deserved.'

I held back a hundred more words. That I cared deeply for her. That I'd walk over broken glass, through rings of fire, to keep her safe and protected. That when she looked in the mirror, I wished she saw what the rest of Ivy Falls did: an incredible woman. A loving mother. The best sister and friend anyone could ask for. But most of all, that she had a heart bigger than anyone I knew.

With a gentle hand, I tugged her in closer. Breathed in every inch of her. This moment was precious, and I wanted to soak in every bit of her touch. We stayed like that for a while until she inched back, ran a finger over my dark stubble, and said, 'I have to use the bathroom.'

I gave her a peck on the forehead and let her go. Laying back against the rug, I tucked my hands behind my head, not thinking about anything else but how I wanted to feel her body against mine for eternity. Take my time finding the little spots that made her moan, giggle, cry out with passion.

'I'm starving,' she said, coming out of the back. She wrapped her beautiful auburn hair into a knot on top of her head and sank down beside me, laying her head on my chest. It was a simple gesture, but after what we'd just shared, it felt intimate. It felt right.

'Did your dad not feed you?' I teased.

She laughed, and I loved how her shoulders sat low and relaxed. That she wasn't running to grab her clothes, regretting what we'd just done. Instead, she eased into my side like she and I had been seeing each other naked for years.

Which I wanted. I definitely wanted.

'I was just tucking into my salad when you called.'

'Yeah, I guess I could have waited.' I moved my gaze over the perfect shape of her breasts. 'But I've got zero regrets right now.'

I leaned in and gave her a slow and gentle kiss. She quickly responded by climbing on my lap and pressing her mouth against the edge of my ear, nipping at the skin on my neck before returning to my hungry mouth. Instinct had me rolling her onto her back, curious to see if I could coax another moan out of her pretty mouth, when a loud screech and crash of metal came from outside.

'What was that?' she yelped.

Instinct had me pulling her to my chest. Listening for any other noise. Another sound like breaking branches rang through the store.

'That's coming from the square,' I said.

We tugged on our clothes quickly. Tess was out the front door, and I was fast on her heels. She sprinted around the limestone fountain, the scent of wet wood and bitter smoke filling the soggy night air. I followed her down the brick-paved sidewalk in the direction of town hall. When we reached its wide fan of a lawn, we found a black car smashed into a century-old oak that shaded the old gazebo in the summertime.

'Call nine-one-one,' Tess yelled over her shoulder.

I dialed, and when the operator answered, I told her to send emergency and fire vehicles to the square.

Tess sped across the lawn, and I caught up to her side. When we reached the vehicle, I yanked open the door, but the driver's seat was empty.

'What the hell?' I said over the downpour that was currently soaking us.

Tess' cheeks lost all their color. She scanned the streets, her gaze darting to town hall before she started running again. She sprinted through the wet grass in the direction of the cement steps that led up to the hall's main door.

A shadowed figure with a hoodie pulled over their head sat on a lower step. I picked up my pace as the sound of sirens filled the air.

When Tess finally reached the bottom of the steps she came to a skidding halt.

The dark figure was bent forward, cradling a small, wet creature – Mrs Vanderpool's dog, Baby.

'Are you all right?'

There was a catch to Tess' voice I didn't understand. She took a few more tentative steps toward the person still hidden in shadow. Rain soaked the ground around us as the sirens drew closer. She bent down slowly, surveying a river of blood that flowed down the person's chin.

With a shaky hand, she pushed back the hoodie, and her voice broke as she said, 'What the hell are you doing here, Billy?'

Chapter Twenty

TESSA

Leverage

I wasn't sure what shocked me more. The sight of seeing my ex again or the fact that a cut sliced through his left eyebrow and a thin stream of blood dripped from his mouth.

'Billy, what happened? Why are you holding Old Mrs Vanderpool's dog?' I said.

Before he could answer, a female paramedic, along with Deputy Ben, rushed toward us. They called for us to move back as Silvio appeared on the lawn holding on to a white-robed Mrs Vanderpool.

'Baby? Baby?' she cried out over and over. 'Has anyone seen my precious dog?'

'Here,' Billy choked out with a flinch as the paramedic pressed at the cut over his eye.

When Silvio and Mrs Vanderpool reached us their eyes went wide.

'What are you doing with my dog, you hooligan?' She moved quicker than I thought possible and yanked Baby from Billy's arms. 'Did you hurt my boy?' She patted the wet dog like she could determine if he had any injuries.

'Hurt him?' Billy gasped as the paramedic cleaned the gash on his lip. 'No. I was driving through the square, and he ran in front of my car. I swerved and hydroplaned into the damn tree to avoid hitting him.'

More people started to fill the square, heading toward Billy's crumpled black Charger that I'd always hated.

Mrs Vanderpool kept patting Baby, but her eyes softened. 'I was taking him out for his late-night potty break. Just ran inside for a minute to get my umbrella. When I went back out, he was gone. There must be a hole in my fence. Been walking the neighborhoods for at least an hour. Didn't think my old boy had it in him to get this far.'

The paramedic checked Billy's eyes with a penlight. Trying to be subtle, Deputy Ben leaned in like he wanted to see if he could smell booze on Billy's breath.

'The cuts on your head and lip are superficial. No stitches needed. Did you hit your head when you crashed?' the paramedic asked, placing a white bandage over his eyebrow.

'No. When I skidded, my phone flew off the console. Popped me in the mouth and head.'

'You're lucky you're only walking away with a few scrapes,' she said. 'That big oak is one tough lady.'

Billy glanced at his car, his pride and joy's front bumper crumpled up accordion-style against the tree.

He stood slowly, and the paramedic watched to see if he was wobbly on his feet. When he looked steady, Mrs Vanderpool stepped in closer.

'Don't like you much, Billy Newton. Never have. But I won't forget what you did to avoid hurting my sweet Baby tonight.'

Her lower lip trembled as she tucked the dog closer to her chest and let Silvio lead her away.

The crowd started to grow around the accident, and I turned back to Billy.

'Answer my question. Why are you back in town?'

He shivered. His clothes soaked to the bone. 'Can we go somewhere warm and talk?' he asked.

He gave a quick glance in Manny's direction. Much to his credit, Manny didn't say a word, but the way he had his arms crossed over his chest said he wasn't too happy about how our night was turning out.

'Do you need to ask Billy more questions or can we go over to the P&P?' I asked Deputy Ben.

He hesitated, scratched uncomfortably at his chin.

Billy held out his arms at his sides. 'Go ahead and give me a sobriety test,' he muttered.

Deputy Ben led him over to another patch of grass as the rain started to taper off.

'Tess.' Manny came up beside me. 'Are you all right?'

'Yes,' I heaved out. 'It's just a shock to see him.'

'What can I do?' he asked.

Make him disappear again. Make him a better man. A better father.

I pushed the thoughts away and said, 'All I need is for you to stay here beside me. To be my friend right now.'

His lips thinned at the word 'friend' after what just happened between us, but in his typical Manny way, he gave a steady nod.

We waited in the wet, dreary night as Ben put Billy through a series of tests, which he passed.

'He can go back with you now,' Ben said when they were finished. 'I need to take some pictures of the scene.' His mouth went grim. 'Make sure his story lines up. Then we'll have the car towed. Once that's done, I'll need to come to the store and take an official statement.'

He started to walk away but paused and turned back to Billy.

'That was a real good thing you did for Mrs Vander-pool. Avoiding hitting her dog like that. Not sure what she'd do without that little mutt.'

Billy gave him a half-smile and followed behind me and Manny to the store. Once we were through the back door, I had him sit in a chair next to my desk. Manny leaned back against the wall. Fists tightened at his sides.

In the light, it was hard not to gasp at the way Billy looked. His frame had always been thin, but now he appeared too bony for his own good.

'Tess, you're shaking.' Manny moved to the desk and pulled a pink cardigan off my chair, laying it gently over my shoulders. I gave him a smile, and he went back to his spot against the wall.

Billy watched us with his lips pressed thin.

'Okay.' I couldn't keep the exhaustion from my voice. 'Explain to me why you're in Ivy Falls.'

'I left Atlanta a couple of days ago. My plan was to come back here. Get my life on track again.' He let out a sigh and winced like he was in pain, which only made Manny's fists clench tighter. 'Drove in past the welcome sign. Started toward the limestone fountain when Baby darted into the street. As soon as I hit the brakes, car started to skid, I tried to control it, but I spun, went up and over the curb and collided with the fucking tree.'

He winced again as he tapped at his lip, the skin already starting to swell.

'Manny, can you get some ice from the refrigerator in the break room? And grab one of those dry towels?'

It was like he didn't hear me, too caught up in leveling his murderous stare at Billy.

'It's okay, Tessa. I've been worse,' Billy mumbled as his lip grew fatter.

'Manny!' This time I put an edge to my voice, and he finally looked at me. 'Ice. Dry towel. Please.'

He pushed off the wall in a sharp move that made Billy flinch. 'I'll be right back.'

Once he was gone, Billy said, 'Tessie, I'm sorry about all this. I wanted to get my life straightened out before I saw you and the girls.'

'I don't get it. The last time we talked, you were looking for work in Atlanta and getting an apartment with...' I broke off because he knew what I was going to say next. 'For months my lawyers have been trying to track you down to give you the final divorce papers. Where have you been?'

'Yeah, about that...' He pushed back his hood, revealing he'd buzzed off most of his shoulder-length white-blonde hair. A new tattoo of a tear was inked into his skin a few inches below his right ear. 'Trini and I broke up. She's too young. Always wanting to go out and party.'

Several caustic remarks flew through my head.

That's what you get for running off with a nineteen-year-old.
How could you be so stupid?

It serves you right, dumbass.

Before I could say any of them, Manny barged back into the office and slammed a bag of ice and a purple towel down onto the desk.

'Thanks,' Billy said, uncomfortably shooting out his hand. 'Seen the show you're doing with Torran. It's good.'

Manny didn't reply, or shake his hand, he just leaned back against the wall and gave my ex the same dead-eyed stare.

Billy had the sense of mind not to say anything more to the guy who looked like he wanted to rip him in two.

'What are your plans now?' I asked.

He shrugged. 'Look for work. Figure out my shit. Honestly, Tessie, this is my home. I miss my girls. All I want is to make things up to all of you.'

'Where are you planning to stay tonight?' Manny's steely voice cut the air like a knife.

'Uh, well, I was gonna stay at a motel outside of town, but now that I don't have my wallet… It's in the car which is being towed…' Billy dropped his head in his hands.

There were a thousand reasons why I despised him, but he was still my girls' father. I couldn't let him leave here tonight without anywhere to go.

'You can stay on the couch at the house, but only for tonight. Tomorrow you're going to figure out your life. A life somewhere besides Ivy Falls.'

He started to protest, but I held up my hand. 'This is my place with the girls. You need to "figure out your shit" somewhere else.'

He gave a defeated nod. 'Guess I deserve that.'

'Tess, can I talk to you for a second?' Manny's fevered gaze said he didn't like my plan.

I followed him out the office door, and he stopped near the mahogany counter where we had the cash registers. He dragged his hands through his hair, and his lips thinned like he was carefully considering what he wanted to say.

'It's not my business to question what you're doing. Why you invited him to stay at your house, but I'm worried about you.' He stepped in and ran his thumb across my jaw. 'Can I be honest?'

'Of course. I want you to be.'

'I think the story he just fed you is bullshit. The way his car was crumpled, that wasn't some leisurely drive through town.'

'I know he's not telling the total truth, but he's beat up, and it's late. I can't in good conscience let the father of my children sleep on a bench in the square.'

He continued to stare at me with a warmth that I loved. That said he was only looking out for me.

'One night only,' I promised. 'Then he's gone and out of our lives.'

'One night,' he repeated like he was trying to convince himself it was all going to be okay.

Which it was.

'Be careful with him,' he whispered. 'He knows he's got leverage in your life. Don't let him use it to make you feel guilty. He's the one in the wrong here.'

'Billy may think he can still sweet-talk me, but I'm a much different person than the last time he saw me.'

Ben knocked on the front door, and I let him in, pointing to where Billy was waiting in my office.

Once he was out of earshot, Manny's mouth went grim. 'You know who's going to hate this more than me?'

I let out a groan and dropped my head in my hands.

When Torran and my father found out Billy was back, all hell was going to break loose.

Chapter Twenty-One

MANNY

Growing An Extra Heart

I tossed and turned all night. Every time I closed my eyes, I saw Tess standing in front of me without a stitch of clothing on. Her beautiful form seared deep into my brain. The heady scent of her rose and spice perfume formed the perfect sense memory.

Even though I wanted that to be my only reminder of the night, I couldn't shake the chill that seeped into my bones every time I thought about Billy's sudden appearance. How Tess had gasped like she was beyond shocked to see him. The warning bells blaring in my head that his return wouldn't be good for anyone in Ivy Falls. And I hated to admit it, but when she called me a 'friend', it felt like a slight, even though she didn't mean it that way.

When the clock blinked four a.m., I finally gave up and stumbled into the kitchen to make coffee. I pulled a notepad off the desk and listed what needed to be tackled today, hoping it would distract me from all the problems Billy was sure to cause. The first thing was calling Ferris and getting his crew straight over to the P&P to fix the leak.

I tugged my hand through my hair, trying to push away the image of Billy following Tess to her car after she locked up. The smirk I swore I saw cross his lips as he eased his body into the passenger seat like it was all part of his plan.

The thought was like a punch to the gut.

I meant what I said about trusting her, but I also saw the way Billy looked at her like she was the answer to all his problems. That he was a total fucking idiot to have left her.

He wasn't the sharpest tack in the box, but at least he got that right.

The coffee maker let out a small series of beeps. I poured myself a giant mug and went to work preparing Lou's lunch for the day. I hoped after a good night's sleep she'd be better this morning or at least ready to talk.

Once I packed up the peanut butter and jelly, chips, apple, and juice pouch, I grabbed my computer and opened YouTube. Maybe if I could figure out that waterfall braid Lou wanted so badly, all would be forgiven.

–

The braid was an epic disaster. I tried over and over to lay the strands right but couldn't get them to stay in place. I finally gave up after the tenth try and smoothed Lou's hair into a ponytail. As I worked the elastic into her hair, I tried to coax her to talk. All I got were one-word answers like the night before.

I made one last attempt by asking her about buying some new toys from the pet store for Fergus who had a birthday next week. That made the little black cloud fade for a moment until I pushed it and asked one more time what was bothering her.

When I dropped her off at school, my teeth rattled at how hard she slammed the door to the truck. I leaned my head against the steering wheel and took in a few long breaths. The parent behind me laid on their horn. Holding up the car line was the least of my problems this morning.

The work crew was waiting when I pulled into the lot in front of the old Thomas Place. Torran's ancient Ford truck was already parked under a nearby tree. I took my time unloading my tools and carried my belt up to the crumbling porch. Torran's voice floated out of the kitchen, and I stopped dead when another voice followed.

Lauren.

I shook my head and glanced at the door. The last thing I wanted to discuss was my follower count, or how she wanted more pictures for the show's website. If I didn't already have so much work to do here, I would have seriously considered taking the day off.

Overhead, the roofers' feet pounded out a solid rhythm as they started working on the gabled roof. We'd decided to pay for the more expensive but eco-friendly slate tiles. Now that I'd seen them in the morning light, I knew they were the right choice. I snuck around the side of the house to check the final framing for the new porch. It was a cowardly move, but the last thing I wanted was to have another discussion with Lauren about 'likes', 'follows' and 'shares'.

A cool breeze blew across the yard, and I let myself get lost in the rhythm of the work. I loved the scent of fresh sawdust. The push and pull of my muscles as I worked a nail out of a particularly nasty piece of rotted wood. But beyond the physical, I loved the measuring and angles of this job. When I was in college at Middle Tennessee State University, I toyed with the idea of being a math major until the summer between freshman and sophomore year. The summer that changed everything.

A buddy from the football team mentioned his father owned a construction company. During the school break, he offered jobs to the players. It allowed them to stay close to campus for summer workouts but earn money during their downtime.

The day I walked into the main office with my application, my life turned upside down. Seated behind the desk was a gorgeous raven-haired woman who looked about the same age as me. When she took my form, she teased me about my name. Asked if I was from the Tennessee city, Manchester, whose claim to fame was hosting the twenty-four-hour music festival, Bonnaroo, every year.

In a horrible attempt at flirting, I jokingly said, 'no', but maybe she could take me to it one time. As if fate intervened, the festival was happening two weekends later. She giggled, introduced herself as Gina, and invited me along with ten of her closest friends. After that weekend, we were never apart again.

Grief mixed with a small touch of shame washed over me. Gina passed over nine years ago, but there were still moments when I woke in the morning and reached for her side of the bed. I didn't regret what happened with Tess last night. I'd wanted to be close to her since the day we'd first brought our girls to the park months after Billy left, but I'd be lying if I didn't say there was a pang of guilt, like somehow I was being unfaithful to Gina. I knew it wasn't rational, but grief didn't make sense. It showed up in the most unexpected moments, knocking every last bit of air from your lungs.

'There you are.' Torran's paint-splattered, steel-toed boots stopped only inches away. I could hear Lauren's voice behind her in what sounded like a business call. I wondered how weird it would look if I just kept working. Pretended I was invisible. 'Have you talked to Tessa today?' she said more as an accusation than a question. 'I keep calling her, and she won't pick up.'

I let loose a low breath. 'No, I haven't.'

'Imagine my shock and surprise when I went to get my coffee at Sugar Rush this morning, and the whole town was buzzing about how Billy hit the old oak near town hall, all in an attempt not to hit Baby. When Barb and Susan looked at me for answers, all I could do was shrug because my own sister won't answer her damn phone!'

With her fevered voice drawing more than a few stares from our crew, I stood and pulled her across the crumbling porch for a little privacy.

'You were at the P&P last night,' she said quickly. 'Did you see him? Did you see the accident?'

I scrubbed a hand over the back of my neck but stayed quiet. She must have seen the guilt on my face because her cheeks went red.

'You're kidding me, right? Tell me you did not walk back into your house last night and not say a word, even though you know how much I hate that bastard!'

If this was a cartoon, steam would have definitely been coming out of her ears. I tugged the baseball cap off my head and rubbed at my already aching temples. 'It's complicated, Tor.'

'Complicated how?' Before I could answer, she said, 'Did he say why he was back? Is he staying?' She lowered her voice. 'Was he with Trini?'

I pressed my lips together. Shook my head. 'Those are all questions you need to ask your sister.'

The harsh set of her jaw eased. 'Crap. Is it that bad?'

I scratched at my hair, wanting to be doing anything but having this conversation with her.

'Talk to her, Tor.'

'I would if she'd pick up the damn phone.' She started to pace until I reached out. Reminded her to breathe.

'Okay. How are you? Was it weird to see him?' she asked.

'Weird?' I cocked my head.

'Yeah, because I know you have feelings for my sister. And seeing Billy must have been, well, weird for Tessa. Weird for you both.'

She had no idea.

'It all happened so fast. We heard the crash. Found the car. After that, police and fire showed up.'

'They said he swerved to avoid Baby, but did they test him for alcohol or drugs? You know he has a DUI.'

'Deputy Ben checked him out fully. Billy was stone-cold sober.'

She chewed on her lip. 'And after that?'

'We went to the P&P. Tess gave him some ice because his lip was swollen and bleeding.'

'He was bleeding?'

'Yeah, but he's fine.'

'All right, you talked. What happened next?'

A question I did not want to answer. I strode back to the place where I was working, and Torran was right on my heels.

'Manny.' Her voice went piano-wire tight. 'Where is Billy right now?'

'Again, Tor. Go speak to Tess.'

'Dammit! Did he stay at her place?' She shoved her hands in her pockets and started to pace. 'How can you be so calm? This is a disaster!'

'There's no use in worrying about things you can't change. Right now I have to focus on what is in my control, which is finishing this porch that we're three days behind on.'

'Manny.' She bent down to look me in the eye. 'What else is bothering you?'

'Nothing,' I said, pounding a nail a little too hard into the new lumber.

'Liar.'

Shit. I could never play poker. I sucked at bluffing.

I set the hammer down and sighed. 'Lou's still mad at me.'

'Really? She woke up last night, and after I got her into her pajamas, we had milk and cookies. When I put her to bed a little while later, she seemed okay.'

'Well then, she must be saving all her anger for me.'

'What did you do wrong?'

'Why do you assume it's always me?'

'Because guys, especially dads, are good at saying the wrong thing at the wrong time.'

'Thanks for the vote of confidence.'

The last thing I needed was a lecture right now. Not when I had at least five plates spinning, and I was sure every single one of them was going to crash and burn.

'Manny.' Her voice dropped like she was sorry. 'This,' she made an imaginary square around the two of us, 'is a no-judgment zone. I'll stay quiet, and you tell me about Lou.'

'She's been quiet and withdrawn lately. When I try to get her to talk, she goes silent. Or worse, she ignores me.'

'You've got good instincts. What do you think is wrong?'

I dragged my hands down my face. 'Honestly, I have no idea. I talked to Tess about it. She said that maybe Lou's having issues with friends at school. Or is struggling with a bully. That maybe she could be behind in her classes. I asked about all those things, and all it did was make her angrier.' I curled my hands around the brim of my hat trying to slow my racing mind. 'I'm screwing this up, and she's barely in double digits. What am I going to do when she's thirteen? Fifteen?'

My voice must have sounded panicked because she reached out and grabbed my hand. 'We all have bad days. You just need to give her time. She loves you.'

'I miss Gina so much that it feels like part of my soul is missing. If she was here, she'd know exactly what to do. What to say to make things right.'

'Lou's growing up. She's going to try and push you away, but you need to hang in there. Deep down she knows you'll always be her safe space to land.'

'I never thought being a parent would be like growing this extra heart. A heart that you would do anything to protect. A heart that would get stomped on and squeezed and kicked, and yet it would continue to grow fuller with each passing year.'

She flopped an arm over my shoulder. 'I don't know much about parenting, but when I watch you and Tessa, you make it look easy. I was a handful for my parents. It makes me wonder if I really ever want to be a mom. That maybe my skills are better at being a super aunt.'

'You are pretty good at the auntie things, but you also have a major capacity for love. If you decided you wanted to be a mom, I think you'd be a rock star at it.'

'Right now, my baby is this house. Fixing up the entry so the film crew can get in and out safely.'

As though she had been listening from around the corner, Lauren came into view with a bright, toothy smile. 'Can we go inside and talk? The network just sent me the contract for Season Three, and it's a doozy.'

I held out a hand to Torran and pulled her up with me.

'Don't let her talk you into any more social media,' she whispered.

'Yeah, that's not happening.'

I followed behind Torran as she chattered with Lauren about the light walnut stain we'd chosen for the hardwood in the entryway.

Two steps over the threshold, my phone rang. I glanced at the screen and quickly answered.

'Hello?'

'Manny, it's Natasha… I mean, Principal Vogel. We've had an incident with Louisa this morning. I need you to come to school and speak with me about it.'

'Is Lou all right?' I sputtered.

'She's fine, but I'm going to have to suspend her for a day.'

'Suspend her? Why?'

My voice must have banked off the bare structure of the entryway because Torran came flying toward me.

'What's going on? Who's getting suspended?' she whisper-shouted.

I waved her off and turned my back. 'Are you sure we're talking about my Louisa? She's never been in trouble before.'

'It's best if we discuss the situation in person. I know you're working on the old Thomas Place. Can you take a break and come to the school right now? Louisa is sitting in the nurse's office. I can't allow her to return to class. After we speak, you'll need to take her home.'

'I'm on my way.'

'Thank you. I'll see you soon,' she said with a tone so sharp it made me clench my back teeth.

'Manny, what's wrong with Lou? Is she all right? Why is she being suspended?'

Torran chased me down the cracked sidewalk. Her questions hung in the air like thick summer heat. I didn't have time to answer as I rushed to my truck, peeled out of the lot and raced in the direction of the school.

Chapter Twenty-Two

TESSA

Heart Of The Matter

The sound of tiny, alarmed voices made me jump out of bed. I grabbed my phone, its screen a dull black.

Oh, crap. I'd forgotten to charge it.

After all the craziness of last night, first the mind-blowing sex with Manny, and then the unwanted reappearance of Billy, I was surprised I'd slept at all.

When I got home with Billy in tow, I thought for sure Dad's head was going to explode. I explained the situation in the square. After he took a few calming breaths, leveled a death stare at Billy, he agreed we could talk about it later today.

The voices in the family room grew louder. I pulled on my robe and raced down the hall. Iris stood next to the couch, her little eyes pinched in the corners. A trembling Rose hovered behind her.

'Girls, it's all right,' I said quietly.

Billy, much to his credit, recognized their confusion and stayed quiet.

'Isn't he… Is that our daddy?' Iris looked him over, her eyes narrowing like she didn't really understand what she was seeing.

'Yes,' I said, pulling a shaky Rosie into my side. 'He's only staying for a short time, but he wanted to see you.'

Billy gave me a startled look, and I held his stare, willing him to follow my lead for the girls' sake.

'Hi, Iris and my Rosie,' he said, keeping his voice soft. 'I've missed you.'

Both girls stared at me with confusion and fear.

'It's okay to say hello,' I said gently.

Iris inched in closer to the couch, her stare fixed on Billy's face. An eggplant-colored bruise bloomed under his eye like a boxer who'd gone too many rounds with a much bigger opponent.

'Why is there a bandage on your head? And what happened to your lip?' Iris asked.

Billy reached up and touched his eyebrow. 'What, this? It's nothing. Just a little scratch.'

Rose moved out around me and, with a full-throated voice, said, 'If you're our daddy, why don't you live here?'

Leave it to my firecracker to get right to the heart of the matter.

Billy gulped down a full breath. Good. He deserved to be in the hot seat. To be pinned in place by the children he'd cruelly abandoned.

'I had to go away for a while. Needed time to think about some things. But now I'm back.'

Iris, my sweet, shy girl, inched forward and climbed onto a cushion beside him. Rose hesitated, looking to me for guidance with wide eyes.

Billy disappeared when she was so little. All she knew of him were the photos that still littered parts of the house. As much as I wanted to scream at my ex for causing this kind of confusion in my girls, I didn't want them to be afraid of their father.

I plastered a smile to my lips and bent down beside Rose. 'It's all right if you want to sit next to your sister.'

She took tentative steps toward the couch and took the spot beside Iris.

Billy smiled at them both. Asked about school. Their friends. The girls were shy at first but eventually told him about their teachers. How they loved soccer and having regular dinners with their grandpa.

He took his time with them. Waited for their cues as to when to ask questions and when to listen. There was so much to be angry about with him, but I'd forgotten how he could slow down, pay attention to his girls when they needed him.

A little gurgle came from Rose's tummy, reminding me of the time.

'Girls, you need to run and get ready for school. We're late.'

'No, Mama!' Iris cried. 'I want to stay here and play with Daddy now that he's home.' The joy in her face nearly tore me in two.

'Sorry, honey, but your teachers and friends are waiting for you at school. Both of you need to get going,' Billy said, thankfully backing me up.

'Will you be here when we get home from soccer practice?' Rose asked, pointing her big brown eyes, courtesy of his DNA, at him.

'Please don't go away again, Daddy.' Iris sniffled like she thought he might vanish at any moment.

Both girls stared at him, their lower lips quivering.

This scene might kill me.

'Your mama's right. School is super important. Go get your clothes on. Brush your teeth. I'll see you again soon. I promise.'

They gave him a sad nod. Iris reached for Rose's hand and together they walked down the hall.

Yep. My heart might actually snap in two.

'Don't do that,' I said once they were out of earshot.

'Do what?'

'Make them promises.'

He had the gall to look hurt.

'Come on, Billy. We both know you can keep your promises as well as you can keep a job – which is not at all.'

'My past behavior has sucked, I know. But give me a chance to prove I've changed.'

Thin yellow light streamed in the windows, casting shadows over his gaunt cheeks. He really was ten pounds past skinny, and his hair was short and patchy in places like it'd been trimmed with dull garden shears. Holes riddled the sleeves of his worn black hoodie. Another new tattoo on his neck was some kind of snake I didn't recognize.

How appropriate for him.

'We can talk about this later. For now, I want you to leave.'

He gave me a look like somehow I was the one breaking his heart, and it only ignited the slow-burning fury that was growing in my chest.

It was just like him to show up right when we were starting to get our feet under us. It was as if he had this sixth sense, knowing when things were going well so he could swoop in and suck all the joy out of things.

Our junior year of high school I was named a National Merit Scholar and couldn't wait to tell my parents. All the way home in the car, he and his friends teased me about being a 'hot nerd'. They swore they were only joking, but there was a cruel dig to their words that stuck with me for days.

After Rose was born, my dad offered to help with a down payment on a house. I was working full-time at the P&P, and Billy floated between catering jobs and bartending. We said yes, both tired of the cramped apartment where we lived.

I loved our little bungalow, but every time Billy drank (which was way too often), he'd make some nasty remark about how my 'daddy and his money' always came to the rescue. He constantly claimed I'd never understand him and all the demons he was fighting. I'd spent ten years trying, but after a litany of excuses, and one too many apologies, my ability to trust him was obliterated by a slip of paper with a few lines claiming he couldn't live with us anymore.

'Once the girls are ready you can say goodbye, but then you need to walk to the sheriff's department. Figure out how to get your car back. When you get settled in another town, text me. We need to discuss signing the divorce papers and how you're going to help me support the girls once you find a job.'

'Tessie, can't you come back after you drop them off?' He glanced at a clock hanging in the kitchen. 'You have a while before the bookstore opens. Give me a chance to explain my plans.'

'Fine, but this better not be more of your games. Another set of lies you're so good at telling.'

'I swear you won't regret it.'

The sooner I heard him out, the quicker he'd be gone from Ivy Falls. I was about to say that when a sharp knock on the back door stopped me.

Great. That could be one of two people: Torran or my dad. I couldn't deal with either right now.

I tightened the belt on my robe, marched to the back door and threw it open.

'Good morning, Tessa,' Mrs Vanderpool said firmly. Her hair lay in tight silver curls against her head. Thick pink glasses were perched at the end of her nose. Baby let out a little bark as he sat tucked under her left arm.

'Is *he* here?' The taut set of her voice told me whom she meant.

'Yes,' I sighed. 'Come in.'

She walked into the house, and her gaze darted around my small kitchen. When her stare landed on Billy sitting on my couch in the family room, she set her jaw. The sudden tic in her cheek said his swollen eye and split lip caught her off guard.

'I wanted to come by and say thank you again for what you did last night. For not hurting my Baby.' The little brown and black dog gave another yip like he agreed.

'Of course,' Billy said, moving from the couch and stopping next to me.

'Are you back to stay or just passin' through?' she spat out.

'Staying. Starting today, I'm going to look for a job and a place to live.' He gave me a determined gaze. 'Begin making up for my bad choices to both Tessie and my girls.'

'Well,' she huffed. 'That's the least you can do.' Baby gave another little yip, and she lovingly patted his head. 'As long as you're staying, I can offer up the small garage apartment behind my house for a month rent-free. It's not much, but it's the least I can do.' Before I could object, say I wanted Billy to find a place somewhere besides Ivy Falls, Mrs Vanderpool added, 'I can also talk to Silvio. He's not a fan of yours, but he's too old to be workin' at the store long hours with only part-time help like he's doing now.'

Billy bobbed his head. 'Thank you, Mrs Vanderpool. That would be great.'

I wanted to stop time. Pull Mrs Vanderpool outside and tell her I didn't want any of this, but then Dr Sheridan's words about her slowing down, how Baby was her whole world, made me clamp my mouth shut. The woman was also the most stubborn person I'd ever met, and no matter how much I objected, she'd never change her mind.

'We're ready for school.' Iris said as she and Rose rushed back into the room.

'I'll be on my way then,' Mrs Vanderpool said. 'You,' she set her fiery gaze on Billy, 'be at my house by three today.' She waved him closer and lowered her voice. 'And if I catch wind of you pulling any more nonsense, you'll be out on your backside quicker than you can blink. This town can overlook stumbles, but you've already blown any grace you've been given because of what you've done to this sweet little family. One more slip-up and it won't just be me kicking your tail across the city line. Got me?'

'Yes, ma'am.'

Without so much as a goodbye, Mrs Vanderpool turned on her heel and left.

Billy went to the girls and tried to help them with their backpacks. Iris let him, while Rose took a hesitant step away, still unsure of him.

She wasn't the only one.

Chapter Twenty-Three

TESSA

Sinister Omen

The car ride to school was a silent one. There wasn't enough time to explain to the girls what was happening. Why their father, who seemed like a phantom in their lives, had suddenly returned.

After Mrs Vanderpool left, I rushed back to my room to change. My clothes from last night were scattered across the floor. I picked them up, and they still smelled of Manny. That heady scent of soap and steel.

I'd never expected things to go as far as they had with him, but I didn't regret a moment. Showing all of myself to him, letting him touch me, caress me in all the places I ached, was like placing the right book with a reader. We fit together perfectly, and, if I was being honest, I knew the moment we decided to let go of our fears, finally touched each other, it'd be hot. But now, I couldn't help but wonder where things stood between us. How Billy reappearing felt like some sinister omen.

Both girls still refused to talk or look at me. They ate the granola bars I'd brought along, their lower lips set in firm pouts every time they swallowed.

We drove past the square, through the single light, and down two more streets to Merriweather Lane. I took a left and proceeded to the end of the cul-de-sac that ended at the school. The small patch of acreage backing up to a big swathe of woods had housed Ivy Falls Elementary since the early 1990s. The school was all cream stucco, and red brick, with a wide front lawn. Behind it was a massive playground, and a large field used for recess or PE during the months when there wasn't ice or snow.

Once inside the office, I bent down and gave each of them a hug. They mumbled something like a goodbye, and my heart shriveled. Damn Billy.

I waved to Miss Marta, the principal's secretary, who'd been close friends with my mom. She and her tiny little legs scurried in my direction. Her favorite color was orange, and she always tried to work a hint of it into her clothes. Today she was wearing a navy sheath dress with a pin covered in orange sequins in the shape of a heart a few inches below her left collarbone.

'Running late today?' she asked.

'Yes. Issues with my phone alarm.'

Her mouth puckered in concern like she already knew about the scene in the square. That my ex was back.

'Have a good day,' I said, turning for the door.

'Tessa, honey,' she called out before I could make my escape. 'Did you hear about Lou?'

That stopped me in my tracks. She glanced over her shoulder to the principal's closed door and waved me forward.

'You just missed Manny,' she whispered. 'He had to take Lou home.'

'Is she okay?'

'Can't say much. Supposed to keep things private around here.'

I quirked a brow at her. Miss Marta loved gossip about as much as she loved her husband of thirty-plus years.

'But you and Manny are…' – her eyes went a little mischievous – '*close*, so I don't feel bad sharing.'

All right, maybe Manny and I didn't hide our attraction very well.

'At recess before school, the playground aide brought Lou in to see Natasha – I mean, Principal Vogel. I guess Lou had a scuffle with a girl in her class.'

'Do you know what it was about?'

'No, but it must have been bad because Natasha had to suspend Lou for the day.'

'Why? Lou's never been in trouble before.'

'We have two automatic suspension policies. One is for bullying,' she said with a shaky breath. 'The other is if you put your hands on another student.'

'Neither of those sound like Lou.'

She pulled off her cat-eye glass and dabbed at her dark lashes with a tissue. 'Lou's teacher,' she sniffled. 'Well, she says Lou's been struggling since the start of the year. She's tried to talk to Lou about it, but apparently, she's as tight-lipped as Barb and Susan when they're creating a new cookie for the café.'

A door creaked open at the back of the office, and Principal Vogel called to her.

'I gotta go, but don't forget I'm waiting on that new Joanna Shupe book. You know how I love those Gilded Age men.'

'It doesn't come out until later this month. I'll be sure to hold a copy for you.'

She smiled, hesitated, and then lowered her voice again. 'I heard there was an accident in the square last night. You okay?'

'Yes,' I sighed, not surprised that news of Billy's return was burning up the Ivy Falls rumor mill.

'Baby means everything to Greta… Mrs Vanderpool,' she went on. 'I think that dog is what has kept her alive all these years after she lost her beloved Leroy. Billy may have a lotta strikes against him in this town' – pity flashed across her watery eyes – 'but finally, for once, that boy made a good choice.'

Principal Vogel walked out of her office. Her stern look swerved between me and Miss Marta like she knew I'd probably gotten some kind of intel out of her.

I said a quick goodbye, and as soon as I was outside, I dialed Manny's number. It rang twice before going straight to voicemail.

Billy was still waiting for me at the house, but I steered my old Volvo in the direction of Manny's. My mind darted between Miss Marta's story about Lou and the situation with my own girls. They'd already been through so much, and now, sadly, that black tide was rising for all of them again.

Chapter Twenty-Four

MANNY

They've Got Nothing On Dolly

Sitting in a paper gown waiting for a prostate exam was more comfortable than the silence in the truck from Lou. Principal Vogel had done her best to be kind about the situation, but I was still in shock.

'Why did you think it'd be okay to push Brittany off her swing? You know we have rules about anger. If someone hurts you, you talk it out – not act physical.'

Lou tucked herself against the door like if she made herself tiny enough she could disappear. A heavy weight of sadness filled my chest. The last thing I ever wanted was for my daughter to feel small.

'Come on, Lou Lou.' I tried to make my voice as gentle as possible. 'You know you can talk to me about anything.'

The silent treatment continued until we pulled into the driveway. She shot out of the truck like lightning and rushed for the front door. Once I had it open, she raced back to her room. Fergus' russet head rose up from his napping spot, but he didn't move. Mr Peepers flapped inside his cage. '*Raisins! Fuck, I want some raisins!*' the bird screeched.

My chest went tight, and my breaths came out in spurts. I reached for a chair at the kitchen table and held on tight. I closed my eyes. Pictured a box. Slowly I pulled in a breath for four seconds until I got to the corner of the imaginary shape, holding on for another four seconds. As I rounded the curve, I exhaled for four. When I reached the next corner, I held my breath for another four seconds. The image repeated itself a couple of times until I felt like my chest wasn't heaving up and down like a ship on a rough sea. I'd read in a magazine that Navy SEALs used the 'box method' to control their breathing in stressful situations.

At this moment doing secret missions under the cloak of night felt just as daunting as raising an eleven-year-old daughter.

The buzzing phone in my pocket stopped the routine. Tessa. Every part of me wanted to answer, but Lou had to be my focus right now. I let the call go to voicemail and walked down the hall.

'Lou Lou,' I called out. 'Can I come in?'

The sound of muffled cries filtered through the door.

'Hey, I'm right here. Please talk to me.'

A sob-filled 'Okay, Daddy' filled the air, and I turned the knob and opened the door.

When Lou was old enough to know her own mind, she'd told me she wanted a pale blue room with daisies painted on the walls. Calling in a favor from a talented artist friend, I had wildflowers, including a dozen daisies, painted across an entire wall.

Lou sat with her knees tucked to her chest under the fairy tent made of opaque yellow tulle in the corner.

Settling down on the edge of her bed, my gaze snagged on a framed picture of Gina on a nearby bookcase. She sat in her favorite rocker with a sleeping Lou tucked against her chest. I'd caught the image late one night after Gina finished feeding her. I'd stood in the hallway, listening as she sang 'You Are My Sunshine' in the sweetest voice. I rushed back to our room and grabbed my phone, instinct telling me I had to capture the intimate moment.

'Lou, this isn't working,' I said, tearing my gaze away from the picture.

She stayed quiet, her sniffles filling the room.

I moved off the bed. When I reached the entrance to the tent, I said, 'Pretty, pretty princess.' Lou had a rule that daddies must say the secret password in order to enter her castle.

Her tear-stained cheeks wrecked me, but I waited for her permission. A slight nod of her head had me hunching down, taking careful steps inside. Soft white fairy lights were strung across the top of the tent. A mound of pillows and blankets covered the floor. Reggie rested his little white and black ferret head flush against her forearm, his favorite napping spot.

'Did you know that I got suspended from school once?' I sat on an oversized navy blue pillow, my body taking up a good part of the tent.

Her beautiful brown eyes went wide. 'What did you do?'

'A few of my friends decided to be funny and drive the coach's car out of the school lot and park it on the football field. We thought it'd be a great prank. The principal did not agree.'

A long beat passed between us until she finally said in a bare whisper, 'Brittany keeps saying you're gonna leave Ivy Falls. That you're famous now and famous people always go to California. That you're not gonna take me with you because you'll be too busy going to fancy parties. Meeting cool movie stars.'

I rubbed my stinging eyes. Pulled in a quick breath. This was what was causing my baby so much pain? I clutched my hands in my lap, trying not to let a dark swirl of guilt swallow me whole.

At first, the show had seemed like a good idea. The extra money let me start a college account for Lou. Helped me pay down our mortgage. But none of that was worth it if it made my only child miserable.

'Is this what's been bothering you lately? Why you've been so grumpy?'

She dipped her head and nodded.

'First,' I said, tilting up her chin, 'I'd never leave *you* or Ivy Falls. This is our home. All the memories of your mom are here. Iris and Rose and Miss Torran and Miss Tess…' I took a thick gulp. 'They're our family too. Nothing on this planet, not even an out-of-control space meteor, could get me to go, Lou. And as for famous movie stars,' I made a *pfft* sound, 'they've got nothing on Dolly Parton. You know, if I was truly famous, she'd be the first one we'd meet. Together.'

That finally got her to crack a smile, and she scooched in close to me. 'Yeah, Dolly was number one on my list too. My teacher says she gives books to young kids all over the state.' Her eyes went mischievous. 'Her Nashville house is an hour and fifteen minutes from here. I googled it.'

'Louisa! You know you're not to use the computer without supervision.'

'I asked Auntie Torran about it one day, and she showed me how to use her phone.'

Oh great. Now my best friend was breaking my rules. That was a conversation for another time.

'Lou Lou,' I brushed a gentle hand over her hair. 'I know the show's been a lot, and it's gotten in the way of the time we spend together. And, although I hate it, I'm aware that kids at school have phones. That they probably show you all the stuff that's being posted. But honestly, none of it is more important than you.'

She leaned into my side. 'Most of the kids have been teasing me.' She narrowed her eyes and gave me an intense look. 'What does "Zaddy" mean?'

I choked on my own saliva. 'Uh, it's an adult term.'

'Like a bad word?'

'It's a word that shouldn't concern you,' I said, desperate to change the subject. 'We're going to be okay, the two of us. I'm busier now, sure, but that will never mean I'm not here to listen. If you need me for any reason, I'll drop everything to help.'

She gave me a big hug. 'I understand, and I probably haven't said it, but it's kinda cool that you're on TV.'

'Thanks.' I ruffled her hair, held on to her for a minute longer until I said, 'So you know the rule about punishment, right?'

'Do I really have to write Brittany an apology letter? Couldn't I just send her an email?'

I swallowed a laugh. 'No. A handwritten note. And it needs to be kind and honest.'

She let out a frustrated huff. 'But she was the one being mean!'

'What do we say about conflict in this house, Louisa?'

She rolled her eyes, but her shoulders gave a little. 'We can't control how other people act, but we can control how *we* behave.'

'And...'

'A clear conscience makes for a happy mind.'

I pulled her into another hug. A big part of me wanted to stay in this spot forever. Keep Lou in this cocoon so no one could tease her or make her feel forgotten again.

'Manny?' A sweet, lilting voice that always made my blood spark to life filled the hallway.

'Is that Miss Tessa?' Lou set Reggie down, jumped to her feet and tore out of the room. I quickly followed and watched as she threw herself at Tess' waist. She let out a small *ooof* before tugging Lou in closer. They stayed like that for a long moment, and I tried not to let my mind race. Think about how if Tess and I could have a future together, there could be more moments like this one where my little girl, who'd been crying only a moment ago, now beamed brighter than the summer sun.

Tess let go of Lou but held on to her hands. 'You okay, Lulubean?'

Lou glanced over her shoulder at me as I leaned against the wall, sure my cheeks were warm from watching the scene. Fergus trotted up, banging into the wall once or twice before he rubbed his head against Tess' side. The dog couldn't see, but he could sure sense how special she was.

'Can I tell her I was suspended?' Lou asked.

I rubbed a nervous hand along the back of my neck. 'I think you just did.'

Tess looked into Lou's eyes. 'Wanna tell me what happened?'

She shrugged. 'Daddy can tell you. I gotta go back to my room and write a 'pology letter.'

Tess ran a loving hand over the top of Lou's head. 'That sounds important. Better get to it.'

Lou bounced back to her room, and Fergus quickly followed her. I waited until I heard the chair to her desk slide out before I went to meet Tess in the middle of the hall. Every instinct in me wanted to reach out and touch her hair. Lean in and press a soft kiss to her pretty pink lips, but things were still new, and I didn't want to confuse Lou if she saw us.

Like she understood what I was feeling, Tess laced her fingers through mine and pulled me to the kitchen. 'Sorry I came in unannounced. I knocked several times, but there was no answer, and I was worried.'

'How'd you know about Lou?'

She gave me a look, waited a beat.

'Miss Marta?' I said.

A faint smile lifted her lips.

'It's fine,' I sighed. 'I'm glad she told you. Happy you're here.'

She reached out and ran a hand down my cheek. Her touch was exactly what I needed in this moment.

'Looks like you need coffee. Lots of it,' she said.

'You have no idea.'

She moved around my kitchen like she belonged here, and I tried not to think how much I wanted that to be a reality.

Chapter Twenty-Five

TESSA

Life Of The Party

By the hard set of his shoulders and shadows beneath his eyes, Manny looked like he'd been through hell. He'd already endured so much with losing Gina, trying to raise Lou on his own. And balancing his time between work and the show couldn't be easy. Now, with Billy back, it'd sort of muddied things between us too.

I started the coffee and sat in a chair at the table. He kicked out a booted foot and tugged it closer. 'Have I ever told you that your hair smells like honeysuckle?' He made his voice lower, sexier. 'That every time I see you, my heart takes off like a damn shot.'

Heat started in my throat and rose up to my cheeks. 'Keep talking,' I teased.

He reached across his lap and took my hand. The sweetness in his eyes was almost too much.

'Hey,' he said with a low thrum that I loved.

'Hey back,' I whispered.

'You okay after last night?'

'Which part are you talking about?' I ran my fingers over the stubble on his jaw. 'The part where I finally got to see you naked or the part where my ex showed up out of nowhere?'

'I'd like answers to both those questions.'

'*Raisins! Fucking raisins!*' his bird screeched out.

I pressed a hand to my mouth, muffling a laugh.

'The vet says to ignore it, and Lou is trying to teach him new words, but so far no luck,' he sighed. 'Just one more issue to tackle.'

I slid my hands up his muscled chest, resting them on his shoulders. 'To answer your question, you and I were perfect last night. Billy, well, that's a different story.'

My phone buzzed, and a picture of Torran and the girls making fishy faces popped up. I quickly turned the screen over.

'How many times has she called?'

'I stopped counting at twenty.'

'She knows Billy is back. At the site this morning, she grilled me about it. You can't keep avoiding her because she'll hunt you down.'

'I know,' I said wearily.

'Talk to me, Tess. What's happening with him? Did he say when he's leaving?'

'I started to talk to him about it, but then...' I was dreading telling him this part. 'Mrs Vanderpool showed up at my door.'

He inched up a brow.

'She wanted to talk to Billy. Thank him for not hitting Baby in the street.'

He scratched at his jaw. 'That was nice of her, but I sense there's more to the story.'

I glanced down at my lap, tension crowding my chest. 'She offered to let him stay in her garage apartment. Said she'd talk to Silvio about giving him a job.'

Manny leaned away, and I shot out a hand to hold on to him.

'She made the offer without warning me. Billy immediately accepted.'

'Well, that's not a shock,' he said brusquely.

'I know this complicates matters, but Billy and I have to clear the air between us. Figure out some kind of plan so we can co-parent.'

He mumbled out a low complaint.

'At first, Rose didn't know who he was. She kept looking to Iris for clues on how to react. The man is her damn father and she doesn't remember him.' I couldn't hide the hurt in my voice. 'I may think Billy is a walking piece of biohazard, but the girls need to build a relationship with him. He used to be a good father. I hope he can be once again.'

He tore his hands through his mop of dark hair. 'And what if he's lying about wanting to change? Hurts you all? It'll kill me to see you or the girls in pain.'

'I won't let that happen. You have to trust me on this one.'

'I do trust *you*. Him… not so much.'

'Manny.' I pulled his face forward, pressed a gentle kiss to his lips. 'I know all of Billy's tricks. If he starts to pull his same crap, I'll make him leave.'

He gave me a kiss back, this one filled with a hesitant sweetness. Like he was holding back all the things he wanted to say.

The coffee maker beeped. I held on to him for a second longer before I stood and poured us both a cup.

'So what's up with Lou?'

'A girl at school told her I was going to run off to be famous in Hollywood. Leave her behind.'

I returned to the table and set the steaming mug in front of him. 'Why are children so cruel to each other?'

'She already has trauma from losing Gina. I can only imagine how crushed she must have felt when Brittany said that to her.'

'You can't save her from the Brittanys of the world. All you can do is make her feel secure. Reassure her that things aren't going to change.'

'But won't they?' I didn't like the hesitation in his voice. 'If Tor and I keep filming, the notoriety will only grow. How can I protect Lou if it keeps getting bigger and more out of my control? Lauren's already pressing us for more out-of-town speaking engagements. And she told me that my full social media presence is written into the next contract.'

'You are the most down-to-earth person I know. They'll listen to you when you tell them you need boundaries. That you have a small child to consider.'

'That sounds rational, but there was a serious tone to Lauren's voice I'd never heard before. Like she thought the network wasn't going to budge on the point.'

I curled my fingers through his and loved how I felt settled inside. Like our hands were always meant to be twined together. 'You're in control here. Hearth and Home is going to do whatever they can to keep the show going. The ratings are major, and that means they're making a lot of money. They won't want to lose such a good thing.'

He clutched my hand tighter. 'Guess you're right. But if they won't lay off the social media pressure, I may have to consider the alternative, and I don't want to think about how that might affect Tor too.'

He let out a low, loose breath. Words weren't necessary. I'd come to know this man so well. He'd sacrifice pretty much anything in his life to protect Lou and keep her happy.

Looking at him made a piece of my heart bloom open. For so long I'd seen him only as a friend. A shoulder to lean on. But the more time I spent in his presence, saw his true nature, the more I wanted to be closer to him. Nestle into his arms and remember what it felt like to have him cradle me in and make me feel safe.

My phone went off with a buzz, reminding me of the time. I called Penny and explained that I'd be late. That the roof had a leak and we needed to put up a sign that we wouldn't be open until later in the day.

'I have to go home. Deal with Billy. See you later at the store?'

Manny gave me a solid look. 'The roof will be fixed by lunchtime. I promise.'

I glanced over my shoulder, and all was quiet in Lou's room. Leaning forward, I planted my head against his chest, loving the steady rhythm of his heart. 'I believe you.'

He tugged me in around the waist. 'Call your sister. She deserves to hear the whole story from you.'

'You're right.'

He brushed his hand over my cheek. It was easy to get lost in the soft caress of his touch, the warm cage of his arms.

I finally pulled away, my own heart stuttering. There was a little girl in the other room waiting on her father. A father who would always be there for her. Who would make sure she was taken care of.

Every part of me wished that for my own girls. Before Billy left my house today, he was going to understand that truth.

—

I ran my hand over the new pane of glass in the back door. It wasn't an exact match, but it'd held. Kept us safe. That was all that mattered.

Two steps inside the house, I came to a rough halt. The kitchen counters sparkled, and the scent of chemicals and lemon filled the air. A low rumble pulled me to the back rooms. Billy stood next to Iris' desk, navigating a vacuum cleaner across the carpet. Both of the girls' beds were made, and the floor was clear of clutter.

'Billy,' I said, but he didn't react. I flicked the lights off and on to get his attention.

He spun around. 'Oh, hey, Tessie.'

'What are you doing?'

He shrugged. Turned the vacuum off. 'Making myself useful.'

I took in a slow, measured breath. 'In all the time you lived here, you never once ran the vacuum or cleaned the kitchen. What are you up to?'

His shoulders sagged, and he faded down onto Iris' soft yellow bedspread. 'Things have gone to hell.' He scrubbed a hand over his buzzed head. The swelling around his right eye reminded me too much of a raw T-bone. He reached out for his old guitar that sat on a stand at the end of Iris' bed. 'Oh, I missed this sweet girl.' His fingers stroked over the strings with a low thrum. 'It was wrong to leave with Trini,' he said in a bare whisper. 'To go all the way to Georgia. I regret every moment I've spent away from you and the girls.'

I barked out a laugh. 'Can't have been too much regret. You've been gone for over two years.'

'I've never been a quick learner,' he mumbled, setting the guitar on the bed. 'While I was away, I learned how good I had it here. You loved me even though I could never love myself. Even though I was a loser who could never hold a job, too caught up in wanting to be wild and free like a stupid teenager. But I swear I've grown up. I miss Ivy Falls. This is my home. Please forgive me.'

This was his apology for running off like a coward? For leaving me alone to take care of our two children? Fury burned in my chest, and I fisted my hands into the side of my skirt, willing my temper to hold.

'Do you know how much you destroyed me when you left? My mother was dying, Billy. I was a shell of a person, and you decided that nothing mattered except yourself. You tossed away our life, our children, like they were nothing. What kind of man does that?'

At least he had the decency to hang his head. 'A scared, dumb and thoughtless man, but I want to prove I can be different. Show you and the girls that I'm worthy of your trust and love again.'

There was a thickness to his voice that shocked me. We'd been together over ten years, and I'd only seen him get emotional a few times. His default was to always crack a joke or be the life of the party.

He'd had a terrible home life. His parents constantly fought. They divorced his senior year, both of them taking off for separate states, leaving him behind to couch-surf with friends until he graduated. He'd made a lot of dumb choices, and every time, I'd let him off the hook because he was dealing with so much.

'Those are hollow words and promises if they don't come with action. You're great at coming up with plans, Billy, but terrible at executing them.'

His shoulders gave a little. 'Yeah, I know.'

The image of the girls smiling at him this morning filled my head. They needed a father. Things between the two of us burned to the ground a long time ago, but just because we were done did not mean the girls had to lose him too.

He gave me a steady stare. 'I know I've let you down so many times in the past. Let my partying and bad decisions make a mess of things. But that all changes now, Tessie. I swear.'

For most of our life together, Billy's personality had taken up the whole room. Even as a teen, I was enamored with the way his loud laugh, wide smile, could draw people in like hummingbirds to nectar. But now, he looked small, broken, with a battered face to boot. He'd done the right thing by saving Baby, and it gave me a glimmer of hope that maybe things had changed for him.

My phone buzzed with another call from Torran. I deliberately turned the screen to him. 'I won't fight you staying at Mrs Vanderpool's, or taking a job with Silvio, if he'll have you, but if you screw this up, you won't only have me to deal with.'

He paled. The only thing Billy was afraid of more than a day without a drink was Torran. If he didn't keep his promises, she'd make his life a lot worse for him than I ever could.

Chapter Twenty-Six

MANNY

Like A Bad Nightmare

Thankfully Ferris Johnson owed me a favor. He showed up at the bookstore at noon with a crew and quickly fixed the small leak. At my request, he'd walked the P&P's roof and confirmed that, except for the small crack between shingles, it was in good shape. When he asked about the tarp, I confessed to climbing on the roof in the rain. I stood patiently as he gave me an earful about how it was a stupid decision. That I was lucky I wasn't in the hospital. I let him grumble on a bit longer before I thanked him again.

My phone beeped with a picture of Lou doing homework at Sugar Rush. A plate filled with cookie crumbs sat beside her electric-blue backpack. So much for total punishment. At least I knew what was bothering her now. It wasn't an easy problem to solve though. As long as I did the show, the social media alerts, the comments, the teasing, none of it would go away.

Tess spent most of the morning in her office. She'd put a note on the door of the P&P that she'd open at one p.m. after I promised the leak wouldn't cost her a full day's business. With Ferris finally gone, I knocked on her door.

Her gaze was fixed on the computer screen. The line of her shoulders bunched up around her ears.

'Hey,' I whispered so I wouldn't spook her. 'Leak is fixed. Penny's taken down the sign and opened up. Ferris says the rest of the roof is in good shape, but you still may want to file a claim for insurance to cover the books you lost.'

Her eyes stayed on the screen like she was in some sort of trance.

'Tess, look at me.'

She pulled in a full, shaky breath as I squatted down beside the desk and cradled her hands. 'What's wrong?'

'Why is all this chaos happening now when I'm finally getting my feet under me?'

I reached out and took her hand. 'You're not alone in any of this. We'll get through it. Together.'

She slid her hand away from me. Her posture going rigid. 'At the house today, Billy told me he's changed. That he wants to be here for the girls,' she said wearily. 'There are a million reasons why I should chase him out of town, but I just can't.'

A dozen worries swam around in my head like fish in a barrel. We'd just decided we wanted to be together and now it felt like that important moment was being stripped away. Like we were driving in reverse when we should be gunning the engine forward.

'Do you believe he's changed?'

'I don't know. There's so much happening, and it feels like it's all getting away from me. Like I don't have any control in my life, and it scares the hell out of me.' She rubbed at her tired eyes. 'The girls, they should have a chance to get to know him. I can't take that away from them.'

'I understand all your fears, but if he's staying, you have to promise me that you'll be honest about what he's doing. If he's not following through on his promises, falling into old patterns, you need to tell me.' I wasn't good at hiding the worry in my voice.

'I will.' She scrubbed at her eyes again, let out a frustrated huff. 'I'm just so angry, Manny. A part of me wants to destroy him the way he destroyed me, but I have to put aside my own feelings right now, and I'm not going to lie, it's damn hard.'

I pulled off my baseball cap, tugged a hand through my hair. 'I know it is, but swallowing those feelings, is that fair to you?'

'Fair doesn't matter. I don't want to look back on this time and feel guilty that I didn't give Billy a chance to make amends. To be an active part of the girls' lives.'

I hated the ache in her voice, but if anyone understood sacrificing for their child, it was me.

'You know what's right. I'll do whatever I can to support you. But I'm also not going to lie to you. I think he's a snake. Sooner or later, he's going to show his true colors again. He may have done a good act for Mrs Vanderpool, but that doesn't mean me, and I'm sure the rest of the town, aren't going to be watching him like a coyote near a chicken coop.'

'I'm counting on it,' she said, giving me a weak smile.

The reappearance of her ex felt like a bad nightmare. One where your feet were stuck in concrete while the one you loved was tied to railroad tracks, a moving train hurtling toward them, and you were helpless to stop it.

I reached out for her again but stopped when a solid thud of footsteps pounded toward the door until it burst open to reveal a very unhappy Torran.

Chapter Twenty-Seven

TESSA

The Right Amount of Severity and Kindness

Torran took two stalking steps toward me and then stopped when she noticed Manny.

'Why aren't you answering my calls, Tessa?'

'It's been a weird twenty-four hours,' was all I could offer.

Torran pressed her lips together like she needed a moment to calm down. 'I heard the rumors that Billy ran his car into the big old oak near the gazebo.'

All I could do was give her a nod.

'And just now, I saw that piece of scum leave the hardware store holding an apron like he worked there.'

'Yes, Mrs Vanderpool offered to talk to Silvio about a job for him,' I said, trying not to cringe. 'And he's going to stay in her garage apartment until he can find a place of his own.'

'He's doing *what*?' Her screech banked around the walls of the small office, before she focused on Manny. 'Is this another thing you kept from me?'

'No. I didn't know about it until a little while ago. And this is your sister's issue to handle. If you haven't noticed, she's a grown-ass woman who can fight her own battles.'

A big part of me wanted to press a searing kiss to his beautiful lips. Thank him for not allying with my sister against me. But how could I explain what was happening between Manny and me when even I wasn't sure what Billy's sudden arrival meant for us?

Torran gripped the edges of her overalls and began to pace. 'After everything he's done, what he's put you and the girls through, I can't believe he'd just show up out of the blue and expect you to take care of him again!'

Manny's gaze swiveled between the two of us. He didn't need to get caught up in this mess. With everything going on with Lou, he had enough on his plate.

'Manny, can you give us a minute?' I said.

'Of course,' he said stiffly. 'I'll go measure the marble on the buffet so I can try and replicate it for the bar. Then I'll head back to the old Thomas Place.'

He walked to the door and whispered something in Torran's ear. The curve of her sharp mouth fell, and she gave a defeated nod.

Once he was gone, Torran sank into the chair near my desk. 'Manny just reminded me that this is your life, your choices, but I need to understand your decisions, Tessa. Billy's been gone a long time. Never bothered to come back and see the girls. Help me understand what is happening.'

I tried not to react to what Manny had asked of her. He was like the calming force in a destructive sea. The lull of his low voice the right amount of severity and kindness that made people listen. When he spoke to me that way, I knew I was safe. He reassured me that things would be okay. But all of this felt like a tornado spinning out of control, and I didn't like that it made me feel untethered.

Like I couldn't quite put all the pieces of my life in the right order.

'This isn't about you or me, Tor,' I said, all the fight going out of me. 'It's about what's best for the girls. All they know is that their dad went away. They don't understand any of the circumstances behind it, and I will move heaven and earth to make sure they never do.'

Torran tugged back on her ponytail and clasped her hands in her lap. 'I need you to talk this through with me. Explain why you're opening yourself to potential pain again.'

'That was not my plan. I was going to ask him to leave. Find a job and a place to live outside Ivy Falls. That he needs to start financially supporting the girls. Showing up for them when he's needed. But then, Mrs Vanderpool appeared at my door this morning and screwed it all up.' I sank lower into my chair. 'That woman means well, but she's devoted to Baby. I'm not sure she would ever recover from losing that dog, so I understand why she made Billy the offer.'

'Why can't this town stay out of people's damn business?' she seethed.

'This isn't the ideal situation, but I have to remove myself from the equation.'

Torran shifted uncomfortably in the chair but stayed quiet – which was a miracle for her.

'Girls who grow up without a father have been shown to have lower self-esteem. They tend to have more physical and mental health issues. Make poor choices when picking a suitable partner. Billy may have been a failure as a husband, but at one time he was a good father to the girls. I can let him have a chance again because I give a damn about Iris and Rose's future, and even though I hate the thought of having him around, their lives will be better if they have a father who is present.'

The stricken look on my sister's face said she was finally hearing me. 'I get it. But how can you be in a room with him and not want to find the heaviest tool and clobber his brain in?'

'It's hard, especially when I think about coming home and finding his note. How in that dark moment, a crushing wave hit me, made it difficult to breathe, especially with what was happening to Mom.' I shook my head like I could erase the awful memory. 'I'll admit, when it comes to Billy, I've always had a blind spot. Since I was fifteen, he's had a powerful hold over me. He was the first boy who ever saw me as something more than a bookworm. I latched on to that. Enjoyed his attention. It was why I put up with his crap for so long. He recognized something in me that I'd hidden. That needed to be seen.'

'I'm sorry,' she whispered. 'Maybe Dad and Mom and I failed you somehow. That you didn't know you were more than that.'

'My issues with Billy have nothing to do with you. He was hot as hell, not to mention charming. Everyone at school loved him, and I sort of fell under that spell. Then I graduated, got pregnant, and it felt like my only choice was to marry him. Settle down in Ivy Falls and be a family.' I leaned back in my chair, all my bones weary. 'There were a ton of red flags with him, and I ignored them all. The way he didn't come home some nights. How people gave me pitying looks in the square, like they knew he was cheating but didn't have the guts to tell me. I pretended it wasn't happening because I wanted to hold on to my sweet little family.'

'Tessa, none of that is your fault. He's the villain here.'

'I have to take responsibility for not being strong enough to see the truth. My eyes are wide open now. That's the only reason he's still here, because I will hate myself if I don't give him this chance to be a father to Iris and Rose. What's between their father and me is dead and gone, but that doesn't mean that the girls can't have a relationship with him. As their mother, I owe it to them to try and make this shitastic situation work.'

Tor leaned back. Scrubbed a hand over her face. 'You're right. The girls deserve to be happy in every corner of their life. I've noticed Iris' stomach issues. Rose's night terrors.'

The pain in her voice tore me in two. She loved my girls like they were her own.

'I will be respectful of your choice. Talk to Dad about it too, but…' She held my gaze. 'This time I need you to look for the red flags. If he does anything that warns he isn't here to make things right with the girls, if he returns to being the same dumbass he's always been, I need to know you'll tell him to get lost for good.'

'I hear you, but the girls, they need him…'

She held up her hand to stop me. 'Manny. Dad. Beck. Those are three men who can be good father figures for your girls. You have to know that Rose and Iris will never be without support and attention from the people in their lives.'

A knot swelled in my throat. My girls were lucky that they were so loved, but they still needed to see that the man who was their father cared enough about them to stick around. 'I swear that if he steps even one toe out of line, he'll be gone.'

Her eyes went soft. 'I'd never argue with you about your choices for the girls. But you have to know that all of you are the beating hearts in my life. It'd kill me to see you hurt again.'

I smiled at her. 'I love you too, Tor.'

Her eyes welled, and then she let that curtain of tough exterior take hold. 'I need to get back to work.'

She moved to the door and hesitated. The cords of stress tight around her shoulders.

There was so much more she wanted to say. To warn me about. But I'd made my decision, and whatever happened next, good or bad, it was all on me.

Chapter Twenty-Eight

MANNY

One Of Their Own

When Torran blew through the door, her temper was already a three-alarm blaze.

'You knew that Mrs Vanderpool offered Billy a place to live, helped him get a job with Silvio, and you didn't say a damn word?'

Two of our flooring crew, who were working in the family room to the right of the main entry, flicked their gazes in our direction. I cinched my work belt and walked to the stairs. The shell of the wood frame stared back at me. I'd rather have spent the next five hours yanking out remainder nails than have to answer her.

'I already told you I didn't know. Tess came over after I brought Lou home from school, and she told me then.'

My phone kept buzzing in my pocket. I glanced at the screen. Damn social media alerts again. I muted the notifications and shoved the menacing device into my back pocket.

'Why was Tess there last night anyway?' She propped her hands onto her hips. Tapped her boot in irritation. 'She was supposed to be having dinner with my dad and the girls.'

I willed myself not to act guilty. Look like I had anything to hide. 'When I got to the P&P last night, I heard a steady drip of water and found a leak in the ceiling.'

I left out the part about me stupidly scaling the roof. If I thought I'd gotten an earful from Ferris, Torran would be ten times worse.

'Wait,' she squeaked. 'A leak? How bad was it? Did it do any damage? Tessa didn't say a word about it to me.'

I gave her a weighted stare.

'Okay, fine. I was a little teed off when I was at the store, but still...'

'It's fine, Tor,' I said, cutting her off. 'Ferris and some of his crew already fixed the problem earlier today.' The tension eased in her jaw. 'Last night I tried to save as much stock as possible, but I knew I had to tell Tess. I called her, and we worked on cleaning up the store.'

I grabbed a hammer from my belt and started to pull nails from the bottom step.

'So you two were rushing around grabbing books and you heard Billy's crash?'

'Something like that,' I mumbled.

My shoulder edged back as I yanked one of the first nails from the bottom step. Torran darted forward, gripped the collar of my white T-shirt and tugged it back.

'Manny!' she gasped. 'Is that a hickey on your neck?'

I slapped a hand over the spot Tess seemed to love last night.

'No.' I definitely sounded guilty. 'It's just a bruise. Caught my neck on an open cabinet.'

'Liar! Did my sister give that to you?'

She laughed and did a little dance, which earned us another stare from the flooring crew. I grabbed a strap on her paint-splattered overalls and dragged her into the living room.

'It happened. Finally!' She did another odd dance that was a weird combination of the Macarena and the Electric Slide. 'That little stinker Tess didn't say a word to me.'

'Why would she? This has nothing to do with you.'

She sobered at the serious tone in my voice. 'Fine, I'll mind my own business, but I'm not going to pretend that this doesn't make me all kinds of happy. That you two being together means Billy has less of a reason to hang around.'

'I wouldn't count on that.'

She went deadly still. 'What do you mean?'

'He knows he's got Tess in a pinch because of the girls. I think he's going to milk that fact for everything it's worth.'

'Did you say that to her?'

'I told her I was worried he might hurt her, but that's all. It's not my decision to make.' I gave her a pointed look. 'It's not yours *or* your dad's either.'

'Yeah, she made that very clear at the P&P. But I don't know if I can stand by and watch this freight train of a nightmare wreck her life again.'

'How did Tess react when Beck came back to town? Did she warn you off? Or did she support you? Tell you to help him save his childhood home?'

'God, I hate it when you make so much sense. Or worse, use an instance from my own life to prove me wrong.'

'She gave you advice, but she didn't meddle. You owe her the same.'

'Doesn't mean I have to like it. Or that I won't be watching every move that bastard makes.'

'You and everyone else in town. I think Billy is going to remember very quickly how people circle the wagons in Ivy Falls once one of their own gets hurt.'

The words made my heart clench. We'd only lived in Ivy Falls a year when we lost Gina. Word spread quietly through town. One by one, casseroles started appearing on my doorstep. Words of sympathy written on pretty cards left inside my mailbox. Kind and soft smiles landed on me at Minnie's Market every time I went to buy milk or bread. It was a little overwhelming at first until I realized it meant that the people of Ivy Falls considered us family.

'What about the crash? Do you buy his story?' she asked.

'No, but he passed a sobriety test, and we did find him holding Baby.'

'Mrs Vanderpool, what the hell was she thinking?' she muttered until my phone vibrated again.

I tore it from my pocket and read the text from Susan saying she'd taken Lou back to my house. After reminding her that screens were off-limits, I put the phone away.

'How's Lou doing?' Torran said, catching Susan's name on the screen.

'She got suspended for a day. I grounded her for a while, but at least she's talking to me.'

'And…' She waited. Drummed her fingers against her hip bones. Whenever the subject was Lou, Torran had a seriously invested interest in the little girl she adored so much.

I explained what Brittany had told Lou. How Lou, in turn, fought back.

A glint of pride tinged Torran's face.

'Physical contact is not okay, Tor. She has to learn that people are going to be mean, and she has to ignore it.'

'It'll all blow over,' Torran said.

'Will it? If we sign another contract, won't things get worse?'

Torran pursed her lips. 'What are you saying, Manny?'

'The constant streams of comments on social media. Lauren's insistence that the network wants more of what little time I actually have.' I pulled my hat off and scrubbed at my hair. 'I'm not sure that continuing with the show is a good thing for me.'

'No… I can't do it without you,' she insisted. 'Look what happened the first time we tried to do a show. I totally ruined things. You need to be around to be the sound, rational voice. To keep me from knocking into another ladder and getting a head full of green paint.' Her voice came out in jagged spurts, and I had to grab her arms, force her to take deep breaths.

'All the attention. It's too much. There's only been one season, and you and Beck are already putting a fence up around your damn house. Women ogle me on the street. Say inappropriate things in front of my young daughter. When I showed Tess all the posts online, she found a picture of Lou the night of the fall festival that some stranger shared. It scared the hell out of me, Tor. None of this is good for Lou. You know it.'

She took a thick gulp. 'What if we kept you off camera as much as possible next season? Drew a line in the sand over the social media issue. Would you still stay on?'

'It's going to take some thought and time. Lou has to always be my first priority. She means more to me than anything else in this world.'

'Lou means the world to me too.' Her voice went soft. 'I'll do whatever I can to protect her, *and you*, even if it means stopping the show forever.'

'No,' I bit out. 'You can't do that. Ivy Falls has too many houses that need saving. And we need to keep interest up in tourism.' I patted her shoulder. Gave a weak smile. 'You are the show, Tor. It can move on with you alone.'

A roaring storm of worry built behind her eyes.

'We've always been a team, Manny. If that can't continue, then we both walk away.'

I wasn't going to argue with her now. It was too hard to reach her when she was this worked up, but the truth was she'd come into her own on camera. She radiated pride as she spoke about her vision for a house. How the subtle choices we'd made, like using green lumber, installing energy-efficient appliances and windows, incorporating low-flow plumbing fixtures, would keep the property thriving for another century.

She wouldn't admit it, but she knew if her star was going to keep rising, she had to continue on with the show, even if it meant doing it without me.

Chapter Twenty-Nine

TESSA

False Hope

The scent of roasted chicken filled the air as I walked in my back door. Iris and Rose scurried around the table, setting down plates and napkins. Purple wildflowers spilled from a glass vase. LED candles we'd used in our Halloween pumpkins now sat in the center of the table, their opaque flames flickering.

'What's all this?' I asked, putting down my purse on a small table by the back door.

Billy stood next to the stove wearing my 'I Use the Smoke Alarm as a Timer' apron. That bruise under his eye was plum-colored now. Those stupid plastic bug-style black sunglasses he always wore dangled from the collar of his denim blue T-shirt.

'Daddy made us dinner.' Iris gave me a megawatt smile.

'And we picked flowers from the empty lot behind the house!' Rose added. 'It can't be a pretty dinner without them.'

Part of me loved the gleam in my girls' eyes. The other part of me wanted to clobber Billy with the cast-iron skillet. What was he doing showing up here unannounced?

I walked to the stove and dragged a towel over the mess he'd made. 'How did you get in?'

'Oh, you mean because my key no longer works?'

I gave him an irritated stare, and he raised his hands in mock surrender.

'I get it. I would have locked me out too.' He tried to give me that grin that used to make me crumble. Not anymore. 'I was waiting here when Torran dropped them off.' He lowered his voice. 'She really let me have it. Which I totally deserved.'

He flashed a look at the girls, who were now playing a game in front of the TV.

'I'm doing my best here, Tessie. Silvio hired me at the store. I've been to the police station. Got all the info about the tow yard and walked the half-mile there to get my car. Called the insurance company to see how to make a claim.'

I gaped at him.

'Yes, I do have insurance. I knew you'd drop me off the policy.'

'Can you blame me?'

'No,' he sighed. 'But I'm making changes, and I want everyone to see it. When Silvio shoved the apron into my hands today, he told me he'd be watching me like a hawk.'

'I'm not surprised. It's not like you have a sterling reputation around here.'

His gaze went to the floor. 'I know.'

'He and Mrs Vanderpool are giving you a second chance,' I added. 'You better not mess it up.'

'I swear I won't.' His gaze moved back to the girls. 'I hope you'll let me show you I'm different now.'

Iris peeled across the room and threw herself at his waist. 'I told Daddy all about soccer practice today. How I scored two goals during my scrimmage.' Rose followed her into the room but hung back. Wary of this man she still didn't know. 'You should have seen it, Mama,' Iris went on. 'It was like I got all this energy, and just dribbled through everyone's legs. My tummy didn't hurt once today.'

I glanced at my rosy-cheeked girl and loved the light in her eyes.

'Is dinner ready?' I asked Billy.

'Sure is.'

He placed the roasted chicken on one of my big white platters and set it on the table.

Once we were all seated, he had the gall to say, 'Should we say grace?'

He reached out and took my hand. The girls looked at us under their fans of dark lashes. Acid coated my throat. We were giving them the wrong idea, false hope, but I didn't pull away because, for one night, I wanted all the worries of the day to be far from their minds.

Rose said a sweet prayer about family and how she liked her teacher. Iris added that she hoped she'd score a goal at her next game, and she was happy her daddy was finally home. Billy couldn't hide his smile as he watched her.

The first time I saw him cry was the day Iris was born. A nurse asked if he wanted to hold her, and Billy nodded. She told him that the best way was skin-to-skin. While he removed his T-shirt, the nurse waited with Iris in her arms. In that moment, I saw a different side to him. How he hungered for the family he'd never had. When he held her, he began to sing a lullaby of his own creation. The tune would transform over the years as Iris grew bigger and then when Rosie came along. It was his special bond with the girls. The last thing they asked for when he put them to bed at night when he was home.

My feelings were like the Christmas lights you unpacked every year. A tangled mess that looked impossible at first, but after time, and patience, you finally separated them into different strings. I wondered if it was possible for me to do that with Billy. To allow myself to still have resentment. Anger. But put aside the past so he could reconnect with our children again.

'Mama,' Iris said, bringing me back to the conversation. 'Do you think I could take guitar lessons? Learn how to play like Daddy?'

'What about soccer?'

She shrugged. 'Maybe I could do both?'

'It'd be good for her, Tessie. There's data that shows music helps kids with science and math.'

I arched a brow.

'What?' he huffed. 'I do read, you know.'

The girls watched us with intensity, and I forced a smile to my lips. 'That's good to hear because you're on story time duty tonight.'

Iris and Rose cheered, and Billy shot me another grateful smile.

—

Once dinner was over, the girls raced around the kitchen with soapy hands, trying not to drop plates as they slid them into the dishwasher. They'd begged to turn on some music and were now dancing through the house to the *Hamilton* soundtrack. They loved all the rapping, but I knew I was never going to get the bridge to 'Satisfied' out of my head.

I pressed their smiles and giggles into my memory. This was how their life should be – not nightmares and stomachaches.

Billy sang along with them in his deep baritone. After high school, he'd had offers to do studio work in Nashville, play at open mic nights. He never followed through on any of those opportunities, because he was too scared, too worried he might prove his father right and fail. Which, sadly, he did anyway.

He spun Iris around, his short, bleached hair looking white in the soft kitchen light. As I watched them, I waited for the anger to come. My questions about how long this would last until he did something stupid again, but I forced them away. For now, my girls were smiling. Happy. And that was all that mattered.

Once the music was over, and there was only one plate casualty, I told the girls it was time for bed. They grabbed onto Billy's hands and tugged him down the hall. He turned and mouthed 'thank you', and the ice around my heart began to thaw a little.

A few crumbs still littered the kitchen floor, and I grabbed the broom and went to work. The sounds of a guitar filtered out toward me. I walked toward the girls' room as Billy sang that lullaby. His voice dipping, churning, crooning as he sang of starlight, moonbeams and being whisked off to a land of sweet dreams.

I pressed the dish towel to my eyes. Shook my head. A swell of worry mixed with a good deal of dread filled my chest. He was so good with the girls when he wanted to be. But despite his claims, I couldn't believe he wouldn't just take off again. Destroy any good memories he'd ever built with them.

Slowly I walked down the hall, another chorus filling the house. A slight knock sounded at the back door, and I expected to find Torran standing there. Probably still fuming over having to leave the girls here with Billy. When I saw Manny standing in the shadow of the faint light, I couldn't hide my smile.

'Hi,' he whispered. 'Can we talk?'

I closed the door behind me and walked down the stone walkway beside the house.

'Everything okay?' I asked when I stopped on a small patch of grass.

'Yeah, I just wanted to check on you. See how your day's been.'

'Billy's here,' I blurted out.

'Okay,' he said in a measured way. 'Are you all right with that?'

'No. Yes,' I mumbled. 'How the hell did my life get this way? I just want things to go back to the way they used to be.'

Manny's gaze went to the ground. 'You mean before you and I…'

'No. I don't have any regrets about that. But this thing with Billy.' I flung my hands back to the house. 'It's making my stomach churn, and I hate every minute of it.'

'What can I do to help?' The loving tone in his voice nearly wrecked me.

'I don't know. To be honest, I'm not sure how I'm going to navigate through all this.'

'Don't take it on alone.' He ran a hand lovingly along my cheek. 'Lean on me whenever you need it.'

'Stop doing that,' I said softly.

His eyebrows went up. 'Doing what?'

'Being so damn good to me.' I took a slow step forward, and he wrapped his arms around my waist.

'This is only a rough patch. A bump in the road,' he said, laying his cheek on the top of my head. 'Things will settle down and get back to normal.'

I chuckled against his warm chest. 'Hate to tell you this, but when Billy is around, nothing is normal.'

He pulled back and gave me a steady stare. 'That was before.' He hesitated. 'Well, before I was present in this picture. I mean if that's what you still want. Me. Present.'

'Of course,' I said, pressing my hand to his cheek. 'I just have to figure out how to keep all the plates spinning, while also making sure Billy's return doesn't cause too much chaos. I hope you can be patient with me as I figure it all out.' I chewed on my lower lip, pushing out the next uncomfortable words. 'That may mean taking things a bit slower with us.'

'Tess, you tell me the pace, and I'll follow.'

He gave me a hopeful smile, and I melted into his arms again. We stood in silence for a moment. I loved the gentle, melodic thump of his heart beneath my ear, reminding me that he was the solid rock I could always lean on.

'Uh,' he mumbled. 'There's one thing I need to tell you.'

The worried tone in his voice made me pull back. He took an uncomfortable gulp and pointed to a reddish-purple mark on his neck.

Oh no. No. No.

'Your sister knows about us.' He pressed a small kiss to my nose and then leaned his forehead against mine. 'She saw that spot. Figured it out.'

'Great. One more thing I'm going to have to explain to her. Did she let out a cheer?'

'No.' His wide chest bounced up and down with a chuckle. 'But she may have done a really awkward dance that reminded me too much of a June bug flipped onto its back.'

I laughed and buried my head into his shoulder. 'It would be nice if I could catch some kind of break one of these days.'

He pulled me into another hug, and for the first time in hours, I relaxed.

'So he's inside with the girls?'

'Yes, he's reading them a bedtime story. He's only here for them, Manny.'

He went quiet, his breath going ragged.

'My guard is up around him. I know every trick he likes to play. Him being here tonight is a one-off.'

'You don't have to explain things to me. I trust you,' he whispered into my hair.

'That's one of the many things I adore about you. The fact that you watch, protect, but never interfere.'

'I'd do anything for you and the girls.'

'We know that.' I pressed a kiss against the stubble on his cheek. 'I'll set firm boundaries. When he can spend time with the girls. How he should start providing for them monetarily.'

The phone beeped in his pocket. He hesitated before pulling it out, his lips going thin. 'I have to go. Susan and Barb had Lou over for dinner, and they're ready to take her home. I want to be there for her bedtime routine.'

'Go.' I pressed my lips to his, meaning for it to be quick, but he wound me in his arms. Deepened the kiss. I let the heat of him wash over me. Pressed my body against his until he threaded his fingers through the back of my hair.

The hinges on the back door whined. 'Tessie, you out here?'

I stepped back from Manny, pressed a hand over his heart, and then walked onto the lighted path.

'What are you doing out here?' Billy asked.

Manny stepped out of the shadows.

'Oh,' Billy mumbled. 'Hey, Manny.'

'Billy.' His stare narrowed on the sunglasses tucked into the collar of Billy's shirt. A tic in his cheek warned something was wrong. 'When did you first get to town?' Manny said with a rough clip.

Billy looked startled. 'I came in last night like I said.'

'You weren't skulking around the soccer fields a few weeks ago? Watching the games? Watching the girls?'

'Manny, what are you talking about?' I said.

He pointed to the sunglasses. 'A couple of weeks ago I saw a guy at the fields. He was wearing those glasses. Same kind of hoodie and dark pants. Even had the same cocky walk. He was hiding behind the trees like he didn't want to be seen.'

I rounded on Billy. 'Were you there?'

Billy took a step back. Held up his hands. 'Not sure what you saw, man, but it wasn't me. And these glasses, I got them at the dollar store on a rack with like a dozen lookalikes.'

'Tess, it was him.' Manny insisted.

'What the hell are you talking about? I just told you I wasn't there.' Billy turned to me. 'I swear, Tessie, until I drove here from Atlanta, I have not been back in Ivy Falls.'

Billy had many tells when he was lying. He never looked you in the eye, often fidgeted, putting his hands into his pockets. He did none of that now.

'Manny, could it have been someone else?' I pressed.

'I know what I saw.'

He and Billy stood in an uncomfortable stalemate until the door opened, and Iris peeked her head out.

'Mama, is something wrong?' Her frightened stare swung between Manny and Billy. 'You were supposed to come and tuck us in.'

'It's okay, Iris. Go back inside,' I said.

Manny's face crumbled. 'I was just leaving.' He leveled a tender gaze at Iris and then back to me. 'I'll see you later, Tess.'

'Good night,' I said as he walked to his truck parked in the driveway.

'Tessie.' Billy started to speak again.

'No,' I said under my breath before going to Iris. 'I'll be there in a minute, sweetheart. Grab Rosie a glass of water and then wait for me in your room.'

'All right.' Her voice hitched before she disappeared from the doorway, the sound of the faucet running a few seconds later.

Billy gave me a pained look, waited for the sound of Iris' receding footsteps. 'Tell me you believe me. We were together for over ten years. You've got to take my word over some guy you barely know.'

The whole situation felt like a bad nightmare I did not want to deal with right now. The girls were confused, and Manny would never make a claim like he had unless he was sure he was right.

'Manny is not some guy I barely know. These last few years he's been here for us when you weren't.'

'Tessie,' he sighed. 'But I'm back…'

I held up a hand to stop him. 'You know the way back to Mrs Vanderpool's.'

His stare went back to the ground. 'Thanks for letting me have tonight. I appreciate getting to spend more time with the girls.'

'Don't…' I started but bit back my scalding words.

'Go ahead,' he said, defeated. 'Say what you want.'

'I'm begging you to not let them down again. They need you in their life. Please, Billy, be the father they deserve.'

His eyes went watery. 'I'm trying. I hope you believe me.'

'Tonight was a good start,' I offered.

'Thank you, Tessie. You always were fair, even when I didn't deserve it.' With a sad nod, he whispered good night and melted into the Ivy Falls darkness.

Chapter Thirty

MANNY

Frustration With A Massive Side Helping Of Pity

Was it possible to miss someone even if they were standing right in front of you? Apparently so, because even though Tess and I had continued to talk over the last two weeks, worked side by side to set up the antique buffet in the store, it was like she was a million miles away.

She walked slowly around the antique piece, the edges of her bright pink skirt swirling around her gorgeous legs. The curves of her beautiful lips pinched tightly as she surveyed the wood and polished marble. I ached to touch her, but instead I stood with my hands jammed into the pockets of my cargo pants, waiting on what she needed next.

'I can't get over what beautiful shape it's in.' She ran her hand over the white marble with the gray veining. 'Does any of the wood need to be treated? How will the marble do with heat? I want to make sure we don't do anything to damage it.'

'A sealant will protect the wood and marble. I'll make sure that's done before you serve your first espresso.'

She gave me a nod, kept her eyes focused on the piece like she couldn't look at me.

From the moment I walked away from her house the other night, I'd felt guilty about accusing Billy. I knew he was lying about when he first came back to Ivy Falls, but I could have handled it in a much better way.

'Tess, about the other night with Billy.'

'Manny,' she sighed. 'It's over. I know you were just looking out for me.'

'I was, but, still, I shouldn't have accused him of anything without proof.'

'After the break-in at the house, and then that rock, I get why you're worried. But Billy is a terrible liar. If he'd been here in Ivy Falls, he would not have been able to keep a straight face.'

'You sure about that?'

'Yes. I was with him long enough to know when he's pulling something shady.'

'Okay. Consider the matter dropped.'

'Thank you,' she said before moving to give the piece one final scan. 'I appreciate you bringing it here. Helping get it set up.'

I stepped forward, needing to be closer to her. 'Is there any way we could have lunch today? The girls are supposed to be with Lou at the babysitter's for another few hours, and we can't do any work at the old Thomas Place while the guy from the city goes over everything that needs to be brought up to code.'

'Wish I could, but there's inventory in the office I need to unpack.' She gave me a wan smile. 'Another time?'

'Sure.'

She brushed past me, and that ache to touch her, let her know everything was going to be okay, swept through me again.

Needing a distraction, I pulled out my sketchpad and went back over the bar design. I stayed busy with measuring and designing new ideas for how the piece should look. It needed a wraparound counter, which meant the lip on the front required enough of an overhang so several barstools could be tucked underneath. I continued to survey the old antique when a damaged bit of wood in the buffet's upper right corner caught my eye.

I walked to the register and waited for Penny to finish with a customer. Even though it was a Saturday, the store only had a few patrons milling about. The scene only made me want to work harder, faster, for Tess so that she could get the coffee bar up and running. Extinguish at least one of the worries spinning around in her anxious mind.

Once Penny was done, she trained her bright eyes on me. 'What can I help you with?'

'Can you tell Tess I'm running over to Silvio's? I need some sandpaper for the buffet.'

'Sure. I'll let her know.' She gave me that lingering smile that reminded me too much of the way women looked at me in the square now.

I rushed out the door and made my way down the brick-paved sidewalk. White twinkle lights lit up store windows. The scent of gingerbread spice and cinnamon filled the air near the Sugar Rush. A few kids rode by on their electric scooters. More than once, Lou had hinted she wanted one for Christmas, which was only a few weeks away. I'd told her that maybe she needed to start with something slower like a kick-scooter and she had reluctantly agreed.

When I reached Silvio's, I pulled back the steel handle on the thick glass door. The smell of fresh lumber and paint thinner filled the small box-like store. In a corner, Silvio talked with Ferris. As soon as they saw me, they gave me that pointed stare. It was the same look I'd been getting from people all over town. Frustration mixed with a massive side helping of pity. Like they all knew how things had changed for Tess and me before Billy arrived and screwed it all up.

I walked toward the back of the store, hoping to avoid Billy, but his voice carried over from the next aisle as he talked to another contractor, Lucas Pride, about wood screws.

'You still drivin' that black Charger?' Lucas asked Billy.

'Yeah, but it's in the shop after my run-in with the old oak near the gazebo.'

'So, you've been back for a bit then? I could have sworn I saw you driving it near the town limits a couple of weeks ago.'

I came to a stiff stop.

Billy's voice went thready as he said, 'Nope. Must've been someone else. I've been in Atlanta until recently.'

'Huh, could have sworn it was you.'

'What size wood screws did you say you needed?' Billy said.

'About a quarter-inch.'

The sound of drawers opening and closing echoed through the small store.

'I know what he needs.' Silvio's unmistakably harsh voice drew closer. 'I have them stored on a higher shelf.'

'I can get it,' Billy insisted.

'No, I'm not too old to climb a damn ladder,' Silvio snapped.

I moved toward the next aisle to make sure Silvio knew what he was doing. He dragged over an old ladder and

219

flipped down the hinges. The soles of his tennis shoes slapped against the steel steps. When he reached the top shelf, he grabbed a small cardboard box with thick black printing. He began his descent with one hand, and only got two rungs down before missing an entire step. The box flung out into the air, sending the screws pinging out in several directions. Silvio tried to make one last grasp for the ladder, but his weight sent the entire thing crashing toward the floor.

I raced forward, but Billy was already there, throwing out his body to break Silvio's fall. The force of the catch threw both of them backward into a display of rakes. Steel pieces ricocheted into the air, slicing Billy across the forearm.

For a few seconds, time stopped before Lucas ran to them, and I quickly followed. Silvio was slightly shaken up. Billy was in worse shape, his blood pooling all over the floor.

'Ferris, call an ambulance.' I grabbed a rag off the counter and pressed it against Billy's arm.

Billy's eyes fluttered and he asked, 'Is Silvio okay?'

'He's fine,' I said.

He gave me a weak smile before he passed out.

As soon as the ambulance arrived, I sprinted across the street to get Tess. Penny looked sick as I ran past her, blood still coloring my hands and T-shirt. Without knocking, I pushed open the door to the office. Tess got one look at me and sprang up from the chair.

'Oh my God, Manny. You're bleeding! What happened?'

'It's not my blood.'

'Who's is it then?'

'It came from Billy.'

She wobbled on her feet, and I caught her by the arms.

'He's okay. There was an accident at the hardware store, and Billy acted like a damn hero again.'

'A hero?' She blanched.

'Yeah. He's on the way to the hospital. Do you want me to take you there?'

'Yes,' she choked out. 'And I need you to tell me every single detail.'

Chapter Thirty-One

TESSA

Stupid, Scared And Selfish

All the way to Memorial Springs Hospital, Manny kept his eyes focused on the road as he told me how Billy helped break Silvio's fall. Everyone in town knew Silvio was getting slower, that he shouldn't be doing any kind of climbing or lifting, but he wouldn't hear any of it. I supposed Mrs Vanderpool had been right to convince him to hire Billy.

When we reached the hospital parking lot, I asked Manny to stay in the truck. He gave me a sad smile and agreed. Said he'd be waiting if I needed anything. He was a good man, and I felt horrible that I was dragging him through all my crap.

Once inside the emergency room, I approached the information desk until the sound of two familiar voices stopped me. Silvio and Mrs Vanderpool shuffled out of the waiting area. Just like Manny, Silvio's shirt was dotted with blood.

'I'm sorry about all this, Tessa. Greta, I mean, Mrs Vanderpool' – his cheeks pinked up – 'she keeps telling me I'm too old to be lifting heavy things, climbing ladders and such, but it was just a box of nails. I thought it was no big deal…' He broke off, pressing a hand to his lips.

'It's all right, Silvio,' Mrs Vanderpool said, comforting him. 'In our heads we all think we're still twenty years old, but our bodies, well, they wouldn't agree.'

Silvio mumbled a quiet agreement before turning his attention to the information desk. 'They won't tell us nothin' about Billy 'cause we're not family.'

'Don't worry. I'll go and check on him now. You two can head home. I'll give you an update later.'

I started to walk away when Silvio reached out his bony hand to stop me.

'That boy's been a terror since he could walk. Always thought he was headed for trouble, because it was the only way he could get his folks to pay attention to him.' He scrubbed a hand over the white whiskers on his chin. 'But what he did today, how he broke my fall...' He shook his head sadly. 'It could have been much worse for me if he wasn't there. I'm not sayin' you should forgive him. What he did to you and your sweet girls was all kinds of wrong. But there ain't a one of us who hasn't stumbled in this life. I guess that's a good thing to remember.'

'The issues between Billy and me run deep,' I said. 'And you two, I know you mean well, but...' I bit my lip, trying to find the right words.

'But we need to mind our own damn business. We hear you loud and clear, missy,' Mrs Vanderpool said with a firm but understanding tone.

'Tell the boy, I appreciate what he did. He can come back to the store full-time when he's ready.'

'Thank you, Silvio. That will mean a lot to him.'

He gave a smile and let Mrs Vanderpool shuffle him out the hospital's automatic doors.

I approached the desk, and a woman with horn-rimmed glasses and a shock of black hair was immersed in something on her computer.

'I'm looking for Billy Newton. He was brought here by ambulance from Hendrix's Hardware.'

'Are you family?' she said with a snippy voice.

'Uh, yes. I'm his soon-to-be ex-wife.'

Her lips twitched, and she shot a thumb to a set of double doors down the hall. 'He's in Curtain Three. I'll take you there.'

I followed her through the doors, the soles of her brown clogs thudding against the dingy yellow tile. We wound our way past hospital beds and movable pieces of equipment that beeped and hissed. The raw scent of rubbing alcohol and urine stunk up the narrow, stark white space.

We'd only walked a few feet when she pointed at a closed curtain. 'He's there.'

I waited until she was gone before I pushed back the thin cotton material hiding the bed. Billy lay against a stack of pillows, eyes closed, his chest slowly rising and falling. A thick cotton bandage wrapped around the space just above his wrist. In the hazy light he looked so much like the young boy I'd fallen in love with. The kid with a quick wit and a knack for making people laugh.

How had he become this? A deadbeat dad with a wandering eye and zero concern for his own children.

I pulled over a squeaky plastic chair, and he inched open his eyes.

'Hi, Tessie.' He shifted in the bed, wincing as he tried to sit up higher against his stack of pillows. 'Manny said Silvio was okay. Is that true?'

'He's fine. A few bumps and bruises, but he's a tough old guy.' I tipped my chin to his bandage. 'Does it hurt?'

'A little. They tried to give me something for the pain, but I said I'd only take over-the-counter stuff. Trying to be good, you know.'

'I understand, but if you're hurting…'

'Been through worse, but, of course, you already know that,' he said quietly.

When he drank too much, he liked to pick fights with guys much bigger than him. I thought he'd learn his lesson after several broken fingers and one skull fracture, but he was like a reckless child, always testing the limits and never caring about the consequences.

'Did they say when you can leave?'

'I'm supposed to stay here for observation for a few hours to make sure I don't have a concussion.' His skin was pale and thin as onion skin. The areas around his cheeks sunken in.

'When was the last time you ate? Had anything to drink?'

All I got was a shrug.

An angry heat slithered up my throat. He was a twenty-six-year-old man still behaving like a little boy. I jumped up from the chair and poured him a glass of water.

He took a thick swallow and shuttered his eyes. 'I know that look. You think I'm an idiot.'

I sat back down and clasped my hands together in my lap. 'You often act like a thoughtless idiot, but not today. What you did for Silvio was brave.'

'I'd do it again. He's always been good to me, even when I didn't deserve it. He was friends with my Gramps if you remember.' He dipped his chin. 'I miss him so much.

Besides you, he was the only one who ever gave a damn about me.'

We stared at each other for a long beat. If I looked hard enough, maybe I could still see small glimmers of the teenage boy I'd fallen in love with. The kid who carried around a nubby pencil and scraps of paper in his pockets so he could jot down a song lyric that came to him. Who sang quietly under his breath during tests to keep his anxiety at bay. But every time I thought I could somehow locate that part of him, remember our good times together, the cruel, hard side of him would emerge, reminding me that the boy I'd cared about no longer existed.

The curtain shook, and a female doctor appeared. Her white coat sat stiffly across her shoulders. Small tendrils of brown hair escaped her tidy bun.

'Mr Newton.' She turned to me. 'Mrs Newton?'

'Yes, for now,' I muttered, which earned me a wide-eyed stare before she glanced at the black tablet in her hand.

'You got lucky today, sir. If that cut had been a millimeter to the left, you would have hit a major artery in your arm. The stitches will have to come out in a week.' She returned to the tablet, tapping at the screen a few times. 'Your CT scan looks normal.' She approached the bed and checked his eyes. 'Any headache? Dizziness? Blurred vision?'

'No,' he said.

'I'm going to discharge you, but you need to be under someone's care for twenty-four hours to watch for symptoms of a concussion.'

'I live alone,' he said.

The doctor's stare shifted to me.

'We're getting divorced.'

The words made Billy flinch.

'Do you have any family nearby, sir?'

His left eye twitched before he released a heavy 'No.'

'If you don't have anywhere to go, then I'll have to keep you here.'

'I can't do that,' he protested. 'The cost for the ambulance, just being in this bed, it's already too much.'

'You can sign out against doctor's orders, but the older friend who came in with you said you hit your head pretty hard.'

The doctor's steady stare moved back to me.

'Tessie,' he said on an anguished breath. 'Please.'

Why was he always doing this to me? Putting me in the most uncomfortable positions? Making it impossible to say no.

'Fine. You can stay at the house tonight.'

'Excellent,' the doctor said. 'I'll get the nurses started on his discharge paperwork.'

Once she was gone, he said, 'Thank you.'

'It's the least I can do since you helped Silvio.'

He played with the sheets again. 'It was nice to hear you say you were Mrs Newton.'

'It's only because I want the girls and I to share the same last name.'

'Don't you miss it though?'

'Miss what?' I huffed.

'Us? The way we used to push the girls on the swings at the park. Take them for ice cream at the Dairy Dip. Tuck them in at night.'

I couldn't help my caustic laugh. 'You mean the few times you decided to be a part of our family? When you weren't out drinking and partying?'

'I did my best, Tessie.' He ran a shaky hand through his cropped hair. 'When I left, I was so lost. I felt like I had nothing to give you and the girls. That you were better off without me. But my time away, it's been like this slow-burning hole in my heart. Coming back has extinguished that fire. Made me want to be a better man.' He let out a slow breath and clutched onto the stiff white sheet. 'Deep down, you know I love our girls.'

'That may be true, but your past actions say otherwise. What kind of father runs out on his own children?' My voice steadily rose. 'Did you know that Rose sometimes has nightmares? That she wakes up screaming? Her entire little body a sweaty and shaky mess? Since you left, Iris has had stomachaches off and on too. None of that started until you left us. You ran because you are a stupid, scared and selfish man.'

'Everything you're saying is true. But can't a man change? Realize his mistakes?' He gave me a solid stare. 'It's been six months since I've had a drink.' He went back to playing with the stiff white sheet. 'I wish I could take it all back. Do better by you and Iris and my little Rosie.'

'I see that you're trying.' I let out a weary breath. 'But it's going to take time to heal all the damage you've caused.'

He gave an understanding nod. 'I'm not going anywhere.'

My head buzzed with all the complications in my life. The failing bookstore. My girls' uncertainty about their home life. How this was the worst possible time to start a new relationship. One of the things in my life had to give before I had a total meltdown. Sadly, I knew which one it had to be.

Chapter Thirty-Two

MANNY

Remember All The Good Times

I can count on one hand the times in my life when I've wanted to climb out of my own skin. The day Gina's dad stared at me from the chair in his study, a wet, suffocating August breeze blowing into the room as I asked on stuttered breath to marry his daughter. When I had no choice but to drop my pants and get a tetanus shot from a young nurse after I stabbed myself with a rusty nail. The first time I met Tess and my words came out jumbled and flustered like I had a mouth full of marshmallows. But nothing could beat the silence in the truck. Tess achingly close enough to touch while Billy sat on the other side of her.

When I pulled into her driveway, Billy swayed as he climbed out. Tess jumped down and helped guide him to the front door. The girls were waiting, and Iris gave him a massive hug before leading him inside. Tess spoke quietly to the sitter, asking her to keep Lou inside for a minute more.

'I'm sorry I've dragged you into this,' she started. 'You've got a lot going on with the house, and the show, and I'm only adding to your problems.'

'Hey.' I lifted her chin. 'Life is never a straight line. We'll get through this.'

'I need you to help me with something.' The heart-break in her eyes stole the air from my lungs.

'Anything,' I replied.

'What's happening with us is special, but...' Tears coated her dark lashes, and even though I could guess her next words, knew they'd break my heart, I reached out and pressed my hand over hers. 'I have to figure out how to handle all the chaos swirling in my life. With Billy back, and the girls not understanding what's happening... plus the store, I don't think I can give you what you need.' She pulled in a shuddering breath. 'It's all too much right now.'

'Tess, this doesn't have to be anything more than what we already have. I understand things are confusing, and I don't want to add to the worry you're already shouldering. I'm here for you whether we are kissing or just hanging out with the girls. Whatever small piece of your life you're willing to give to me, I'll take it.'

She shook her head. Took a step back. 'You deserve more than that.'

'It doesn't matter what you think I deserve.' I closed the space between us. 'It's what I want. And all I've ever wanted is you.'

'Mama, can we have some lemonade?' Rosie stood in the doorway. Her small hands on her hips like she needed an immediate answer.

'I better go,' she said.

'Tess, I mean it. Things don't have to change between us.'

She gave me a weak smile, glanced at Rose. 'Don't they though?'

I'd be an idiot if I said I hadn't seen this coming. Like a car crash happening in slow motion, I had watched helplessly as Tess began to unravel. How when we were in a room together she kept her distance. Even today, she tried to put on a brave face as we talked about the coffee bar, but there was a shakiness to her demeanor that warned a lot weighed on her mind.

I meant what I said about things not changing between us, but I also knew Tessa. Once she set her mind to something, there was no chance of changing it.

–

Lou was my little emotional sensor. Her instincts acute whenever things were off with me. Even when I was struggling with my own mental health, I never kept the truth from her. She'd give me space, a moment, when she heard me start my breathing routine. It often cut me to the core because, as a child, the last thing she needed to worry about was her father's state of mind.

Silence filled the truck as we drove the short distance home. Before we reached the turn for our street, she said. 'Why did my mommy leave us?'

I almost crashed straight into the curb.

'She didn't leave on purpose, Lou Lou. You know that.'

'But why did she have to get sick?'

I pulled to the side of the road. Once the truck was stopped, I turned to face her, and my heart split into a dozen pieces as I took in my child's broken stare.

'Climb up here,' I said.

Once she was unbuckled and on the seat next to me, I tugged her into my side.

'I'll be honest, Lou, sometimes I don't understand it either. People in our lives get taken from us, and, at first, we're sad. Slowly that sadness goes away, and we're allowed to remember all the good times we had with them.'

'It's not fair. All I know about her is what you've told me. What I see in the pictures around our house. The things Grammy and Papa say when they visit.'

'That's my fault. We should talk about her more. Go through your baby books and look at the pictures of you two together.'

'Do you think I look like her?'

I pulled in an achy breath. 'With each passing year, you grow just as beautiful.'

She looked at me with wide eyes. 'I do?'

'Yes. Your hair is the exact same color as hers. A rich ebony like a moonless night,' I said, plopping a kiss on the top of her head. 'Your mama always separated out her vegetables from the meat on her plate the way you do. She wasn't a real fan of broccoli either.'

She gave a little laugh.

'And your giggle. It reminds me of her in so many ways.'

She snuggled in closer to my side.

'We can keep her alive by remembering her in all these ways. Talking about her more,' I said with a promise.

She went quiet and then said on a whisper, 'Do you think Miss Tessa could be my mama one day?'

I forced myself not to crumble. Not let my voice shake when I replied. 'What makes you ask that?'

She inched back and gave a good roll of her eyes. 'I'm not blind, Pop. Whenever she's around, you're happier. I see it in the way she treats you too. Both your cheeks get all pink when you're near each other.' She gave me a mature look that reminded me she was growing up too quickly. 'Plus, you tried to hide it, but I saw you hold hands when we went apple-picking. Brittany, well, she said before we stopped being friends, that's what people do when they like each other.'

'Things are complicated between us, honey. In fact,' I said, trying to keep my voice even, 'we may not see Tess for a little bit as she tries to get the coffee bar ready for the store.'

She crossed her arms over her chest and went painfully silent again. Every part of me wanted to confess that I wanted exactly what she did, but too often things we wanted slipped out of our grasp, and there wasn't a damn thing we could do about it.

Chapter Thirty-Three

TESSA

The Opposite Of Drama

For the last week, Manny and I worked together in a brittle sort of agreement. Every conversation between us was short questions and even shorter answers. He'd asked if I'd ordered the Italian espresso machine I'd had my eye on, and I'd given a quiet yes. When I'd asked if we'd receive the marble slab for the top of the bar before Christmas, all he'd given me was a simple nod.

I hated every minute of it, but it was the right choice. It wasn't fair to build things between us when I couldn't dig my way out of the complicated issues swirling in my own life.

'Hey.' I looked up to find Billy staring at me from the threshold of my office, a paper bag clutched in his hand. 'Still like the chicken pesto sandwich from McCrearys?'

'Yes, but that's like fifteen minutes outside of town.'

'Silvio gave me an extra-long lunch.'

I glanced at the spot on his arm where his seven stitches appeared to be healing well.

'It's not that far,' he said, noting where my stare lingered. 'I actually think he wanted to close the store for a bit. Heard him on the phone this morning with Mrs

Vanderpool. Sounded like she was inviting him over for lunch.'

I tried not to smile. 'They're spending a lot of time together.'

He shrugged and sat in the chair in front of my desk. 'No matter our age, guys always like the attention of a gorgeous woman.' His gaze lingered on me a little too long before he handed over the sandwich that was still warm. 'What are you working on?' he asked between bites of his BLT.

'I want to throw a small party to celebrate the opening of the coffee bar. I'm thinking the second week of February.'

He pointed to the pad on my desk and smiled. 'Is that your "Tessa Do" list?'

'Maybe,' I said with a laugh.

Ever since I was a kid, I loved making lists. I had one for my morning routine. The girls' schoolwork. It was a nightmare when my parents took Tor and me on vacation because the packing list was endless. In high school, I made one at the beginning of the year for all my classes. Instead of a 'To Do' list, Billy called them my 'Tessa Do' lists.

'You know me. Trying to be organized, because I need this all to go smoothly.'

Billy gave me a long look.

I finally met his gaze and gave him an irritated, 'What?'

'I owe you an apology.'

'For what exactly? There are so many things that require one.'

He blanched but gave me a slow nod. 'True. In this case, it's for doubting you and your ability to handle this store.'

I nearly choked on a piece of chicken. 'Excuse me?'

'There are a lot of shitty things I said and did to you, Tessie. The minute I questioned if you could handle the work here, I knew it was the wrong thing to say. You've always loved this place. Your mom knew that.' His words weren't more than a whisper. 'She was right to will it to you.'

'Well, thank you,' I said, tapping the edges of my mouth with a napkin. 'But I'm not going to lie. It's been a struggle for me.'

'You may not be outwardly strong and outspoken like Torran, but you have a quiet power that I think is more potent. That people also respect.'

'That may be the kindest thing you've said to me in a long time.'

'I know.' He tipped his chin down. 'That's just one more thing I should apologize for.'

I didn't know how to handle this contrite side of Billy, so I went back to eating and focusing on my list.

He leaned in and looked at it as I wrote notes about checking our application for the food service permit and needing custom napkins with the P&P logo. I added a line about asking Barb and Susan about plates for the signature pastries they were making. And a reminder to go to the bank to have extra cash on hand in the hope that business might be brisk that night.

Billy watched me with interest. 'Anything I can do to help you out? Silvio has me working from nine to three, but I'm available after.'

Again, I had to take another beat, not used to this new and responsible version of him.

'When it gets closer, I may need you to do more carpooling. Take the girls to school or soccer practice.'

'Whatever you need, Tessie. I'm here.'

He gave me a warm gaze that held so much promise. When we were a family, I'd wished for these kinds of moments. When he'd act like a real husband and father.

For the life of me, I couldn't figure out how we'd gotten here. After Rose was born, he did all the fatherly things. Changed diapers. Took the girls on walks in the double stroller when they were fussy. Once they became more self-sufficient, he began to fade away. Like he had his own plans and none of them included his family. Now we stood in this odd place where he was equal parts stranger and longtime friend. It made me wonder if he really did have the capacity for change. To become a different person after making such a terrible mistake. Maybe at some point we could be friends. Co-parent the girls successfully. Even in light of all that, there was still one thing we needed to settle.

I reached into the top drawer of my desk, skimming my hand over an extra set of keys before clasping onto a large gray envelope. The name of my attorney stamped in the corner in deep blue ink. I slid the envelope across the desk to him.

Billy took a full swallow. 'Is that what I think it is?'

'Yes,' I said, pulling a pen out of the old coffee cup on my desk. 'This is as good a time as any to sign the divorce papers.'

His skin went ashen as he slid the documents out. The room stayed quiet as he read page by page. When he was finished, he put the papers down and shook his head. 'You want full custody of the girls?'

'Of course. The last time we talked I told you that was the plan.'

'I just thought with me coming back, showing you how I've changed, we could work something out.'

'Billy, be serious. You abandoned them. Abandoned all of us.'

His shoulders quickly sank.

'I see that you're putting in a real effort, and I will continue to allow you to see the girls, but I won't give you any kind of custody, at least not right now.'

He began to wrap up his sandwich, his eyes still focused on the floor. 'I understand.'

A sharp knock thankfully broke up the uncomfortable moment. I moved around Billy and opened my office door.

'Tess, we need to talk…' Dad stomped inside and stopped at the sight of Billy, who stood up quickly.

'I was just leaving. See you later, Tessie.'

My father stood with his back ramrod straight. If a look could turn someone to ash, Billy would be incinerated right now.

Once he was gone, my father stared at the papers on the desk. 'Did he sign them?'

'We were just talking about it.'

'Tessa.' The lines in his forehead bunched together. 'Put that pen in his hand and make him do it before he disappears again.'

'Dad, I've got what feels like a million things going on, and I'm not in a place where I can push him right now. It'll get done soon, I promise.'

He must have heard the catch in my voice, because the tight set of his jaw went slack.

'I get that you're worried. That you want to protect Iris and Rose.' I dragged in a stilted breath. 'But he's got a job, a place to live, and he's trying to make amends.'

'I still do not know what Greta Vanderpool was thinking,' he huffed.

'That Billy swerved his car, hit a tree, all in an attempt to not hurt the one thing she holds most dear in this world.'

'Yes, I get that,' he said wearily.

'We're finding our way, Dad. It will all work out.'

He crossed his arms over his chest. 'I worry that he's going to hurt you all again.'

'I'm not going into this blindly. We just discussed how I am asking for full custody. How his time with the girls will be carefully monitored. I've also told him, several times, that the minute he steps a toe out of line, he'll be out of their lives for good. But, for now, he's doing what he's promised, and it's been good for the girls to spend time with him.'

'A chameleon can change to whatever he needs his environment to be.' He glanced back in the direction Billy left. 'Those tattoos can be covered up. That mop of bleached blonde hair can be shaved off, but he can't hide the crimes of his past, no matter how hard he tries to look or act like an upstanding citizen.'

'You have every right to be worried, but your job as a grandfather is to think of the girls first.'

He closed his eyes. Dragged a hand down over his face. 'It's times like these that I need your mother. She'd know the right way to calm me down. Help me see reason instead of red.'

'Dad,' I said softly. 'I know you love Iris and Rose. That love is bigger than what you feel for Billy. Lean into that. *Please*.'

He pulled me into a hug. 'What effect does this have on Manny?' he asked quietly.

This was one topic I did not want to discuss with him.

'Tessa.' He pulled back, and the loaded look in his eyes said he'd heard the gossip about Manny and me.

'We've agreed to give each other space.' I pulled my braid over my shoulder and fiddled with the elastic. 'Between the store, the girls, and now Billy, I don't know how much more room I have in my life for drama.'

'Is Manny drama?'

'He is the opposite of drama,' I confessed.

'I've tried very hard this last year to listen to what you and Torran need. To not interfere. But these past months, I've watched you bloom back to life. When Manny is around, you light up brighter than all that neon inside the Dairy Dip. He pays attention to your needs. Wants to make your world fuller. Is it worth risking all that because Billy is back?'

'There is only so much I can handle right now. Manny needs someone who can be fully engaged. Give him their undivided attention. I feel like a piece of taffy being yanked in twenty different directions, and there isn't enough time in the day to build something good and solid with him – which is what he deserves.'

Dad furrowed his brow. 'Do you think he'll wait until you've got this all figured out?'

I gave a sad shrug. 'That's an answer only he can give.'

He pulled me into another hug, and I tried not to think about how every second I spent away from Manny felt like a long string of stormy days without a chance of sunshine in sight.

Chapter Thirty-Four

MANNY

Blotting Out The Ache

All afternoon Lou begged me to take her to the Dairy Dip for a milkshake. As I supervised the final installation of the flooring at the old Thomas Place, she sat on a box in the corner quietly watching a movie on my phone and had not complained a lick. That may have also been because she'd finally been granted access to screens after a long break.

Before I'd released her from her punishment, we had another talk about Brittany and the other girls at school. She admitted the teasing had not entirely stopped, but it'd settled down, especially after she told all the girls that my newfound status would make it easier for her to meet her idol, Harry Styles (never gonna happen).

When the plumber finished in the kitchen, I double-checked the measurements for the cabinets that were due to be delivered next week. The film crew had worked in the space earlier this morning, shooting B-roll for the interior and exterior of the home, but, thankfully, they were gone now.

Torran spent most of the afternoon working upstairs in the master bathroom. We'd spent hours going over whether or not to include a built-in soap alcove in the shower. If the flooring was a good match for the marble slab we'd selected for the countertop. The low creak on the staircase and solid thud of footsteps said she might finally be coming up for air.

She walked toward me with her phone pressed to her ear. Her voice low and tense.

'Issues?' I whispered.

She put her hand over the mouthpiece. 'Lauren wants us to go to Atlanta to meet with the network. They want to discuss final details about the contract for Season Three in person.'

'Not unless we can come to some kind of tentative agreement about the publicity and social media.'

Torran tapped the speaker icon and Lauren's voice filled the room.

'Manny, can you hear me?'

'Atlanta? Really, Lauren?' I said.

'Yes. We need you both at the corporate office to meet with the head of the network to work out the final contract details.'

'Fine. When do they want us there?' I said.

'The second week of February,' Lauren answered.

'That's right around the time the coffee bar will be finished. Tor, didn't you say Tess was planning a small party to celebrate?'

My voice caught on Tess' name. Much to her credit, Torran didn't jump on it. She'd seen how I'd spent all my time focused on this house in hopes of blotting out the ache I felt by not spending time with her sister.

'I swear this won't interfere,' Lauren said.

After I agreed, Torran went over a few more filming details before she hung up.

'I know you weren't expecting this, but Lauren swears the network is willing to negotiate with us.'

'All right, but I'm driving to Atlanta because that tin-can truck of yours won't make it ten miles past the city limits.'

'Hey.' She feigned hurt. 'Don't talk about Sally Mae that way. She's a classic.'

'A classic wreck,' I mumbled.

She jokingly punched my shoulder before beelining her way toward Lou and swinging her around in a circle.

'When you're done making my child dizzy, we need to talk about where you want the appliances in the kitchen.'

She gave Lou a quick squeeze and followed me into the shell of a room that had once been banana yellow and avocado green. We went back and forth before agreeing on the placement for the new stainless steel fridge, double ovens and wide farmhouse sink.

Her phone beeped, and when she glanced at the screen, her shoulders sagged.

'Lauren again?'

'No, it's Beck. He canceled dinner tonight.'

'Guess he's busy, huh?'

She shrugged and shoved her phone into the front pocket of her overalls a little too sharply.

'Tor,' I urged. 'Something wrong?'

'Beck...' She shook her head and walked to the framing where we'd decided to put the stove.

'What's up with him? Haven't seen him around lately. He must be working hard.'

'He's been distracted lately.'

'Distracted how?'

'Not answering texts right away. Staring off into space like he's miles away. I'm worried he's keeping secrets from me.'

'What makes you think that?'

'He talks on the phone, but when I come into the room, he hangs up quickly. When we were at Sugar Rush last week, he had all these quiet side whispers with Barb and Susan.' She tapped at the phone in her pocket. 'This is the second time in ten days he's canceled dinner on me.'

I gave her a pointed look. 'You know what I'm going to say.'

'Talk to him,' she said with a hint of frustration. 'Our life has been good this last year. Piper is settled. We're working on this house, which has always been a dream of mine. I don't want to think about anything interfering with how smoothly things are moving along.'

'Open and honest communication,' I said firmly. 'If you don't talk, your mind builds up all these dire scenarios, which are probably all wrong. If you know the truth, your brain can't think the worst.'

She arched a brow. 'Is that what you've done with Tess?'

'Tess and me,' I sighed. 'We're complicated.'

'Billy,' she seethed.

'I'm not going to lie, being away from her, giving her space, is one of the most painful things I've ever done. But I also need to respect her wishes. Wait until she's ready to try with me again.'

'And how long can you wait?'

'I can't answer that, but she has to find her way through this. Figure out how she can incorporate Billy into her new normal with the girls. That's something I understand.

I had to swim through the muck after losing Gina, and it took me a while to figure out a rhythm for Lou and me.'

'I know what he did for Silvio when he fell from that ladder. How he's been helping to care for Mrs Vander-pool's yard on the weekend. Doing odd jobs for her around the house. But I've also known Billy most of my life. There is a selfish side to him, and that doesn't change overnight. Some way, somehow, he's going to hurt Tess and the girls again. I can feel it in my bones.'

My thoughts flickered to that night at the house when I accused Billy of being at the field. For a moment I considered asking Tor about it, if she thought he was lying, but then I pressed my lips together. The last thing Tess needed was another person doubting her choices.

'That's not what I want. Not what you want either,' I said quickly. 'The best outcome is that he figures out his purpose. Keeps a job, pays child support, and stays out of all of our lives as much as possible.'

'Pop.' Lou appeared in the doorway to the kitchen. 'My show is over. Is it time for a milkshake?'

Torran shuffled across the kitchen, her worried look morphing into joy as she reached out for Lou's hand and spun her in another circle.

'Dragging your dad to the Dairy Dip?' she asked.

'Yes. Some kids at school say they have a new milkshake that tastes like peppermint.'

'Oh, that sounds delicious.' Tor hesitated. 'Things good at school? Your Pop told me you were having trouble with one girl.'

Lou swapped a look with me. I nodded, telling her she could say whatever felt comfortable.

'Yeah, she was being mean.' Lou leaned in. 'But I think she's jealous 'cause I told her Pop could introduce me to Taylor.'

Torran cackled. 'As in Swift?'

Lou nodded, and Torran gave me an amused smile.

'Lou Lou, we've talked about how saying things like that is not okay,' I said.

'I know, but it was kind of fun to watch Brittany's eyes bug out for a second.'

Torran muffled a laugh with her hand. 'You know, Lou, I've seen your Pop do some amazing things. Taylor's not totally out of the question.'

'Really?' Now Lou's eyes went wide.

I let out a groan. 'Please do not encourage her. And Lou, that's not something we should be spreading around. I'm just a guy working on a TV show with his annoying best friend.'

Torran gave Lou another spin and had the gall to wink at me. 'Come on, Manny. With you, anything is possible.'

–

The only spots open at the Dairy Dip were two seats at the counter. The place sparkled with red and green twinkle lights. Foil trees in gold and silver hung from the ceiling. 'Sleigh Ride' blared from the whimsical jukebox set in the corner of the shop.

A neon sign above the counter was lit up with blue and yellow lights, advertising a dozen types of milkshakes, ice cream bars, cookie sandwiches, as well as regular sundaes and thick mixed desserts with crushed candy bars inside.

Lou climbed onto a red leather stool, and I took the one beside her. A teenage boy took our order. Lou asked for the 'Peppermint Kiss' shake while I opted for the caramel and vanilla swirl.

The song changed to 'Jingle Bells', and Lou hummed along. A friend of Piper's, Maisey Bedford, sat at one of the wrought-iron tables near the door with her husband, Joe, a local lawyer, and her two small kids. When she saw us she gave a warm wave.

The teenage kid at the counter slid a glass mug and a silver cylinder with extra shake toward Lou. Her face lit up as she took her first sip.

'This is so good.' She held out her mug. I took a drink and tried not to shiver. The sweetness made my jaw ache. My thoughts immediately went to Tess and her worries about cavities. Yeah, we'd definitely have to thoroughly brush Lou's teeth tonight.

'Pop, we need to talk about something serious.'

I froze. She'd been good about not asking about Tess and the girls, like she sensed how it was hurting me. But it'd been a while since we'd spent any time with them, and I sensed Lou was at her limit.

She straightened her shoulders. Tipped up her chin. 'Is there any way I can talk you into putting a motorized scooter back on my Christmas list? Kick ones are for babies.'

I held back a laugh as she set her small mouth in determination.

'Nope. We start slow. You show me how you can ride a kick one safely, and then we can talk about a motorized one later on.'

'Okay. Like when I'm twelve?'

'Maybe thirteen,' I said.

She started to protest until Iris and Rose sped toward the counter calling her name. I'd tried to hide my feelings when I was around Tessa at the store, but my traitorous heart went light at the sight of her racing in after them. She wore jeans and a sky blue sweater that set off the red in her hair. It felt like torture not to reach out and touch her. Kiss her. Tell her how beautiful she looked.

Lou excitedly pulled Rose onto her lap. I moved to let Iris take my spot at the crowded counter. Tess gave me a hesitant smile. The curve of her beautiful pink lips tense.

'A mom and daughters outing?'

'No,' she said on a brittle breath as Billy walked in the door.

'Oh, okay,' I managed to say even as my heart cracked straight down the middle.

'Lou says the peppermint shake is the best. Can I get one, Mommy?'

Joy made little Rose practically vibrate. I guessed that was what happened when you finally saw your family as whole.

'That's a lot of sugar, sweetie. What about a vanilla cone?'

'Ah, come on, Tessie.' Billy tucked those stupid black sunglasses into his shirt pocket and pulled Rose off Lou's lap, propping her on his hip. 'I think this one time we can let our Rosie have what she wants.'

Rose giggled, and Tess shot Billy an annoyed look. Iris quickly added she wanted the same milkshake.

'Fine.' Tess reached into her purse for her wallet.

'That's okay,' Billy said, grabbing a few bills from the back pocket of his jeans.

Tess double-blinked as he paid for the drinks and went back to his conversation with Iris and Rose.

Even though I tried, I couldn't pull my gaze away from Tess. Worry filled the lines around her mouth. She'd said she needed space, but I had to know what made her look like she wanted to tear her own hair out. I motioned for her to move farther down the counter, and she inched my way.

'What's wrong?' I asked.

She scrubbed a hand over her mouth. Shook her head. 'Long day at the bookstore. The warehouse sent the wrong order for the church's book club. We had a kid get sick on the rainbow carpet after story time.' She muttered something about regurgitated blueberries. 'But' – her eyes finally filled with light – 'most of the coffee and tea I ordered arrived. The leather stools came in too, and they're gorgeous.'

This is what I wanted for her. Joy in her voice. A warm smile brightening her entire face.

'That's good. I'll be by tomorrow to check out the crew's final work on the bar.'

'But it's Sunday. I thought that was your "no work" day?'

'Torran and Beck offered to take Lou to the movies.'

'Oh, that's good.'

I hated the sudden weight that returned to her shoulders. The way she cocked her head left and right as if she was carrying the weight of the world. My fingers twitched, wanting to reach out and smooth out that knot in her neck again.

My gaze kept moving to her pillow-soft lips, and her eyes narrowed on my face. She could ask for all the space she wanted, but there was no mistaking the ache in her eyes too. I wanted to protect her. Let her know that I was always here for her, but my mind kept going back to those damn sunglasses. How Billy insisted to Lucas in the hardware store that he hadn't been driving around town a month before he hit the tree, which was impossible because no one else in Ivy Falls had a car like his.

'Tess, don't you think it's weird that since he's been back there haven't been any more incidents?'

She glanced over her shoulder, watching Billy poke Iris' side and making Rose laugh.

'Halloween night was a prank. And the window...' She hedged like she was trying to talk herself into the next thought. 'Well, that could have been the wind.'

'Tess.' I moved in closer. 'Do you really believe that?'

'Please, Manny. Not now.'

I took another step, wanting to reach for her, convince her of the truth, but a loud crash stopped me. The steel container holding the rest of Lou's milkshake spun on the floor. Spilled ice cream oozed across the tile like a pink river.

'What happened?' I said, pulling Lou into my arms.

'It must have fallen off the counter when I wasn't looking.' Her eyes went watery. 'Can we please go home?'

'Sure, yeah, okay.' I glanced at the teenage kid behind the counter and mouthed, 'Sorry'. He waved a hand at me like it happened all the time.

Tess came over to comfort Lou, reaching out to rub her back.

'Don't touch me,' Lou snapped.

'Louisa! Apologize to Tess right now.'

Iris, Rose and Billy watched the scene with concern.

Lou struggled out of my arms and rushed for the door. I made more apologies to Tess before I went after Lou.

The Saturday afternoon sidewalks around the square were crowded with people doing their holiday shopping. A few tourists pulled out their phones and took pictures while I chased after Lou. She sprinted past Sugar Rush and the hardware store. Just as she was about to dart into the street, Silvio stepped off the sidewalk and grabbed her before a massive truck rolled past.

'You gotta watch where you're going, kid,' Silvio said.

Lou burst into tears, and when I reached her, she flung herself into my arms.

'What's happening, Lou?' I said, choking on the words, my entire body vibrating with fear.

She mumbled a few words into my shoulder. I pulled back, and with a sob-crowded voice, she said, 'Miss Tessa is going to live with that man.'

'You mean Iris and Roses' father?'

She nodded. 'Iris said her mama and daddy were happy now. That they were going to be a family again.'

'Oh, honey. That is more about what Iris wants than what is true.'

'But Iris wouldn't lie. She's my friend.'

'She's not lying, but I'm not sure she understands the situation.'

'How do you know? She could be right. That would mean they wouldn't need us anymore. Want to spend time with us. I love Miss Tessa and how she makes wonderful chicken Parmigiana. How she can do all the wonderful voices from *The Lorax*. We lost Mama. We can't lose her and my friends too.'

She threw herself back into my arms, and I held on as her sobs rang in my ears.

The shuffling of feet made me look up. Tess raced toward us and stopped only inches away.

'Is she okay?'

Lou didn't deserve any of this. She needed to have a carefree life. To run and play with her friends. Not worry about the unraveling of her world.

'Silvio grabbed her before she ran into the street and got hit by a truck,' I snapped.

'Oh, Manny,' she gasped. 'What can I do to help?'

'I can't do this with you right now,' I flung back.

'Talk to me,' she pushed. 'We're friends.'

'Are we?' I said bitterly.

She flinched, and I held onto Lou tighter, knowing the last thing she needed was to hear me argue with the woman who'd been like a mother to her this last year.

'I can handle this. Go back to your family, Tessa.'

She blinked back tears and gave me a broken nod. 'I'm sorry,' she whispered before walking away.

Lou continued to sob in my arms. I shouldn't have snapped at Tess, but what was happening was confusing for someone as young as Lou. Hell, it was confusing for me.

I wanted to convince Lou that what Iris said and what was actually happening weren't the same thing. But after watching how Billy had insinuated his way back into Tess' life, I wasn't sure I could promise her that anymore.

Chapter Thirty-Five

TESSA

Olive Branch

Christmas Day announced itself quiet as a whisper. A small layer of snow coated the front and backyard. Miraculously, the girls were still asleep at seven a.m., leaving me enough time to catch my breath, have a quiet cup of tea and ready myself for the day.

We'd spent the night before with Beck and Torran at Huckleberry Lane. Piper, Isabel and Dad rounded out our group. The girls squealed with delight when Torran set up their gift in the backyard: a miniature soccer goal that they put to the test right away.

I plastered a smile to my face. Cheered when Iris sent the soccer ball straight into the net, even with Beck playing goalie. Inside though, I was aching. None of the scene felt right. Manny should have been chasing after the girls and Lou. Sitting next to me at the dinner table, brushing his fingers ever so lightly over my hand.

Sadly, I'd made my choice, and so had he. Billy's arrival, his slow transition back into our lives, had sent what we'd been building off track. Lou almost getting hit by a car was only proof of how far things had spun out of control.

The plodding of small feet filled our bungalow. Iris appeared first, her auburn hair a tangle atop her head.

Rose followed right after. They looked adorable in the matching red and green plaid pajamas Isabel gifted them last night.

I wasn't expecting their muted behavior as they took seats at the table. For sure, I thought they'd come tumbling into the room, wondering what Santa Claus had left for them. Instead, Iris gave me a hopeful stare. 'Are we seeing Mr Manny and Lou today?'

'Lou asked Santa for a scooter,' Rose added. 'Can we go see her ride it after breakfast?'

My heart ached at the anticipation in their voices. They weren't the only ones who were missing Lou and Manny. Before I could answer, there was a quiet knock at the door.

'Is that Grandpa?' Iris asked.

'No. We're supposed to see him later today.'

I tamped down the hope that one beautiful, slightly stubbled face would be waiting on the other side of the door. When I pulled it open, I did my best not to show my disappointment.

'Mornin',' Billy chirped, his arms filled with presents covered in shiny silver and gold wrapping paper – which I was sure was courtesy of Mrs Vanderpool. Since his return, she'd taken Billy on as her pet project like he was a puppy that needed training, which, honestly, he did in many ways. 'Look what Santa left at my place. Must have known you were both good girls this year. That you deserved extra.'

He gave me a hesitant smile as he crossed the threshold and walked into the family room where we had our small tree. He moved with a cocky glide, his body not so bony anymore. Had to be all the home-cooked meals Mrs Vanderpool kept leaving at his doorstep.

'I thought we'd agreed that you'd come over later this afternoon for dinner,' I said in a whisper.

'Sorry, I couldn't wait.' He said without an ounce of regret. 'Let me drop these off, give the girls a hug, and then I'll go.'

'Billy,' I sighed as he laid the gifts onto the red and gold skirt surrounding the tree. He was buying the girls presents, and yet he still hadn't paid a penny in child support.

As if he could read my mind, he said, 'I have something for you too.' He reached into the pocket of his black leather jacket and handed me a small white envelope. Inside sat three one-hundred-dollar bills. 'I know it's not much, but it's a start. Really, Tessie, I want to do right by you and the girls.'

'Thank you. Every little bit helps.'

'I swear I'll keep paying as much as I can.' He reached out, brushed his hand over the top of mine, and I took a quick step back.

'It means a lot that you're finally taking your responsibilities seriously,' I said, ignoring the way his stare stayed fixed on me.

The girls squealed and pointed out each gift tag that said their name.

'Daddy!' Rose grabbed his hand and yanked him toward her growing pile. Billy's face grew into a wide smile. It was the first time she'd called him that since he'd been back.

The girls continued to scramble around the ridiculous mound of gifts. My dad had gone overboard this year. He'd told me in a quiet moment last night that he'd picked things he was sure my mother would have bought for the girls if she was still alive. It was impossible to argue with that and the way he beamed brightly as the girls watched him set their gifts around the tree.

It was Iris' turn to show Billy her loot. She giggled and danced on her toes. Threw her arms around his waist for a big hug.

He glanced in my direction again. The joy on his face was clear as he returned her embrace. It'd been two years since the girls had a Christmas with their father. They deserved this special moment with him.

'Want coffee?' I asked.

'Yes, please,' he said before scooping up Rose and tickling her side, her delighted giggles filling the air.

In the kitchen, I set the machine to brew. The wind picked up. Winter frost rained down from the trees in a sparkling veil. A slow strum of notes said Billy had grabbed his guitar from the girls' room. Now the three of them sang 'Jingle Bells' at full volume.

The scene should have made me happy, but my mind went back to Manny, wondering what he and Lou were doing this morning. How even as the girls crooned along with their father, the house still felt empty without them here.

–

In a flurry of hugs and kisses, Torran and Beck arrived at my house for our traditional Christmas dinner that I'd held ever since Mom passed. The girls tugged Beck back toward their room, anxious to show him the new books and toys they'd received from Billy.

'How's Beck doing? Still acting weird?' I asked Torran.

She gave a small shrug. 'He keeps saying he's got a lot on his mind. I get it. We're both really busy right now.'

As I worked on basting the turkey, Torran poured herself a glass of wine.

'Number?' she asked.

Since we'd lost our mom, we'd agreed to this check-in with each other, asking on a scale from one to ten how we were feeling. If we were having a particularly rough day, the number was low. On a good day, it could be in the high range. Tor even had the number eight tattooed behind her ear as a sort of goal for every day.

'I'm about a five,' I said.

Her mouth drooped. 'I was hoping for higher.'

'It's hard, but I'm trying for the girls' sake.'

'It's okay to miss him, you know.'

'Tor, not today. All I want is to get through it. Not think about who will be missing from the table tonight.'

'He told me about the Dairy Dip and the truck.' She sucked in a low breath. 'If the two of you would just sit down and talk—'

'Stop. There's too much going on, and the way he looked at me after Lou almost got hit…'

'Hey.' She reached for my hand, trying to calm the way I was trembling. 'He doesn't blame you for that.'

'I keep seeing his face. The raw hurt and fear. It was like he could never forgive me.'

'This is all going to pass, Tessa. Things will go back to the way they used to be.'

'Can they though, with Billy here? He's making such an effort with the girls, and the coffee bar is nearly done, but I'm still terrified it won't be enough to save the store.' The worry spinning through my brain was like a loud and unending scream. 'I don't have the bandwidth for much more, Tor.'

'Maybe…' She closed her mouth. Shook her head.

'Maybe what?'

She pinned me in place with a steady look. 'You could talk to someone again.'

I let loose a bitter laugh. 'Yeah, maybe, but when would I have time for that?'

'Let's be clear about something,' she huffed. 'There are a dozen people in this town who would watch the girls. Help at the store if you needed it.' The corner of her mouth twitched. 'You could even ask Billy. He seems to be helping now.'

'Wow. Was that you saying something nice about him?'

'Let's be real. I'm never going to forget what he did to you and the girls. But if anyone in this town gets the need for a redemption arc, it's me.'

She tapped her finger slowly against the glass. A hint of blue paint still colored her skin.

'I've been watching him these last weeks. Seen how he's helped out Silvio. Hell, the other day I saw him taking Baby for a walk around the fountain. And you know how Mrs Vanderpool feels about letting that dog out of her sight for more than a minute.' She took a slow sip of her wine, pressed her lips thin again. 'There's also no denying that Iris hasn't complained of a stomachache lately.'

'And Rosie has slept soundly through the night for the last few weeks,' I admitted.

'If he's going to be back in our lives, I'm willing to accept it. But don't think that he's ever going to be off the hook for his past indiscretions.' She chewed on her bottom lip. 'What about you? How are you feeling about him?'

'Conflicted, for sure.' I reached out and took a large gulp of her wine before handing back the glass. 'He's slowly earning back my trust. When he says he's going to pick up the girls at the store to take them to soccer practice, he arrives on time. He even gave me money today to help support the girls.'

Torran gave a firm nod. 'As he should.'

'It's just…' A part of me was too afraid to say what was on my mind.

'Tessa, what is it?' she pressed.

I closed my eyes. Pushed out the words that had been swimming in my head since I'd seen Manny at the Dairy Dip. 'Do you think it's odd that the weird incidents, the break-in, the rock at the P&P, nothing like that's happened again since Billy's been back?'

She took a beat. Tapped at the glass. 'It's odd, yes, but also maybe a coincidence.' She gave a small shrug. 'Look, I am the last one to give him the benefit of the doubt, but I also know that everyone in this town is a damn busybody. If anyone had seen Billy lurking around, they would have spoken up.'

It was a good point, so why didn't it make me feel better?

The girls raced into the room and excitedly asked for a pen and paper.

'What for?' Torran asked.

'We're playing a game with Beck and keeping score,' Iris said.

'You should come and play too, Auntie Torran,' Rose said, clasping her hand and dragging her forward.

'All right,' she said, taking the pen and paper from my outstretched hand. 'Love you. Don't worry so much.' She smiled as Rose tugged her down the hall to the girls' rooms.

I continued to baste the turkey, boil potatoes, needing a good distraction from my racing thoughts. A half-hour later, Isabel and Dad arrived. He wore his regular plaid Christmas bow tie, and Isabel had on a skirt that matched. It was her first Christmas with us, and I could feel the nervousness wafting off her as she set her bright red wool coat on the peg behind the door.

Dad leaned in and gave me a peck on the cheek. When there was another knock on the back door, his jaw clenched as Billy stepped inside, shaking small bits of snow from his hair that was starting to look normal after that terrible buzz cut.

He hung his leather jacket near Isabel's coat, ignoring Dad's stare. Billy had put in an effort, wearing dark-wash jeans and a gray Henley. He gave a nod of acknowledgement to Dad. They'd sort of grown into a mutual agreement that they'd tolerate being in each other's space, but that didn't mean they had to speak.

Billy walked to the cabinet under the sink, pulled out an apron, tied it around his waist, and said, 'What can I do to help?'

Dad blinked twice, and Isabel smiled.

'Drain the potatoes, please, and get started on mashing them,' I said.

Much to his credit, Dad pulled out a colander from a lower cabinet and set it in the sink for him.

'Where's the hand mixer?' Dad asked. 'Might as well work together.'

The tense set of Billy's shoulders relaxed. He'd always been afraid of my dad, but he'd also said more than once how much he respected him.

Dad grabbing the mixer from a lower cabinet, offering to work beside him, was as much of an olive branch as Billy was going to get.

When dinner was finished, and the girls tore through the last of their presents, Billy asked if we could talk outside.

I pulled on my white wool coat, and he grabbed his leather jacket and followed me. As we stood in the cold, our breaths turning into a misty fog, he said, 'I want to talk to you about something important.'

'Good. I want to talk to you about something too.'

He arched a brow. 'All right, you go first.'

'Tell me why you came back to Ivy Falls.'

'This again?' He had the nerve to act irritated. 'Things were bad in Atlanta. I wanted to come back to my home. It's that simple.'

'Why return at night? Why come through the square if you were planning to sleep at a motel off the highway?'

'Nostalgia, I guess. Wanted to see the spots where you and I had spent the most time. Holding hands by the fountain. Having our first kiss at the park when we were teenagers.'

'And you hadn't been back before then?'

His lips thinned. 'I know what Manny is accusing me of, and the answer is no. The night of the accident was the first time I'd driven past the city line since I left.' He looked me in the eye. 'I swear, Tessie.'

The candor in his voice made me believe him.

'Can we get past this now? Talk about the reason I asked you to come outside.'

'Sure. Go ahead.'

'These last weeks, being here with the girls...' He paused. 'With *you*, has made me do some major soul-searching.'

He took a gulp. Shoved his hands into the pockets of his jeans. The tic in his cheek warned what was coming. He was leaving again.

'What I'm trying to say is that, well, I was hoping, praying really, that you'd take me back.'

I shook my head, not sure I'd heard him right.

He must have seen the confusion on my face because he quickly said, 'We've been together practically our whole lives, Tessie. You know me better than anyone else. The forgiveness you've shown me, the way the girls are so much happier now, all of it is a sign that we're meant to be together.'

I stayed mute, stunned, as he rambled on.

'It'll be easy. I can move back in. Take on more responsibility. You can focus all your time on the store. On the coffee bar. It makes perfect sense.'

He gave me a wide grin like he had it all figured out. Like he thought that somehow, in just a few weeks, I'd forgotten the pain he'd caused. The grenade he'd thrown into our lives at the worst possible time ever.

'What do you say?' He reached out and gripped my cold hand. 'I love you. You love me. What happened to us was a blip. A bump in the road. We both made mistakes. But now we're back on track and can be a family again.'

All my life I'd considered myself to be a kind, calm person. Someone who, even in the worst situations, could take a breath, take a beat, react rationally, but in this moment, the only thing filling my body was white-hot rage.

For months after he left, I'd gone without sleep. Held my girls as they sobbed at the loss of him. Confused about why he was at the table one night for dinner and gone the next. Since he'd returned, he'd made an effort to do better, but that didn't erase the pain he'd caused. The days I'd lost to grief and anger. How every morning and evening I looked at his side of the bed and wondered what I'd done wrong. Tortured myself over what I could have said, or changed, about our relationship so he would have stayed.

Seeing him standing in front of me now, his face filled with expectation, there wasn't an ounce of me that felt guilt or responsibility for what he'd done. He'd made his choices, and they were never about us.

I wrenched my hand away and took a firm step back. 'We *both* made mistakes? Are you fucking *kidding* me?'

Even with my entire family inside, it was hard to temper my fury.

'You think I can forgive and forget what you did to me? To the girls? How I had to mourn my mother alone while you were off screwing a waitress you met at the Pool and Brew? No,' I seethed. 'For months, I tortured myself. Wracked my brain over what I'd done to push you away. You've always been a selfish man who has never thought about his actions or how his choices affect those around him. The issues between us were never about me, Billy. All of that was YOU!'

'Hey.' His gaze moved to the house. 'Keep your voice down. You don't want the girls...'

'Want the girls to what?' I bit out. 'Hear the truth about their father?' I started to pace, even as the fire burned me from the inside out. 'Let me make this clear to you. I may have let you back into our lives, but that was all for the girls' sake. They deserve to believe that their father loves them. That he'd never do anything to hurt them. That is the *only* reason why I have put one of the most important things in my life on hold.'

'So this is about Manny?' he sneered.

'We're not talking about him right now. This is about *you*. How for years I swallowed down, tucked away, all the things I've wanted because I didn't want to rock the boat or hurt you. I'm falling into that same pattern again, and I won't let it happen. I'm not that small, scared girl anymore. You can be in our lives, spend time with Iris and Rose, but you and I are over for good.'

His skin went pale. The edges of his fingers trembled as he pulled the leather coat tighter around him. 'I understand you perfectly, Tessie. All I've ever wanted is for you to be happy. If that means being with Manny, then I guess I get it.'

'God, you don't get it,' I shot back. 'I don't need someone in my life to make me feel fulfilled. It's taken me too many years to realize that the woman I am, the mother I've become, is a success in its own right. Never again will I need validation from anyone to feel worthy of recognition or love. My triumphs, my fails, will all be because I had enough confidence in myself, in my own judgment, to live a full and healthy life.'

His phone made a loud squawk. He glanced at the screen, his jaw going firm before he shoved it into his back pocket. 'When I came here today, I thought for sure we were gonna get back together. I'm sorry I got it wrong.'

'Stop apologizing, Billy. You need to realize the life you left behind here no longer exists. I've moved on. You should too. That means figuring out how you can be a solid and steady force for the girls. That is what matters.'

His shoulders wilted as he said, 'I'm gonna head to Atlanta tomorrow. There's a few loose ends I need to tie up. When I get back, I'd like to do as you say. Be that important part of their lives. Can I start by taking the girls to soccer practice on Fridays? Picking them up from school on a designated day?'

'Yes, we can work something out.'

He gave a quick glance at the house before starting down the steps.

'You aren't going to say goodbye to Iris and Rose?'

He tipped his chin down, kicked at a frozen weed popping up on the sidewalk. 'I need some time to think. Give them a kiss for me. Tell them "Merry Christmas".'

I gave a small nod and let him do what he did best. Walk away.

Chapter Thirty-Six

MANNY

Cold Turkey

For the last few weeks, I'd done everything I could to stay busy. All the walls were primed and painted in the old Thomas Place. The house did not originally have heat or air conditioning. It took over a month, but we worked out the lines to put in two new HVAC units. The Hearth and Home crew were in a rhythm now, moving from room to room as the house became shiny and new.

Christmas and the New Year passed with an aching chill. We got a small dusting of snow, but I made a point of clearing our driveway so Lou could take her new scooter for a spin. She tried to smile, pretend she was having fun, but we'd spent the last two Christmases with Tess and the girls, which made this one feel hollow. Void of light.

Lou kept asking about playing with the girls. Having sleepovers or dinners together. I made excuses about Tess being busy with the new additions to the bookstore, but we were already into early February, and I wouldn't be able to hold Lou off much longer.

'Manny!' Torran's insistent voice broke through my thoughts. 'Did you hear anything I just said?'

She stalked across the conference room at Hearth and Home's corporate headquarters and planted herself in front of me. She'd been good about not pushing the issue of Tess. Not meddling. By her restraint, it was clear that Tessa had also warned her to leave me alone.

'I asked if you've looked over the contract? If you were happy with how Maisey's husband and his law firm renegotiated the terms?'

I blew out a long breath. 'Everything's fine except for...'

'The social media and promotion parts,' she finished.

'Yes. I want to step back. Do the work but not be on camera. The audience loves you more anyway.'

She gave me the stink eye. 'Since when do you start fibbing like that? You know damn well that the show works because we're a team.'

I tugged a hand through my hair, and it got stuck on the parts that Lou insisted she gel into place. This morning, as she was helping me pick out a button-down and the only pair of dress pants I owned, she gave me a lecture about trying to look my best. How her teacher said that making a good first impression was the key to people liking you.

I corrected her by pointing out that people liked you if you were kind and honest. She waved me away like her teacher knew better than I did.

I was going to be in so much trouble in a few years.

'We can be a team, and I can still be off camera.'

Tor gave me a hard look that quickly softened as her gaze ran the length of me. 'Are you sleeping? Because you look like shit.'

'Thanks. That definitely puts me in the mood to nego-tiate.'

She pointed to one of the expensive leather chairs at the table and then pulled out her own until we were facing each other. 'I know things with Tessa are difficult right now…'

So much for the restraint.

'Can we not talk about it? I have too many other things on my mind.'

She steamrolled ahead in her normal way. 'How is Lou doing with the time away from Tessa and the girls?'

'Not good. She's confused about Billy and why we're not seeing Tess and the girls like we regularly do. After two years of spending so much time together, it's hard to go cold turkey.'

Her jaw ticced. 'Are we talking about Lou or you?'

I dragged my hands down my face. 'Both of us,' I admitted.

It was no use lying to her. We knew each other's tells, and I wasn't good at hiding my feelings anyway. After years of therapy, I'd learned it was best to talk about my feelings, or I'd get lost in a spiral of darkness.

I pushed back from the table and walked to the wall of windows that faced the sprawling Atlanta skyline. Black storm clouds threatened from the east, and the forecast predicted heavy rain and ice. I wanted to get this meeting over. Hightail it back to Ivy Falls before the storm swallowed the city.

'Where is Lauren? Wasn't the meeting set for nine?'

Torran pushed back the sleeves of the green blouse she was wearing and glanced at her watch. 'It's still two minutes till.'

She approached me, moving uncomfortably in the skirt and flats she was wearing.

'Don't smirk like that. I know I look ridiculous.'

'You don't, actually. It suits you.'

She rolled her eyes. 'I do my best work in overalls, you know that.' There was a taut tone to her voice I didn't like.

'Things still weird with Beck?' She ignored me but knew I wouldn't let this go. 'Did you talk to him?'

'He told me he's busy at work. That he and Pete are targeting another big account.'

'And you don't believe him?'

'I do, but there's something weird happening that I can't put my finger on. Even Piper's been quiet around me lately, which always makes me nervous.'

'I know you and Beck have had some rocky patches, but there needs to be trust there too. Are you leaning a little too much into your past?'

'Maybe.' She looked at her fingernails like they were fascinating. 'I think there must be something wrong with me.'

'Well, I already knew that,' I joked.

'Shut up,' she muttered. 'What I mean is that I can't relax even when things are going well. It's like I'm Wile E. Coyote just waiting for the next anvil to drop.'

I pressed a hand to my mouth, trying not to laugh at the dire way she saw every aspect of her life. 'First, I need you to take a breath.'

She gave me that annoyed look that said I should move on.

'I'm not going to diminish what you've been through, Tor. The last couple of years have been rough, but not everything has to be doom and gloom. You have to live for the moments right in front of you. Both of us know that, especially after losing someone we loved with our whole hearts.'

She reached out and tugged me into a firm hug. 'I wish there was something I could say to make you feel better about Tessa.'

'It'll work itself through,' I offered, even though I wasn't sure I believed it, especially after the incident at the Dairy Dip, and now the long weeks we'd gone without an honest conversation.

'I hate Billy.' She pulled back, her face morphing into a hard mask. 'He may be attempting to change, act all contrite like he did over Christmas, but it doesn't erase all the destruction and mayhem he's caused. Tessa has to see that.'

'Your sister is an adult. She can make her own decisions, and if you get involved…' I broke off, not wanting to say my next thought.

'What? She'll be angry? Well, too damn bad. I've been protecting Tessa my whole life, and I'm not about to stop now.'

I was about to remind her that she needed to let her sister figure out the truth about Billy when Lauren and an entourage of suits entered the conference room through a wide glass door.

'Good morning!' Lauren practically vibrated, and I didn't want to think about how many Nitro Cold Brews she'd had this morning.

She introduced the group of four executives, which included the head of the network, Mr Adler. He was easy to pick out, standing straight-backed with neatly trimmed white hair. His tailored gray suit with monogrammed cufflinks was a perfect fit to his thin frame.

We sat at the table and exchanged small talk until Mr Adler cleared his throat.

'I want to start off by saying how thrilled the network is with your show. The ratings are some of the highest we've seen for a debut.' He spun in the expensive leather chair and tapped at a panel on the table which opened. After pulling out a small black remote, he pointed it at a large screen on the far wall, and the contract for Season Three appeared. 'By now you've probably read most of the boilerplate copy.' His voice was thick with a gentle southern twang. 'The payment per episode details. As I'm sure Lauren has told you, one of the things we've been thrilled about is the show's social media numbers. Likes and comments are extremely high when we feature each of you individually and share more personal details. We'd like to see more of that in the next season.'

Adler nodded to a woman who sat across the table from him in a navy blue suit. Her hair was pulled back into an elaborate braid, and I quickly wondered if I could find a tutorial for it on YouTube.

'Torran and Manny, it's wonderful to meet you in person. I'm Hollis Barnhill, director of marketing and public relations. As Mr Adler stated, we see great potential in the show, and the audience loves you.'

She stood and moved around the table, taking the remote from Adler's outstretched hand. Clicking it once, a slide appeared, showing the rising increase in the show's viewership. I couldn't be reading the numbers right.

Torran let out a small gasp and said, 'Is that how many people watched our final episode?'

Ms Barnhill clicked the remote and highlighted a multicolored bar chart. 'Yes, your numbers steadily rose each episode, eventually quadrupling by the end of the season. It was like people found *Meet Me in Ivy Falls* early on and spread the word like a grassroots campaign. It's something we haven't seen before at Hearth and Home. It usually takes at least two seasons before a show hits its stride.'

She clicked the remote again. The next slide showed impressions and likes from the big social media platforms. My throat went drier than the rough sandpaper I used to smooth off the edges of the custom furniture I made. The numbers were much higher than I expected – which didn't bode well for me.

'I pulled this data yesterday,' Ms Barnhill went on. 'Every week we are seeing an upward trend in followers for the show's accounts. A lot of that is due to the early photos Lauren and her team took of the house on Huckleberry Lane.'

Lauren smiled and nodded along.

'For the next season, as mentioned in the new contract, we'd like to see your follower count grow even higher. We think we can get there through a little more personalization of your posts.'

She moved to another slide. Torran and Beck's smiling faces from the final day of shooting Season One appeared. Beside me, Torran shifted uncomfortably in her chair. Ms Barnhill clicked to the next slide, showing a screenshot of the post with the likes and comments highlighted in bright yellow. They were both in the double-digit thousands range.

'As you can tell, your fans love it when we share personal images like this.'

Ms Barnhill directed her steady gaze at me, and my heart raced at what I knew was coming next. She clicked the remote again, and a picture of me holding Lou on my shoulders at the preview party we'd had in the square filled the entire screen. It was a candid snapped by one of

Lauren's assistants. When I noticed her take it, I immediately asked that it not be made public. I was involved in the show – my daughter was not.

'Manny, this picture is precious. It shows how much you adore your daughter. Our viewers would love to see more of her.'

'No.' I spat out the word like poison.

Ms Barnhill batted her eyes at me. 'What do you mean "no"?'

'My daughter will not be part of any sort of promotion for the show. She deserves her privacy. I refuse to be one of those people on the internet who monetize their children.'

'Manny.' The quiet grace was gone from Adler's voice. 'It's part of this deal. We need more people to fall in love with the show. To see that, in addition to being a master carpenter, you're a good single parent. The audience will eat it up.'

I gripped the edge of the table. Pulled in a slow breath. It was rare that I lost my temper, but when it came to Lou, I wasn't messing around. I'd promised Gina as she lay dying that I'd do everything in my power to keep Lou safe. This was a moment where I felt that promise most keenly.

'I've already spoken to Lauren about this. I'd like to be more in the background of the show. Torran is better on camera anyway,' I said, doing my best to keep my voice even. 'As far as promotion goes, I will not do anything more than what I committed to this season. My daughter is already having issues at school because of the publicity. Hell, Torran had to put a fence up around her house because fans were bothering her at all hours of the day and night. I won't subject my little girl to any of that bullshit.'

Mr Adler clasped his hands on the table and stared Lauren down. 'Well, this was not anticipated. We'll have to think about our next steps in regard to the future of the show.'

It was a dagger meant to change my mind, but my choices shouldn't hurt Torran.

'Why don't you do the next season with Torran? You can say I had other commitments. She's always been the real face of the show anyway. The fans love her.'

Adler's cheeks went red. 'You can't walk away, Mr Parks. Not when we've had a successful debut and are planning for the next seasons already. Perhaps I need to involve our lawyers.'

'Do whatever you need to, but my daughter will always come first. That is non-negotiable.' My stare clashed with Lauren's as I pushed away from the table. 'Excuse me. I need some air.'

Torran gave me a sad smile, and I squeezed her shoulder before striding out of the room.

A part of me should have felt some loss at walking away from the kind of money and opportunity Hearth and Home was offering, but there was too much uncertainty swirling in my life, and it was causing Lou pain.

Once I stepped inside the elevator, I rested my head against a cool steel panel. The walls of my chest ached. I did my breathing technique as visions of Tess filled my head. Her smile. The way her touch loosened the stress in my jaw and back. How she was always ready to fight for Iris and Rose. Not until this moment did I realize that the decision I'd just made to put Lou first was exactly the same choice Tess had made for her own girls.

Chapter Thirty-Seven

TESSA

Thanked The Fates

When my dad called this morning and offered to take the girls to school it was clearly subterfuge. He was making an excuse to come over so he could talk to me about Billy, who'd been gone for several weeks now.

We were only a day away from the opening of the coffee bar, and Manny and I were now in a space where all we did was nod and swap one-word answers. Even though things were so tentative between us, it was hard not to stare at how his muscles flexed under his tight white T-shirt as he finished the final touches on the bar. How when he chewed on the corner of his lip, I wanted to replace his teeth with my own lips.

Basically, things were a complete shitstorm between us, and I hated every minute of it.

Like Ivy Falls could feel the tension too, everyone moved around me with a mixture of pity and disdain. Not that I blamed them. Manny was practically the hometown hero. When he'd moved into the little house on Petunia Avenue, word quickly spread about the retired college football player who could build almost anything with his hands. People loved his sweet wife and their baby girl who had the biggest brown eyes anyone had ever seen.

After Gina passed unexpectedly, Ivy Falls rallied around him. He'd told me that he'd received over a dozen cards, flowers and enough cornbread to feed a small nation. He'd also said that he'd never felt so much love in his entire life.

I walked to the back door. Looking at the new pane of glass felt like a taunt, reminding me of how Manny had swept in and protected me and the girls on Halloween night without a second thought.

Dad came up the small path. As soon as I opened the door for him, Iris zoomed past me.

'There's my girl!' Dad crowed. 'Where's my other sweet pea?'

'Here!' Rose hopped into the room with one sock on and one sock off.

He picked them both up and held them tightly to his chest. My heart twinged. Torran and I had been at odds with him for a long time, but we'd all learned over the last year to bend a little. To accept that none of us were perfect. That family meant more than holding grudges. Had Dad been the perfect father? Nope. But he was trying.

I stood and watched him snuggling the girls and reminded myself that I was giving the same kind of grace to Billy.

'Hey, girlies, go grab your school gear. I need to have a little chat with your mama.'

They slid from his arms and hurried back to their room.

'Brush your teeth too,' I called. 'And Rosie, put on your other sock and shoes!' Once they were out of earshot, I held up my hand before he got a word out. 'I don't want to hear it.'

Dad's lips thinned. 'Hear what? I haven't said a word yet.'

I stuck out my finger and circled it around his face. 'You don't have to. The way your lips are puckered and the deep crinkles around your eyes warn you're about to dole out a lecture, and I'm all out of patience right now, considering that's all I've been getting from Torran.'

He stepped farther into the kitchen and leaned against the counter where a chipped piece of tile fell to the ground. My first thought was to text Manny and ask how to repair it. I'd found myself doing that a lot lately. Reaching for my phone to tell him a funny story or send him a video with a panda bear rolling down a hill, which always made him laugh. Torran called it 'old people' flirting, and she wasn't wrong. It was how we'd communicated, gotten to know each other, become fast friends, and now I'd put that all in jeopardy.

'I only want to know how you're doing. You've got a lot on your plate right now, hence me taking the girls to school.' He paused. 'And maybe a quick donut beforehand.'

'Dad,' I sighed. 'You can't get them all sugared up before school.'

He tapped at his chin. 'Can't I? I think it's in the grandparent handbook that I can take my granddaughters for treats whenever I want.'

I quirked an eyebrow.

'Fine, I also came by to ask about Billy. He seemed to make himself right at home over the holidays, but then he disappeared. Silvio said he agreed to give him some time off but hasn't heard from him in a while. Are you all right?'

'Dad,' I sighed. 'I'm fine. Billy's texted a few times. He's still in Atlanta figuring some things out. It's just taking longer than he expected.'

He glanced over my shoulder to make sure the girls weren't returning. 'Are you sure that's all this is?'

'He said he'd be back. That he wanted more time with the girls. That's all I know.'

I kept all the other worries I had about Billy to myself. This pattern felt all too familiar. While I'd been able to distract the girls from his absence, I wasn't sure how much longer I could make excuses for him to Rose or Iris, or to anyone else in town.

He crossed his arms over his chest. 'I don't like any of this, Tessa. You should have sent him packing the moment he returned.'

'How would you feel if someone took away your rights to see Tor and me? Kept you from having any kind of relationship with us?'

His tight shoulders gave a little. 'I'm not sure you'll believe this, but it would have gutted me.'

'Oh, Dad, I do believe you,' I offered quietly. 'But this is where we're at right now. Billy is back in our lives and the girls are happy. The past hurts, but I'm trying to move forward. We all are.'

'And you can't do all that and still be on speaking terms with Manny? I saw you looking more than once at the end of the table where he and Lou usually sit during Christmas dinner.'

'It's not like we are totally ignoring each other, but it's complicated. He's got things happening with Lou, and I have to think about Iris and Rose.'

He must have caught the catch in my voice. 'People say parenting is about sacrifice. How mothers and fathers should always put their children first. That's good in theory, but adults need companionship, love and affection, too. Just because you have children does not mean

278

you still don't have...' He cleared his throat and his cheeks went pink. '...certain needs.'

I dropped my head in my hands. 'I am *not* going to take sex advice from you.'

'No,' he said quickly. 'What I'm trying to say is, uh, well, yes, you need that too, but you also need to see yourself as an individual. A woman, as well as a mother.' He gave me a weighted smile. 'Make me a promise that you won't lose yourself on the way to making a good life for your girls.'

'You sound like Mom.'

He took a thick gulp. 'I do?'

I wrapped my arms around him. 'Yes. She'd be proud to know you're still fighting for us. For our family to be whole.'

He ran a hand down over my hair and then pulled away, his eyes watery. 'She used to say that parenting never stops. That even when your little birds fly the nest, you still worry. Want what's best for them. More and more every day, I'm finding that to be true.'

Iris raced back into the room with Rose hot on her heels.

Dad quickly swiped at his cheeks and said, 'Your mama says we can stop at Sugar Rush for donuts before school!'

The girls cheered as I helped them slide their lunch totes into their backpacks. My dad held out his hands, and my babies each took a side.

'Grandpa.' Rose dipped her voice to what she thought was a low whisper. 'Can we have hot chocolate with whipped cream and sprinkles too?'

My dad looked over his shoulder and gave me a devious grin. 'Of course. Anything for my sweet peas.'

I started to object, but he promptly closed the door on me.

A low bubble of laughter escaped my lips until I looked down and saw the piece of tile. A part of me knew he was right about what I needed, but I'd only think about that once I was sure Rose's night terrors were truly gone. That Iris' mysterious tummy aches had finally subsided. Then, and only then, would I consider what came next for me.

—

Penny was already in a tizzy today, her arms loaded down with books as she raced between the shelves and the front counter.

'What are you doing?' I asked, setting my bag and purse next to the several tower-like stacks she'd made.

'If we're going to make the coffee bar a success, I thought it'd be smart to make a display in the front window about all things... well, coffee.'

She picked a book off the stack she'd assembled and handed it to me. A bright blue coffee mug filled most of the cover.

'I've pulled books on roasting techniques. How to make the perfect espresso or latte. There is also this.' She handed me a tome of a book with at least 300 pages. 'It's a coffee-table book about coffee.' She giggled at her own joke.

'I think it's a great idea,' I said, handing the book back to her.

'There's also the sign outside to consider. What do you think of "*Problems? Come inside, and we'll let you venti*"?'

I wrinkled my nose.

'Okay, what about "*Why did the mocha call the cops? Cause it'd been mugged!*"'

That made me laugh, but I shook my head. 'Keep working on it.'

Penny nodded and went back to her array of books. I pulled in a breath and surveyed the store. Tomorrow night the space would be filled with my closest family and friends, sipping coffee and tea. Testing the new desserts Barb and Susan had created specifically to sell here.

All of this was a risk, but I had to put the worry out of my mind because this venture had to be a success. Even with my small business loan, my bank balance was still much too low. I was willing to do anything to save this store, and if I had to sling coffee day and night, I was willing to do it.

While a few customers moved around the space, I made my way to the back corner. The bar Manny had built to match the buffet was beyond exquisite. His eye for detail, the intricate woodwork, the elegantly shaped spirals that mirrored the original antique took my breath away. Even the special piece of white marble he'd ordered blended seamlessly with the original gray vein.

My memories raced back to that day at the apple orchard. How he'd seen my vision right away and never second-guessed me. Our entire relationship, he'd given me nothing but comfort, kindness and love. I pressed a hand to my mouth to hold back the sob building in my throat.

'When I came in at eight thirty to start unpacking boxes, he was doing a final polish on the counter,' Penny offered quietly. 'He looked at his watch a lot, like he was expected to be somewhere at a certain time.'

Or watching the clock so he could avoid me.

'Have you tried working with it?' I tipped my chin to the massive silver espresso machine sitting on the marble server.

'No, but don't worry. Manny said he already talked to Piper. She's planning to stop by later today to give us a tutorial on running the espresso machine and the industrial coffee makers.'

The relieved sigh I let out made Penny shake her head.

'I don't have the right to comment on your personal life, but I'm pretty sure that man would walk naked through a burning building, holding a full gas can, just to ensure your life was beautiful.'

A tear slid down my cheek, and she handed me a tissue. 'Sorry. Must be allergies.'

She patted my shoulder. 'Sure it is, boss.'

After giving me a sad smile, she went back to her display. I composed myself before heading to my office. Once I reached the doorway, I stopped dead. My chair was pushed to the far wall. Papers littered the floor. The top drawer in the desk was open, and one of the file cabinets was ajar.

'Penny,' I called out. She came and met me near the door. 'Was my office like this when you came in?'

'Yes. I thought things were moved around a bit because we've been getting so many deliveries.' She must have seen my cheeks lose color. 'Is there a problem?'

I moved farther into the room, glancing to the far wall where we kept the safe. Nothing looked out of place.

'I guess I didn't realize how messy it was because we've been so busy getting ready for the party.'

The alarm on Penny's phone went off. 'Forty-five minutes until opening. Do you want me to handle the tills?'

'I'll take care of it.' I waved her away. 'Go back to whatever you've got brewing out there.' She laughed at my coffee pun and went back into the store.

My hands moved over the stacks of paper on the desk. I bent down and picked up delivery receipts and pieces of scratch paper where I'd written my to-do lists. Underneath the desk sat the envelope with the divorce papers. When Billy returned, that was the first thing we were going to settle.

Using my shoulder, I shoved the file drawer shut and assessed the room again. My heartbeat slowed. The office may have looked like a tornado had hit it, but nothing was missing. All the earlier issues, the break-in, the rock, were now making me paranoid about simply a messy space.

I had to get it together.

For the next ten minutes, I worked on getting the office in order. I was filling the last of the trash bags when Penny's voice saying 'hello' floated through the store. Torran filled the threshold a second later. The look on her face warned something was terribly wrong.

'I've spent the last twelve hours trying to calm down, but I'm not having much luck,' she fumed.

'Uh-oh. So is your number like a two?'

She pursed her lips, her face going a shade close to crimson.

'Ohhhkay,' I said. 'What's got you so mad?'

The creases around her mouth hardened. 'You.'

'Me? Why?'

'Because Manny is totally off-kilter. Yesterday, he blew up our meeting with Hearth and Home. Told them he was no longer going to be part of the show.'

I blanched. It was clear he was uncomfortable with all the media attention, and how it was affecting Lou, but I never thought he'd totally walk away.

I wasn't ashamed to admit that, over the last month, I'd watched all the show's episodes on repeat. Needing to see his face. Hear that low grumble I loved. He was so good at being Torran's foil, working the room easily, explaining in simple terms how certain repairs could be done. He was the calm to her storm, and the fans loved it.

'I know he's been worried about the publicity. How he's been trying to protect Lou.'

'It's that, yeah, but his head is also too stirred up with other things, like you, to make good decisions.'

'Are you kidding me? That's like saying I can control what you do. Or what Dad does. The last time I looked, Manny was a grown man who could make his own damn decisions.' Heat filled my chest and I pulled in a slow breath. 'Manny has not been happy with things with the show for a while. He hates that he can't walk around the square without someone filming his every move or taking a picture of him, or God forbid, Lou. Did you know she's being bullied at school because of the show? That kids are showing her posts about Manny that are all kinds of inappropriate?'

The color fled her cheeks. 'I knew she got suspended. That a girl in her class was being mean, and Lou fought back. Manny never told me the full story, and I let it go because he's got so much going on.'

'It's been hard on her. Hard on him,' I said, sinking down into the chair behind my desk. 'So before you blame me for this, why don't you go and talk to your partner?'

She quickly deflated. 'I'm sorry. There's no reason for me to take any of this out on you. I'm worried and admittedly a little scared. I've never seen Manny blow up like that before. He was furious, Tessa.'

I dragged a hand along my messy braid and dropped my head. 'I miss him, Tor.'

She walked behind the desk and knelt beside my chair. 'Give it time. You'll work things out. Billy will build his own life, and the girls will be okay.'

I swiped a tear from my cheek. 'I'm not sure about Billy. After Christmas dinner, he asked if we could reconcile.'

Her lips thinned. 'And what did you say?'

'No, of course. I didn't have to hesitate. Even give it a minute's thought.'

'Because...' she said, leading me.

'Because he's an asshole, who left me for another woman. Who then tried to claim that we'd both made mistakes.'

'And is there another reason?' she pressed.

'You are just like Mom. Always trying to wheedle the truth out of me.'

She gave me the same steady stare.

'All right, it's also because I've already given my heart to someone else.'

She bit the corner of her lip, trying to hide a smile.

'I never expected...' I broke off, not able to find the words.

'To fall in love with Manny?' she finished.

'After Billy left, I couldn't see beyond the next day. All I could do was push forward, trying to keep myself and the girls in one piece. But then Manny came to the park that day. I loved how sweet he was with Lou. How he didn't hesitate to jump in and play with Iris and Rose. Chasing them in a game of freeze tag or shoving his hulking body down a twisty slide. For so long, I relegated him to the friend zone. When I finally allowed myself to feel something for him, my ex shows up.' I closed my eyes, willing back more tears. 'I've been so scrambled with trying to save this store, torn between what's right for the girls, that I pushed him away. But in that moment, with Billy begging for a second chance, I knew the only thing that made sense for my life was a future with Manny.'

She pulled me into a hug, and for the millionth time in my life, I thanked the fates, or whatever you wanted to call the forces of the universe, that they'd given me a sister.

'Manny isn't going anywhere, Tessa.'

'He was angry about what happened with Lou after the Dairy Dip. And then Christmas came and went, and neither of us reached out,' I said on a weary breath. 'Do you think he can forgive me for making such a mess of things?'

'You'll have to talk it out, but I know deep down all he wants is a chance to build a future with you.'

'Okay,' I said with a determined huff. 'I'll do everything I can to make it work with him.'

Torran gave a nod, but there was lingering hesitation in her eyes.

'What aren't you saying?'

'It's not anything about you. This conversation just reminds me of a talk Manny and I had about Beck.'

'Really?'

'Yeah, Beck's still acting distracted. He keeps telling me it's work. The stress of trying to bring in a new account.'

'That makes sense, but how does that relate to advice from Manny?'

'He said Beck and I should have open and honest communication. That our minds can invent all sorts of dire scenarios, but the only true way to have a relationship is to talk things through, no matter how uncomfortable it may be.'

Now it was my turn to grimace. 'Sounds like good advice.'

'Work it out with him, Tess. You'll feel better.'

She gave me another hug, and for the first time in months, I felt like things were finally shifting in a positive direction. That while one path was ending, a new and brighter road was straight ahead if I could just find the courage to take that first step.

Chapter Thirty-Eight

MANNY

Stuck With Me Forever

Half an hour was too damn long to stand in front of a mirror. A pile of button-down shirts and chinos in an array of bland, business-like colors lay across my bed. Tension built in the back of my neck. It was just a small party to celebrate the opening of the coffee bar. It didn't have to be a big deal, but my brain was in overdrive. I kept wondering if Tess and I would ignore each other at the store tonight. Or even worse, if we'd do that uncomfortable and awkward nod where we recognized the other's presence, wanted to be brave enough to say hello, but instead turned back into the crowd to make small talk with all the other residents of Ivy Falls. Residents who I was sure would watch the whole scene and give me a pitying stare that said, *Hey Manny, sorry that crush you've been nursing for over two years doesn't seem to be working out.*

I let out a small huff, grabbed the denim button-down shirt and slid on the khaki pants. There was no use in looking in the mirror again. I'd only see the disappointment and ache of rejection etched deep into the lines around my eyes and mouth.

'Pop,' Lou called out from her room. 'Can I wear my pretty pink shoes?'

'Those are for special occasions, Lou.'

The sound of her footsteps filled the hall until she appeared in my doorway. Fergus trotted up beside her and nudged her into the room. 'Please can I wear them? They match perfectly with my flowered skirt, and Miss Tessa's new coffee thing sounds like it's special.'

She spun in a circle, the long fishtail braid it'd taken me over an hour to complete swinging like a rope behind her.

'You're right, Lou Lou. This is a special occasion.'

She rushed forward and gave me a crushing hug. 'Thank you.'

'*Raisins!*' Mr Peepers screeched from his cage in the kitchen.

No F-word. That was a first. Maybe Lou's training was finally paying off.

'Did you give Fergus his dinner?'

'Yes. And before you ask, Reggie's cage is clean, and he has new water.'

'That's my girl.'

She gave me an appraising gaze. 'That shirt looks good. I think Miss Tessa will like it.'

The bright look in her eyes said she still believed there was a chance something might happen between Tess and me. That things would go back to normal. Town gossip, as much as I hated it, said Billy disappeared after Christmas, and no one had seen him since. More than once I'd considered just picking up the phone, breaking the unbearable silence between us, but I wasn't sure what choice Tess would make next, and I'd also been doing a lot of thinking of my own.

Late at night when the house was quiet, the bird no longer squawking, Fergus snoring quietly at my feet, I'd paged through the scrapbooks Gina had made of our first years together, and then after Lou arrived. I loved Lou's little gummy smiles. The infectious light emanating from Gina as she held her newborn in her arms.

For so long, I'd held on to the memory of her. The laughter. Tears. But most of all the love that felt like it was larger than every constellation in the sky. Tess had broken the barrier I'd built around my heart. With her gentle smiles, quiet laughter, she'd made me see that it was time to move on. To not let go of Gina, but to put my love for her in a separate chamber of my heart. To open up a new place for the right person. Was that person Tess? I hoped so, but whatever came next, I was ready to start a new chapter not only for me but for Lou too.

I sank onto the bed and patted the spot beside me.

'Lulubean, we should talk about Miss Tessa and the girls.'

She scraped the toe of her pink shoe against the carpet before trudging toward the bed.

'Iris and Rose's father is going to be a bigger part of their lives now.'

The confused look in her eyes warned she still didn't understand what was happening. 'I don't get it. Where has their daddy been all this time?'

I took a moment. No child should ever have to hear that a parent could, and would, walk away from them.

'He left for a while, but he's back now and wants to be part of their lives.'

Her lower lip quivered. 'Can daddies do that? Just go away?'

I pulled her in closer to my side. 'There are many complicated things that happen to adults.'

She looked up at me with watery eyes. 'It's just like Brittany said. Parents *can* leave.'

'Oh, sweetie, no. You're stuck with me forever. You'll have to take care of me when I'm old and gray. Help me find my teeth when I lose them.'

'Your teeth? Why would you lose your teeth?' Her voice bordered on panic.

'It's only a joke, honey,' I said, trying to reassure her. 'This is all very confusing, and I know that being away from Tess and the girls during the holidays was rough. But you'll see them all tonight, and slowly we'll all figure out what happens next.'

I said the words, not knowing if they were a hundred percent true, but Lou needed this. Needed some kind of confirmation that she wasn't losing both Tess and the girls all at once.

'Okay,' she said hesitantly like she still didn't understand the situation.

'There is one other thing we have to talk about.'

'I know what you're gonna say,' she sighed. 'I need to do a better job of feeding Fergus and Reggie on time.'

'Yes, but that's not what I mean.'

Words tossed around inside my brain, and I knew the best way to handle the situation was to say it simply.

'I've decided I'm not going to do the TV show after this season is over. Miss Torran and I will still work on houses together, be partners, but I won't be involved in the production anymore.'

'Why? I thought you and Miss Torran were good at it. That's what everyone in town says, even Old Mrs Vanderpool, and you know she doesn't always say nice things.'

I stifled a laugh. 'It's kind that she said that, but I think it's better if I focus on you and me more. This way things won't be so uncomfortable on the street too. People bothering me for pictures.'

'So no Harry Styles? No Dolly?'

I patted her head. 'Afraid not, honey.'

She deflated like a balloon with a small leak. 'Okay, but will you miss doing it? Showing off your work?'

'That was one good part of it, but the rest was a little too much.'

She shrugged. 'I was getting used to the staring. It was also kind of cool to see how excited people got when they took a selfie with you.'

I must have visibly flinched because she set her small hand on my shoulder.

'Being an influencer is a big deal, Pop. Brittany says those people get free stuff sent to them. They also get vacations to anywhere they want just for talking about a hotel on their channels.'

'You're speaking to her now?'

'Yeah. At recess yesterday, we sat down at the lunch table with our friends and talked it out. We're all good now.'

If only life was as easy as having an honest talk around a school lunch table.

'I think you should keep doing the show.' She paused, her eyes flashing with regret. 'Not because I want anything free, or to meet celebrities, but because you're good at it. I think people need to see all the hard work you and Miss Torran are doing for Ivy Falls.'

'*Raisins! Raisins! Raaaaaaisins!*' Mr Peepers sang.

She bounced off the bed and gave me a wide grin. 'Before you even say it, I'm going to get him some water. Go over the phrase again.'

Once she was gone, I moved back to the mirror. Those small spots around my ears were even whiter now. I tugged at my shirt and smiled, thinking about Lou. The way she'd figured out how to fix her own world without my help. I only wished things could be that easy for me and Tess, but she had to make her own choices. I'd carved out a special place in my heart for her, and I couldn't imagine Tess and the girls not being part of our lives, even if it was just as friends.

In the end, Tess would have to decide what was best for her and her family, and I hoped that somehow, in some way, Lou and I would be part of that plan.

Chapter Thirty-Nine

TESSA

Eight Bordering On Nine

I paced in between the biography and self-help aisles. After months of preparation, and too many sleepless nights, this was finally happening. That small idea shared between Manny and me in the streets of my beloved town was now a reality.

People were going to come to my store to hang out again, buy a coffee or drink tea, and relax among the stacks. Pick out a new book and remember why this little place was an important part of the community. Why they should shop here instead of one of the chain stores, or one of those big online websites that not only sold books but twenty-five rolls of toilet paper, a gallon of peanut butter, or a thousand other items you didn't need.

I kept pacing until Torran stalked down the aisle toward me. 'Why doesn't it surprise me to find you back here?'

I shook out my hands and feet, willing my nerves to settle.

'Hey.' She reached for my shoulders. 'Number?'

'A negative two,' I said with a caustic laugh.

'There is no reason to worry, Tessa. Beck is helping Dad bring in extra chairs. Piper and Penny are behind the bar handing out free samples of that blonde roast you recommended. Mrs Vanderpool and Miss Marta spent the last few minutes drooling over the baked goods Barb and Susan made, and Isabel has the girls corralled over in the children's section.'

'Tell me again why I agreed to say a few words. I hate public speaking. It's only in the last few months that I've finally gotten used to reading during story hour.'

'You've got this. All the people here love you. They are not expecting anything grand. Go out there and show them your normal warmth. Introduce them to your new offerings and then cut the ribbon. That's all you have to do.'

Everything she was saying was true, but I wished my heart, which was currently doing the conga, would get the message.

Torran looked over her shoulder at where Beck was having a conversation with our dad.

'Did you ever figure out what was up with him?' I asked.

'Work is stressing him out, and I'm making too big of a deal out of it.' She closed her lips tight, looking a little bit guilty.

'What did you do?'

'I cornered Pete. Told him I'd make Manny unavailable for a lot longer for that client, Teddy Ray, if he didn't tell me what was up.'

'So you're blackmailing people now?' I laughed.

'It's not blackmail. It's subtle coercion.' She laughed too. 'Anyway, he admitted that they've been working long hours on some new medical equipment account that has a pretty big budget.'

'See, you were making up too many dire scenarios in your head. Exactly like Manny said.'

'I know. Just when I think I'm getting over the part of me that's terrified Beck will run again, that I have to trust him, I'm reminded I've still got things I need to work on.'

'Don't we all,' I sighed.

'How are things with Manny? Did you call him? Is he coming tonight?'

'Why wouldn't he come? The reason this is happening is because of his help.'

She pointed that ornery stare at me. 'Tessa, did you call him?'

'No,' I confessed. 'But he knows he's invited.'

She flapped her hands at her sides. 'I thought we talked about this. He needs to hear from you.'

'I know, but what if it doesn't work between us and I lose him? That I already have because of the mess my life has become.'

Torran held my gaze for a long beat. She only did this when she wasn't sure how I'd react to whatever was spinning through her head. 'Don't get mad at me, but I think it's more than that.'

'What do you mean?'

'You're hesitating because you're scared. It's easier to let things get in the way, avoid an uncomfortable conversation, rather than facing the chance of getting hurt again.'

I both loved and hated that she knew me so damn well. 'What if he doesn't want me? If he's realized all of this is too complicated?'

She held on to my hands like she understood I needed to be steadied. 'All you can do is be honest. Tell him how you feel. That's what Mom would say.'

I nodded, even as the waves of nerves still spun through me. 'Have you heard anything from Hearth and Home?' I said, desperate to get my mind off the fear and sense of impending doom rattling my bones.

'Lauren texted me. Said she was coming tonight but nothing about the contract.' She let go of my hands and chewed on her bottom lip. 'I've decided to tell her I'm out if the network won't agree to Manny's terms.'

'Tor,' I gasped. 'Are you sure? The show has helped the town and your business so much.'

'None of that matters without my best friend beside me. Finances might get tight again, but all I wanted was to bring people back to Ivy Falls. Remind them what an amazing place this is. I've done my part. Now it's up to the mayor.'

Right on cue, Dad strode down the aisle toward us. He looked handsome in his deep green dress shirt and charcoal pants.

'Tessa, honey, people are asking for you.'

'You done hiding?' Torran teased.

'Yes,' I grumbled.

I followed her and Dad to the center of the store and came to a stumbling stop. Our friends were packed shoulder to shoulder in the small space. A crowd pressed against the coffee bar. The overstuffed chairs and sofas were filled with the people I knew and loved in Ivy Falls.

'This night should be an eight bordering on a nine,' Torran said. 'You've put in the work. Go and mingle. Enjoy your victory.' She gave my shoulder one last squeeze before heading toward the coffee bar where Beck stood with Piper.

Tonight, Piper was wearing a soft pink blouse and black skirt. Looking at her was a positive reminder that you could rise from the ashes. Make a good life if you focused on what was important. Didn't let fear take hold.

These last months had felt like I was standing on the edge of a rocky cliff. That with one wrong move, the ground beneath me would easily give way. In this moment it was like the wind gave me a gentle nudge back. Spun me around and sent me in the right direction. Whispered that I knew what to do.

I set my chin and went in search of Manny, hoping he was here. After saying hello to Dr Sheridan and his wife, as well as Maisey and her husband, I found him planted on the rainbow rug in the children's section. Iris sat crisscross applesauce in front of him. Manny was laser-focused on her head, giving her the same kind of fancy braid as Lou. Rose bounced on her toes nearby, waiting for her own turn.

How did I ever think I could have space from this man? His actions never had an underlying motive. When he gave me his word, there was no doubt he'd keep it. And when his hands moved across my skin, a warmth shifted over me like my body understood that every moment spent in his arms was precious.

Penny stepped beside me, and a devilish grin slid over her face. 'Do you think if I sat in front of him, he'd do my hair too?'

I hip-checked her with a laugh. 'No, ma'am, you have customers you need to ring up,' I said, tipping my chin to the growing line at the register.

'Fine,' she mumbled. 'And for your information, everyone adores the sign.'

After a few rounds, Penny had finally come up with: *Thank you, Ivy Falls. We love you a latte!* It wasn't as funny as some of her other suggestions, but it said exactly how we felt about this town.

'It's a good one.'

'I know,' she clucked happily. 'Before I go back to that' – she flailed her hands to the growing line at the register – 'we need some smaller bills. Tens and fives.'

'I'll take care of it.'

As I made my way to the office, Isabel stopped me. She looked beautiful in her yellow skirt and matching cardigan. Her snow-white hair swept back in an elegant bun.

'The coffee bar was a genius idea. You should be proud of what you've accomplished.'

'Thank you for being here.'

'I would not miss it for the world.' Her gaze scanned the room.

'My dad was going to check out the new books I got in on gardening.'

Her lips twitched. 'Hmm. He was talking recently about growing tomatoes.' She started toward the non-fiction shelves, and I couldn't help but smile at how she practically danced all the way there.

I was almost to the door of the office when Mrs Vanderpool stepped into my path. Tonight, Baby was wearing a sweater that looked very similar to the traditional Burberry pattern. Where did she find them?

'Child.' Mrs Vanderpool's voice didn't have its usual steely tone. It was soft and almost watery. 'Your mother would be proud of you. This store has been the beating heart of this community since the day she opened the doors. I believe she is looking down upon you with a warm smile and a grateful heart for all you've done to save it.'

I swallowed back the thickness in my throat. 'Thank you. That means a lot to me.'

'I must also apologize for overstepping with Billy. Sometimes I let my mouth run off before I think things through. I should have checked with you first before I offered him the apartment. Talked to Silvio about that job.' Her lips went tight. A warning that Billy hadn't checked in with Silvio lately.

Mrs Vanderpool glanced over her shoulder to where Silvio was laughing along to some story Ferris was telling about his prized roses.

Wait. Was that a blush on her cheeks?

'It's all right, you only meant well, Mrs Vanderpool,' I said, not hiding my grin.

'Please, call me Greta.' She tore her gaze away from Silvio. 'You're a grown woman now. No formalities are needed.'

'That'll be hard. You've always been Mrs Vanderpool to me.'

'Don't you mean "Old Mrs Vanderpool"?'

I shifted uneasily on my feet, and she cackled.

'It doesn't bother me,' she said, stroking Baby's head. 'In fact, I'm glad I have a nickname. It means I'm seen. And when you're an old widow with no kids, it's good to know people still think of you enough to whisper your name out like a curse sometimes.'

She patted my hand and went to greet the rest of her friends in the book club, who'd already confirmed they'd be returning to the store to have their meetups from now on.

The chatter continued to rise in the store, and I took in the scene.

This was my hometown.

My family.

They'd shown up for me in so many ways. Yes, they were nosey. Knew way too much about my private life. But they were also what made Ivy Falls home. Why my mother had wanted to build this store in the first place. So we all had a place to gather. To rest. To escape the worries of the world and get lost in a good book. I'd never stop being grateful that she'd put the care of this place in my hands.

Penny waved at me from the counter and mouthed 'change', reminding me of my task.

I walked to the office, laughter ringing in my ears. When I reached the door, I turned the handle, but it wouldn't give. Penny must have locked it because of all the people moving around the store. I pulled out my key and let myself in. Only a few steps over the threshold, a hand slammed over my mouth, and the door swung shut behind me.

Chapter Forty

MANNY

Talk A Tough Game

Most days you could easily move in and out of the aisles, linger in front of the bookshelves, at the P&P. Tonight that was impossible, because almost every resident of Ivy Falls packed the small store. I sucked in a breath, inching my way around the tables and small couches set around the space. People crowded around the coffee bar. The shrill *whoosh* and *hiss* of the espresso machine matched the rising volume in the room.

No matter what was happening between Tess and me, I couldn't keep the smile from my lips. When you asked Ivy Falls to show up, they did it with a wild kind of zeal.

Near the front door, Deputy Ben stood with Miss Cheri. Their conversation floated my way, and I smothered a laugh.

For weeks Miss Cheri had been prodding every able-bodied person in town about becoming the director for the upcoming production of *Mary Poppins Jr.* at the children's theater. So far, she hadn't talked anyone into the voluntary role.

Like the good person he was, Ben listened intently before making an excuse about wanting to try another flavor of tea.

My eyes scanned the room for Tess, but I hadn't seen her since Lou and I arrived. I started to walk to the coffee bar when a rough tap on my shoulder stopped me.

'Manny.' Beck's business partner, Pete, stared at me with intense eyes. His dark hair was slicked back, and his sleeve of tattoos was a sharp contrast to the starched white polo shirt he wore. 'You've been avoiding my calls.' Pete's lips thinned. 'We still need to make an appointment with Teddy Ray to talk about the plans for his restaurant.'

'Sorry, with the work we've been doing on the old Thomas Place, I've been a little distracted,' I confessed.

'Distracted by other annoyances too.' Lauren pushed into our small circle and eyed me like a painful thorn in her side. 'Don't think that you can run away from the show. You're too important to it.'

Pete stared down his nose at her. 'Excuse me, we were having a conversation.'

Never to be intimidated by anyone, Lauren squared her shoulders. 'You're excused,' she said in that sweet Georgia voice before latching on to my arm and pulling me away. Once she had me cornered in a quieter part of the store, she lost most of her vibrato. 'Manny, I swear you're going to give me gray hair before I reach thirty.'

'I never meant to put you in a tight spot with the show, but you know how I feel about my daughter.'

She held up a finger to stop me. 'Before I leave tonight, I need you to write down every detail you want in the contract. Parameters around social media. How many, if any, public appearances you're willing to do. If you want security cameras at your house or a fence. Mr Adler and the network have agreed that whatever is required to make this work for your family, they'll make it happen.'

'How the hell did you pull that off?' I chuckled.

'I don't think you realize how valuable you and Torran are to the network. Your reruns have the highest ratings in the afternoon time slot. Mr Adler might talk a tough game, but your show is a hit, and he's not letting you go.'

My gaze moved to Lou sitting with the girls at a nearby table, reading them her favorite picture book, *Knight Owl*.

'And they'll agree to all my terms, including little to no social media?' I asked, needing to confirm I'd heard her right.

'Yes. At this point, I think Adler would let you write your own damn contract if it meant you'd stay.'

I hid my smirk as she continued to tap her pointed heel anxiously.

'There is one other thing I might want.'

'Okay. Anything,' she said.

'Could you get Lou an introduction to Dolly Parton?'

'Uh, well, that might be hard. I suppose we could track down her PR person...' Lauren sputtered until she watched me grin. 'You idiot. Don't tease me like that!' She swiped at my shoulder.

'Go get yourself a coffee. You've earned it.'

She let out a caustic laugh. 'Make that list, Manny.'

'Yes, ma'am,' I said, pointing her in the direction of the bar.

She stalked off, and I searched the room for Tess. My gaze moved over the growing crowd and landed on Piper Townsend who sat alone on a couch near the front window.

'Hey,' I said, approaching her. 'Thanks for helping Tess with the espresso machine. I owe you one.'

'You don't owe me a thing. Happy to share my barista skills.'

I tipped my chin to the space beside her, and she moved to make room for me.

'You did amazing work on the bar,' she gushed. 'That custom counter designed to match the buffet is incredible. Tessa is really lucky to have you as a fr—' She broke off quickly. 'Well, she's lucky to have you in her life.'

She smiled, gave a wave to Beck, who always seemed to be checking in on her.

'I never really had a chance to make a ton of friends. Well, not since we had to leave Ivy Falls when I was a kid.'

'This place sort of gets into your bones and settles in deep. Once you're a resident, you become family. Everyone in this store, including me, is your friend, Piper. Whatever you need, support you might want, it's here if you reach out and ask for it.'

'Beck tells me that often, but thanks for the reminder,' she sighed. 'I wish I could do more. Actively take part in the community.'

Just at that moment, Miss Cheri's booming laugh filled the room.

'I heard the Ivy Falls Children's Theater needs some help.'

Her eyes went alight.

'Why don't you go talk to Miss Cheri about it?'

Her arms flung out and she gave me a quick hug. 'Thank you, Manny!' She jumped off the couch and raced in the direction of Miss Cheri.

I took a minute to look for Tess again. Why couldn't I find her at her own damn party?

Penny walked by, and I said, 'Have you seen Tess?'

A knowing smile crossed her lips before she tipped her chin toward the back office. 'She went to grab change for the registers.'

I moved across the room, waving to Deputy Ben who was chatting with Dr Sheridan and Silvio. When I reached the office door, it was locked. I knocked, but the store was too loud to hear if Tess answered. I knocked again, pressed my ear to the door. The sounds of shuffling feet and Tess' voice, sharp and frightened, bled through the door. Warning sirens blared in my head. Using all my strength, I jammed my shoulder against the door until the frame splintered and the lock popped open.

Tess stood behind the desk, her eyes wild. Billy stood next to the open safe. I'd only met her twice, but I was sure the woman with burgundy hair standing only a foot away from him was Trini. I blanched at the bank bag she clutched against her pregnant belly.

'What the hell is going on here?' My roar vibrated through the room.

Billy's body tensed, and Trini rounded on me with wide eyes.

'I came in to get some change and found them in here,' Tess said quickly. 'Yesterday, I thought things looked out of place.' Her stare narrowed on Billy. 'He must have taken the spare key hidden in the desk drawer. Thought he could come in the back door without being noticed.'

I hated the brittle tone of her voice. The way defeat colored her eyes. She'd given him a second chance, and here he was stealing from her. Breaking her heart again.

'Tess, tell me what you need, and I'll do it.' I said the words as a vow because I meant it. I was done letting this asshole hurt her.

She clutched her fists at her sides. 'Close the door. Stand there and be my witness.'

I gave her a firm nod, but my stare stayed on Billy. In my head I had visions of making him pay for what he was doing to her, but giving him a black eye, a broken nose, wasn't what Tess needed right now, and it flew in the face of what I'd always told Lou about not getting physical with people – even if they deserved it.

'I'm done with you, Billy.' Tess kept her voice level, but it was threaded with venom. 'Time and time again you've let me down. Broken my heart. Made the girls confused and sad. All that ends now.'

'Please, Tessie. Let me take this money. Go off with Trini.' His gaze flicked to the open back door and the black Charger idling outside. 'I'll never come back to Ivy Falls.'

'You don't have to beg,' Trini spat out.

Billy rounded on her. 'Quiet. I've got this handled. I know Tess. She won't fight me on this.'

Tess gripped the edge of the desk. Every instinct to protect her flared in my body, but I planted my feet. She'd clearly communicated what she needed, and I wouldn't let her down.

'Is this why you came back? Pretended to change? All because you wanted to rob me? Steal from our children?'

'I came back because I missed you.' His gaze slid in my direction. 'But then I saw you two from inside *our house* on Halloween night. You were supposed to come in the door, and we'd have this great reunion, but it wasn't hard to see how you felt about him. How you looked at each other. The way Rosie was so content asleep on his shoulder. It wasn't the right time to let you know I was here in Ivy Falls, so I took off.'

Tess' gaze went murderous. 'You bastard! I should have known it. You left that damn box of your favorite cereal on the counter! You never could put anything away.' She took a forceful step forward. 'The park. Were you there?

Have you been sneaking around so no one would see you? Was Manny right about that too?' Billy's lip twitched as Tess said, 'You've gotten to be a much better liar. Let me guess, you threw the rock at the window too?'

He gave a brazen shrug. 'I was angry. It was me who should have been here with you. Not him.'

'That makes no sense. You made your choice, Billy. You chose her.'

'We broke up.' Trini snapped. 'He left, and then I found out I was pregnant.'

Tess' beautiful eyes went wide. 'That's why you went back to Atlanta? She's your "loose ends"?'

Trini gave him a heated stare.

'Yes,' Billy breathed out. 'Trin said she needed me. That this is a chance for us to start fresh. We're headed to California. I'm going to get some gigs playing music, but we need cash to make that happen.'

'And you thought stealing from me was the answer? You couldn't just get a job like a normal person? What about the money you made working for Silvio?'

'Used it to fix the car. What was left went to you for the girls.'

'What? That was only a few hundred dollars.'

'Come on, Tessie. Let us take the money. Five hundred bucks means nothing to you. Right now you're throwing a party for a new coffee bar.'

'You asshole,' she fumed. 'Why do you think I built the coffee bar? This place is bleeding money, and I'm literally a few bad months away from losing it. If you ever gave a damn about me, or our family, you'd know that I'm doing everything I can to save my mother's store!'

He had the gall to laugh, and I about lost my fucking mind. I took a step forward, but Tess shook her head at me.

'You'll never lose this place,' Billy scoffed. 'Your *daddy* would bail you out. Hell, this whole town would give you money if you needed it. Me and Trin, we're alone.'

'Alone by choice,' she flung back. 'You had a life here, a family, until you threw it all away. Hell, even after all that, this town was still willing to give you another chance.'

'Yeah, a family, and an entire town, who did nothing but judge me. Belittle me. I tried to change, but even then, you wouldn't take me back.'

The bastard had actually made a play for her, even after everything he'd done?

'That's your fault,' Tess blasted at him. 'The life you built, the people you let down, that was your doing and no one else's. For God's sake, Billy. Stop blaming the world for your problems, and for once in your life, grow the hell up.'

The shock on his face said he'd never seen this side of Tess before, and I couldn't have been prouder of her.

'Let us go.' Billy's tough veneer crumbled. 'Please. Trin and I need this.'

Tess yanked an envelope off her desk, pulled out a few sheets of paper and slapped them down. 'Sign the divorce papers, and maybe I'll think about not pressing charges against you both.'

'Do it,' Trini hissed as she rubbed at her belly. 'You've got your new family to think about.'

'We don't need you here, Billy. Move on, and we will too,' Tess added in a voice so concrete there was no room for misinterpreting her message.

Billy's mouth tensed as he stared at her. It took every ounce of willpower I had not to punch him in the face.

'I have rights, Tessie. I bet I could find a judge to agree to joint custody. Ask for whole summer vacations. But…' A disgusting smirk lifted his lips. 'If you let me take the money, I'll sign whatever you want, giving up any rights to the girls.' He rolled back his shoulders. 'Then you and him can do whatever the fuck you want.'

All the things I'd worried about, how he'd lie, hurt her again, made the rage rise up in me. She didn't deserve any of this. And the way he could just toss away Rose and Iris made me bite the inside of my cheek, hold back all the curses I wanted to fling his way.

To her credit, Tess' face stayed an unemotional mask. On a barely audible breath, she said, 'Look up.'

Billy's gaze moved overhead to a small white ball and a little black camera I'd installed after the rock came through the window.

'If you don't leave now, I'll call Deputy Ben in here. Show him the recording, proving your intent. I'll press charges for theft, trespassing and whatever the hell else I can think up.'

'You wouldn't,' Billy challenged. 'Think what that would do to our girls. They'd hate you for sending me to jail.'

'They are *my* girls,' Tess said roughly. 'One day I will tell them that you chose yourself over being a real father. That they have many other men in their life who love and care for them.' Her gaze darted to me and then narrowed back on Billy. 'They'll understand eventually that their lives are much better without you around. Iris and Rose are young. Over time you'll fade from their memory, and one day, it'll be like you never existed.'

'You wouldn't dare. It'd tarnish that "Little Miss Goody Two Shoes" persona you have in this town.'

A thin smile crossed her lips as she lowered her voice. 'You don't know me. You've never really cared enough to get to know me. These last ten years of my life have been tainted by your presence. That's over now. Everyone in this town knows who I am and loves me for it.' Her gaze went heartbroken as she looked at Trini and her round belly. 'Sadly, you've never loved anyone in your life except yourself.'

Tess reached out and tugged the bank bag away from Trini, who took a startled step back.

'Sign the papers, or I'll go to the police. I'd hate to do that to your poor baby.' Her voice quivered for a moment. 'But if you don't do as I say, I'll make both your lives miserable.'

Pride flooded through me as I watched her go toe to toe with Billy and Trini and not flinch. She didn't need me to break his nose or yell at him. She had enough force and strength to take him down all on her own.

'You'll regret this, Tessie.' He scratched out his signature and tossed the pen onto the desk.

'The only thing I regret is trusting you. Letting you back into our lives. Now leave, before I have Manny throw you out.'

Billy hesitated until I took a step forward, curling my fists as a warning.

'Let's go, Trin,' he said, towing her out the back door.

With a roar, his car sped out of the parking lot, leaving a hazy cloud of brown dust in its wake.

I waited two full breaths before I said, 'Are you all right?'

She gave me a weak smile. 'Yes. I'm relieved, actually. Having him here only caused chaos. His stupidity and callousness just made it easier for me to get him to leave for good.'

'Hey.' I started to reach out my hand to her and then dropped it to my side, unsure of where we stood. 'I'm proud of you. Standing up to him took guts.'

She pressed her warm hand to my cheek, and my aching heart did a double beat. 'Thank you for letting me handle the situation. It couldn't have been easy to stand by and watch that unfold, but I appreciate you trusting me.'

'Tess, you're strong and brave. There isn't anything you can't do if you set your mind to it. I want to be here for you in any way I can. In any way you'll let me.' I leaned into her touch. 'That day, after the Dairy Dip, I was wrong to lash out at you. I need you in my life in whatever way you'll have me.'

'I've made so many mistakes.' Her lower lip trembled. 'Part of me was scared. Afraid of getting hurt again. But I know now that the most certain thing in my life is what I feel for you. I hope you can forgive me for being so terribly wrong.'

'You were doing what you thought was best for you and the girls. And I understand being scared. The steps we are taking are fucking terrifying, but I want you to know that I'll take things as slow as you want. That no matter what, I will always support you. Believe in you. I care for you, and all I want is for us to figure out a way to be together.' I hesitated, pulled in a long breath. 'To make our families one.'

'That's what I want too.'

Her mouth found mine in a hungry, desperate kiss. I pulled her in close, needing to feel her body next to mine.

I moved my tongue around the edge of her lips until she opened for me. We stumbled back against the desk, and I lifted her up onto the corner. Our kisses became more frenzied, like we were trying to make up for all the weeks we'd been apart.

She moaned against my neck as she worked kisses down along my throat. I tugged her in against me, wanting her to feel what she did to me every single time she touched me. She ran her hands down my back and tugged out the hem of my shirt, tracing the waistband of my pants before her hands slid lower.

A low growl left my throat as I plunged my tongue deeper into her mouth. As I was tugging up her blouse, running my fingertips over the top of her lacy bra, the sound of voices outside drew closer. I stepped back quickly, my heart nearly beating out of my chest.

I loved the wicked smile dancing across Tess' lips as she slid off the desk. A second later, Piper came in the door with Torran on her heels. Neither of them noticed the damaged doorframe as they took one look at us and burst out laughing.

'Sorry to interrupt,' Torran said with a sly grin as she stared at her sister's crumpled blouse and tousled hair. 'But you've got a room full of people waiting on a ribbon-cutting ceremony.' She gave us another long look. 'We can stall them for a while if you two' – she gave an annoying wink – 'want to continue whatever was happening in here.'

'Change,' Tess blurted out. 'We were getting change.'

Piper gave a full-throated laugh. 'Sure you were. Come out when you finally find the "change".'

She threaded her arm through Torran's and dragged her out of the room.

Once they were gone, Tess tucked in her blouse. The pink flush to her cheeks made me pull her in again. I reached up and smoothed out the hairs that had escaped her braid.

'I can fix that for you,' I teased.

'Let's make a promise to each other,' she said, straightening out my shirt, her hands lingering on my chest. 'Whatever is happening between us, we consider it a partnership. I don't need you to fix everything for me. To swoop in and be a superhero.' She grinned.

Yeah, she'd never let me forget that costume.

'I can't learn that way,' she went on. 'And I'm tired of people seeing me as meek and helpless.'

'After the way you just eviscerated Billy, that will never be my assumption.' I pressed a quick kiss to her forehead.

'I'm serious, Manny. If we're going to be in a relationship, I want to be equals. I help you and you help me. We support each other whenever and wherever we can. Listen and respect each other's opinion. I've spent too long relying on other people for help. I need to be an active participant in my own life. Going through hell with Billy has taught me that much.'

'I'll agree to whatever terms you lay down as long as I get to kiss you.' I gave her a full-watt smile. 'Wherever and whenever, and of course, in any spot I want.'

Her cheeks flushed that delicious pink again. 'That, Mr Parks, is a deal I can definitely agree to.'

I pressed another hungry kiss to her mouth before she finally tore herself away and pulled me back into the store.

When things quieted down, we'd have to talk more about what happened with Billy. How she'd have to explain his sudden disappearance again to her family, and probably the entire damn town. But, for now, I wanted Tess to enjoy this victory because, in so many ways, she'd earned it.

Chapter Forty-One

TESSA

Speechless

I pressed a hand against my kiss-swollen lips. At any other time I would have been embarrassed to face the residents of Ivy Falls, but I no longer cared about what people thought. I'd spent too much of my life trying to be a mediator, calm uncomfortable situations, so I'd never really learned to battle for what I wanted. To tell the people I loved when I needed space to learn things on my own.

Billy returning to town had been a nightmare, but it'd also taught me that I was tired of operating from a place of fear. That if I wanted to have a happy and fulfilling life, I'd have to take control of my future. That began now with welcoming the entire town to my new and improved store.

Moving to the coffee bar, I pulled out a mug and admired the P&P logo etched against its center. I clanged the glass with a fork and drew everyone's attention. My head started to spin until I thought of Mom. How she would have loved every moment of this. How her beloved store had once again become the gathering spot for all of Ivy Falls.

'Thank you for joining me and my family tonight to celebrate the opening of the Pen & Prose's new coffee bar.'

The room exploded in applause.

'Like a doting parent, this community has always wrapped me in love and support. Been there for me in good times. Surrounded me during the bad.' I took a thick gulp over the growing knot in my throat. 'My hope with this new venture is that all of you will come here when you need a little peace and quiet. That once you're in the door, you can shut out the world for a while and get lost in a good story.'

Dad gave me a loving smile, and Torran kept nodding along with my speech.

'And,' I laughed, 'maybe buy a book or two and a really good espresso.' The crowd chuckled along with me. 'My point is that tonight, and, well, every single day, Ivy Falls makes me feel cherished. That is all because of the people who fill this community. No words will ever be able to express how grateful I am to have each one of you in my life.'

From the back of the crowd, Mrs Vanderpool, Isabel, and even Silvio dabbed at their eyes.

'I'd like to ask Manny and our girls, Iris, Rose, and Louisa, to join me.'

The girls did a happy little dance as they pulled Manny up to the bar. His loving smile lit up every inch of my skin.

'Let's all try to hold the scissors together and make one big cut,' I said.

My loves, my family, put their hands on top of mine and together with a firm snip the yellow ribbon strung across the front of the bar sliced in two.

A loud cheer shook the room. The girls hugged my waist as Manny pressed a kiss to the top of my head.

Barb and Susan brought out more treats. After a long discussion, we'd decided to start selling a specialty coffee cake, German chocolate brownies and raspberry scones. As partners, we'd agreed to talk every few weeks about what customers were buying. Go over any new items they might want to concoct for the store.

Manny stayed next to me as we tried several varieties of coffee and tea. Piper worked side by side with Penny, filling each and every request with a smile.

'Hey, Piper,' I called over the counter. 'When you're not working at Sugar Rush, do you think you might want to manage the coffee bar?'

Her big brown eyes went wide. 'Um, yes!' She hesitated. 'But are you sure you want to trust me?'

I leaned over the bar and squeezed her hand. 'There's no one I'd trust more.'

'Then I accept if Barb and Susan agree.'

'We do.' They stood behind us, holding hands. Like me, they saw so much potential in Piper.

Manny pulled me in close, pressed his warm mouth next to my ear, sending delicious shivers through my body. 'Congratulations! If the turnout tonight is any indication, the coffee bar is going to be a success.'

I spun around and pressed my cheek against his wide chest. 'Thank you for believing in this dream. For helping make it happen.'

'You're capable of amazing things, Tess. I'm proud I get to stand by your side and watch all the wonderful moments to come.'

Not caring who was watching, I stood on tiptoe and pressed my mouth to his. The kiss lingered for a few minutes until a chorus of giggles made me pull away.

The girls had their arms wrapped around each other's shoulders. With a satisfied smile, Lou said, 'We all approve. Does this mean we'll be sisters?'

'Let's just say we are going back to our regular routine for now.' Manny's wide smile brightened the entire room.

Lou beamed, but a puzzled look crossed the girls' faces.

'What about Daddy?' Iris asked.

My heart tugged, and I bent down to look both of my babies in the eye. 'We'll have to talk about that later. Right now, I want you all to go play and have fun.'

Lou, as if she understood the seriousness in my voice, took each of the girls' hands.

'Why don't we read that new book called *Nerdy Corn*. It looked fun.'

My girls nodded and let Lou lead them away.

'Damn Billy,' I whispered under my breath.

'Hey.' Manny tilted my chin toward him. 'It'll be hard for a little bit. But we will give them all the love we have until the sting of him being gone becomes a distant memory.'

I pulled him in closer and gave him another kiss. He held on to me as the frenzy in the store continued around us.

'I have something to say, and I want you to hear me out before you argue.'

He inched back and gave me a puzzled stare.

'*Meet Me in Ivy Falls* is an important show. You and Torran together are what make it special. If you go back to the network, make your demands firm, I bet they'll cave in an instant.'

His lips twitched. 'They already did. Lauren said I could pretty much write my own terms.'

The relief in his voice, the heat of his breath against the tender skin on my neck, made my body go electric. I laid a gentle kiss against his lips. Here and now it was mostly chaste, but when we were alone it was definitely going to be a four-alarm fire.

The party continued around us. Barb and Susan doled out their sweet treats while the hiss of the espresso machine filled the room. I leaned back against Manny and took in the scene. For the first time in months, there was a looseness to my shoulders. A boulder the size of a house no longer sat on my chest. The warmth filling my body was peace, and I was going to hold on to it for as long as possible.

Piper called us back to the bar, handing me my favorite Colombian dark roast, when a quick little scream, followed by a boisterous laugh, filled the room. Piper's eyes lit up, and she swapped a weighted look with Pete, who stood talking to Ferris a few feet away.

'What's that all about?' Manny said.

Like a wave, the room shifted toward a back corner of the children's area, and we followed the crowd. Small whispers began to rise as Manny and I turned a corner to the long wall of windows where we kept the picture books. A gasp filled my throat, and Manny clutched my hand.

Beck was down on one knee. A blue velvet box sat in the palm of his hand. My sister stood as still as a statue.

'Torran Elizabeth Wright, I've loved you ever since the day your mother brought me to this spot, and I saw you sitting in a patch of sunlight looking like a real-life angel. Our road over the last years has been rough, but a while ago I promised I'd do everything in my power to make a good life for us. To show you that my love is eternal. This is the next step in proving to you that whatever the world throws at us, we can get through it if we're together.'

For the first time in my life, I watched my big sister become speechless. The only sign that she was still breathing was the rough rise and fall of her chest.

'To some it may be a silly, old-fashioned tradition, but I know you've been through a lot, so I not only asked your father for his blessing, but I went to the cemetery and spoke to your mom too.'

Barb and Susan sniffled next to me. Manny handed me a napkin to wipe away my own tears.

'Will you do me the great honor of becoming my partner in this life?'

If I hadn't seen it with my own eyes, I would have never believed it. Beck Townsend had rendered most of the town silent. Mrs Vanderpool clutched Baby to her chest. Isabel held on to my father's shaky hand. Piper swiped at her cheeks as Pete patted her shoulder. Manny slid his arm around my waist and held on for dear life.

'Well, are you gonna answer him?' Rosie propped her hands on her hips and tapped her toe, clearly frustrated with her aunt's silence.

Torran blinked several times. I moved to comfort her, but Manny held me back.

'Wait,' he whispered.

It hurt to see her stand there alone. To know that in this moment she would have looked to our mom for strength.

Torran slid down to her knees and placed her hands against Beck's cheeks. Ever so quietly, the quietest I've ever heard her speak in my life, she replied, 'I love you with all my heart, Beck Townsend. Yes, I will be your partner in this life.'

The crowd cheered so loudly the windows shook. Rose, Iris and Lou beelined in their direction and knocked them over in a hug. Everyone laughed and went to congratulate the couple once they'd managed to extricate themselves from the pile of girls strewn across the top of them.

Manny pulled me away from the scene and into the aisle where everything had changed for us.

'Did you know?' I asked.

He shook his head. 'I guess that explains why he's been distracted and secretive lately.'

'Are you upset he didn't tell you beforehand?'

'Are you?' he volleyed back.

'No,' I laughed. 'I'm not sure I could have kept my mouth shut.'

'It's a credit to Beck. He knows when it comes to Torran, neither of us can keep a secret.'

'You are a good man, Manchester Parks,' I said, tugging him toward me until we were hip to hip.

'As long as you think so, that's all that matters to me.' He pressed a gentle kiss to my lips, and I slid my arms around his neck.

It'd taken me so long to figure out what I needed. What I had to sacrifice to keep my girls happy. Manny had been there for the entire ride, never wavering. Never failing me.

'What are you thinking?' he asked.

'That I'm going to have to tell Dad and Torran about Billy, and there will be a round of "I told you so".'

'I think they might surprise you. The good thing is he's gone now, and if he's smart, he'll never be back.' His thick arms circled me tighter, and I sank into his warmth.

'I hope this party is over soon.'

He lifted a thick eyebrow. 'And why is that?'

'Because there are many more places in this store that have soft rugs.'

That devious grin of his was going to be my undoing. 'Yep. We should make it our mission to test them all.'

At first, I'd been afraid of what would happen to us if we admitted how we truly felt, but now I couldn't imagine anything but having our lives completely intertwined.

Manny gave me a tender look. The light in his eyes spoke of days, months, years, and I wanted them all.

A Letter from Amy

Dear Reader,

Thank you for returning to Ivy Falls and going on this ride with me.

It's often said that writing the second book in a series is the hardest, but telling Tessa and Manny's story came to me like water gushing out of a spout. Early on in my plotting, I knew they were going to be my second couple. Some days I could not type fast enough, because both their voices were so loud and clear in my head. It was apparent from the earliest drafts that whenever they were on page together, it was special. But, of course, I couldn't let their road to an HEA be easy.

Tessa arrived on the page broken and world-weary, and my job was to allow her to grow, change, and learn how to speak her truth, even when it wasn't always in her nature. I have many people in my life who are quiet, but when challenged rise to the occasion with fervor and fight. I wanted to reflect that in Tessa's journey, and I hope you enjoy it.

Manny was an absolute joy to write. He may have a voice like a bear, but he has the sweetest cinnamon roll of a heart. I once read a social media post where a reader said they wanted to see stories where widowers openly grieved the loss of their spouse while still forging a new life for themselves. My goal with Manny's story was to balance his loss alongside his hope for new love. I will also admit that my favorite part of doing research for this book was watching videos of men learning how to braid their daughters' hair. Dads can do fishtail braids like bosses, I'm telling you!

One last note...

Grief in small yet recognizable ways tends to be a theme in my books. For both Manny and Tessa, grief informs how they act, not only toward each other, but to the people in their lives. Losing a spouse, or going through the breakup of a marriage, can be difficult. If you find any of these topics uncomfortable, please take care while reading.

To learn more about the Ivy Falls series you can check out my newsletter, True Writing on Substack.

You can also find me online at:

Website: amytruebloodauthor.com
Instagram: @atruebooks
Threads: @atruebooks
TikTok: @atruebooks

Acknowledgements

Writing acknowledgements never gets easier. There are so many people you meet along your publishing journey who make what can often be a whirlwind experience so much easier.

First, many thanks to my editor, Jennie Ayres, who continues to push my craft and absolutely gets the stories I'm trying to tell. A big shoutout to my agent, Kristina Pérez, Isabel Lineberry, and the whole team at Pérez Literary and Entertainment. I can always focus on my writing because I know you all have my back one hundred percent. Also, a massive thank you to the team at Hera, including Ross Dickinson for insightful copyedits, my publicist, Kate Shepherd, and Diane Meacham for another gorgeous cover design.

I will always be grateful for my huge support network, which includes David, Olivia, and Ryan, as well as my siblings and entire extended family. You are my biggest cheerleaders, and I'm incredibly grateful to have all of you in my corner.

To my Arizona writing network – this job is so much easier because I have all of you to lean on. Special thanks to my critique partner and good friend, Kelly deVos, for challenging me to make my craft better every single week. To Joanna Ruth Meyer, who is one of the first people I text when I'm having a writing crisis or when

I need a rational opinion on the wild things happening in the publishing world. Thanks for always being there and listening. To the SCBWI Arizona PAL crew for letting me still be part of the party, even if I'm dipping my toe into the adult world now. And to my library buddy, Kaitlyn Carlson, who has listened to me ramble on for months about this book. Your insight and thoughtful feedback are appreciated more than you know!

Last but certainly not least, thank you to booksellers everywhere who genuinely care about the written word. I continue to be in awe of how you've supported my books over the years. You are the unsung heroes of this industry. And, as always, to the readers. Your positivity and kindness mean the world to me. Hope you'll stay on this adventure with me into Book Three!

Amy's Playlist for Finding Love in Ivy Falls

'Tightrope' – Young the Giant

'Deep End' – Holly Humberstone

'Daydreamin'' ' – Ariana Grande

'hate to be lame' – Lizzy McAlpine, FINNEAS

'Breathe Me' – Sia

'Labyrinth' – Taylor Swift

'Trouble' – Cage The Elephant

'Sleep Tight' – Holly Humberstone

'You Broke Me First' – Conor Maynard

'Let Me Down Slowly' – Alec Benjamin

'You Should Be Sad' – Halsey

'I Found' – Amber Run

'Surrender' – Natalie Taylor

'Make You Feel My Love' – Adele